ALSO BY JERAMEY KRAATZ

The Cloak Society
Villains Rising
Fall of Heroes

COMING SOON:

Space Runners: The Dark Side of the Moon

SPACE RUNNERS
THE MOON PLATOON

JERAMEY KRAATZ

HarperCollins *Children's Books*

First published in Great Britain by HarperCollins *Children's Books* in 2017
HarperCollins *Children's Books* is a division of HarperCollins*Publishers* Ltd,
1 London Bridge Street London, SE1 9GF

The HarperCollins website address is: www.harpercollins.co.uk

1

Copyright © Full Fathom Five, LLC 2017

ISBN: 978-0-00-822640-4

Typeset in Optima by Palimpsest Book Production Ltd, Falkirk, Stirlingshire

Printed and bound in Great Britain by Clays Ltd, St Ives plc

MIX
Paper from
responsible sources
FSC® C007454

FSC™ is a non-profit international organisation established to promote
the responsible management of the world's forests. Products carrying the
FSC label are independently certified to assure consumers that they come
from forests that are managed to meet the social, economic and
ecological needs of present and future generations,
and other controlled sources.

Find out more about HarperCollins and the environment at
www.harpercollins.co.uk/green

For anyone who has shot for the Moon,
ended up in the grass, and tried again.

Congratulations,
2085 Scholarship Winner!

On behalf of the Elijah West Scholarship for Courage, Ambition, and Brains (EW-SCAB), I am pleased to inform you that, out of the millions of applications we received this year, *you* have been selected to receive an all-expenses paid two-week trip to the Lunar Taj — the galaxy's first (and only!) off-world resort. Located on five hundred acres of prime Moon real estate overlooking the Sea of Tranquility, the Lunar Taj offers countless opportunities for adventure, including zero-gravity sports, scenic Space Runner treks across the dark side of the Moon and access to the latest in cutting-edge virtual reality technology. Ever wonder what it would be like to play weightless basketball? You're about to find out! Itching to explore craters no human has ever set foot in? Join one of our off-resort expeditions! There may even be an opportunity to meet the legendary adventurer and inventor Elijah West himself!

And, of course, the fun doesn't stop on the Moon: upon completion of your two-week holiday, you'll receive an EW-SCAB trust fund of one million US dollars!

To begin the enrolment process, we'll need a biometric signature from your parent or guardian. In addition, please upload heat-scan measurements so we can begin work on your custom-made space suits right away! Don't delay – your Space Runner will be launching soon!

Congratulations on this once-in-a-lifetime opportunity,

Pinky Weyve
Executive assistant to Mr. West

ABOUT THE SCHOLARSHIP

Since 2080, Elijah West – philanthropist, innovator, and *Time*'s Man of the Millennium – has opened the doors of his preeminent Lunar Taj to the best and brightest of Earth's youth. Recipients of the EW-SCAB have gone on to earn early acceptance to top-tier universities, find success in burgeoning Space Runner racing leagues and even land coveted positions as full-time staff members at the Lunar Taj. Despite the amount of entries received every year, Mr. West alone selects each scholarship recipient.

CHAPTER 1

Benny Love was three quarters of the way to the Moon when he discovered his holographic spider was missing.

"Aw, man," he murmured into his open rucksack, "I had such big plans for you!"

He'd been practising with the spider for the better part of a year. Or, more specifically, mastering the controls of the tiny hover-mech that flew around projecting the arachnid onto whatever surface Benny saw fit – most of the time someone's shoulder or the ceiling of his family's RV in the middle of the night. He was *good* at it, and had hoped to show off his skills by pranking some of the other scholarship winners. So much for that idea. He wondered which of his little brothers had swiped the spider from his bag the night before, because he *definitely* remembered packing such vital gear. They were probably playing around with it now, getting sand in the hover-mech's delicate parts.

He made a mental note to figure out a way to repay them when he got back to Earth. Maybe with a terrifying story about the three-headed child-eating aliens he encountered at the Taj, or by infecting them with an incredibly contagious case of imaginary lunar flu.

He tried not to dwell on the spider and instead looked out of the passenger window just in time to see a satellite fly by – a shining speck against the black backdrop of space that quickly disappeared among the pinpricks of stars located light-years away. He glanced at the readouts on the dashboard. His Space Runner was travelling at just under fifty thousand miles per hour.

Benny was a very long way from home.

He hadn't quite wrapped his head around the fact that he was riding in a car capable of blasting off from Earth and travelling to the Moon. A luxury vehicle sleeker than any sports coupé ever imagined, crammed full of next-generation artificial environment systems and touch-operated holoscreens and powered by one explosive gravity-manipulating fission hyperdrive under the hood. A total beast of a machine. It was the type of car Benny had seen in ads and news stories on his HoloTek datapad but never in person. At least, not until today. Certainly it wasn't the type of vehicle he'd thought he'd ever have a chance to ride in. His caravan back on Earth – like every other roaming pack of cars and mobile homes in the Drylands – was made up of sand-battered rust-buckets cobbled together from bits and pieces of old wrecks and whatever salvageable parts the members of his group had come across in their travels. The RV that he and his brothers and grandmother lived in was so old that it ran partially on fossil fuels.

And yet, here he was. Not only was he riding in a Space Runner, but he'd probably get the chance to meet the person who'd invented them eight years ago. Elijah West. Benny had read all about him online. The man was an adventurer who'd redefined space exploration. Who drag raced across Mars on weekends. Eccentric, certainly, and maybe even a little crazy (he *did* live full-time on the Moon and, according to some reports, spent millions of dollars a year having cargo ships full of his favourite fizzy drink shipped to the Taj).

But he was also the world's biggest philanthropist. The fact that Benny was currently shooting through space and would have an unfathomable amount of money waiting for him when he came back to Earth was proof enough of that. Benny had never met Elijah, but the man had already shaped his future. The EW-SCAB trust fund he'd come home to in two weeks represented more than just the latest datapads and hologram tech. A million dollars wouldn't make him rich compared to a lot of people, but it *was* the promise of a real home, a way out of the Drylands and all the dangers and struggles he and his family faced in the desert wastes that had once been the West Coast of the United States.

In fact, Elijah's very existence was kind of comforting to Benny. Every biography or profile of the trillionaire mentioned that he'd been born with nothing and became the mogul he was today because he simply refused to believe in limitations. That anything was impossible. Late at night, when Benny told his little brothers that they wouldn't have to live in the Drylands forever, it was Elijah he was thinking about.

Benny tossed his rucksack to the floor and dragged his hands across the front of his space suit a few times, trying to wipe off the dust and grit he'd got on him while rummaging through it – nothing from the caravan was ever *really* clean, no matter how often you washed it. Eventually he just accepted that he'd be a little dirty when he got to the Taj, and propped his feet on the dashboard. The shiny black surface under his boots lit up in a flurry of colours and holograms. He realised his mistake a split second before a mixture of drums and instruments that sounded like laser pistols blared through the cabin. He bolted forward and tapped at what he thought might be an off-button, but that just caused the lights inside the vehicle to pulse along with the thumping bass.

All the noise woke Drue, the kid in the seat next to him. The first thing Drue had done when he met Benny was claim the pilot's chair, even though the trip to the Moon was completely automated by an onboard guidance system. Then he'd fallen asleep before their Space Runner took off. He'd stayed that way, mouth open and head lolling back and forth, for the past few hours. Not that Benny really minded. It gave him a chance to quietly stare out at the stars and the forty-nine other gleaming Space Runners holding the rest of the scholarship winners that were all heading towards the Moon like a fleet moving in for invasion.

"Aren't we there yet?" Drue asked, blinking sleep away. He didn't wait for Benny to respond. "Ugh, why aren't we moving faster? What's the point of having a hyperdrive if they aren't going to push it?" He leaned forward and drew a half-circle anticlockwise on the dashboard in front of him, the blinking lights reflecting off the gold buttons on the cuff of his space suit. The music died down to a faint pulse.

Benny watched this carefully. He wasn't sure what Drue's deal was, but there was something about him that seemed off. Maybe it was the way his brown hair was so perfectly slicked over to one side, unlike his own black hair that usually stuck out in all directions thanks to a mixture of sweat and dust. Or maybe it was Drue's space suit. Benny's had been made for him by the people at EW-SCAB – close-fitting, dark blue coveralls made out of some rubbery, radiation-blocking substance. A thick band around the collar contained an emergency force-field helmet and oxygen supply, should he find himself outside of the artificial atmosphere of the Taj. His last name was stitched in silver over his heart. It was the first brand-new piece of clothing he could remember getting in years – not counting the stuff his grandmother made for him – and the same suit everyone else had been wearing before take-off. Except Drue's. His suit was just a little bit shinier, and his last name, Lincoln, was spelled out in gold on his left chest pocket. It looked expensive. Like something Benny would be thrilled to find in an abandoned farm or town back on Earth because he could probably trade it for a decent hover-scooter, or at least new tyres for his dune buggy.

Drue looked at the dirt smudged across Benny's space suit and crinkled his nose.

"What have you been doing while I was asleep?" he asked.

That's when it clicked – Drue looked at him like a lot of

people did on the rare occasions when the members of his caravan would buy supplies in the cities bordering the Drylands. Such places had grown more and more over-crowded and expensive as the ongoing drought forced people to abandon their homes and move further east. Those who could afford to live in the cities didn't seem to want people like him and his family hanging around for too long. He could tell that from the way they avoided eye contact or clutched their bags close when he walked by. On a few occasions, shop owners had even told him that he should go back to the desert if he didn't have any money to spend.

"Nothing," he said to Drue, crossing his arms over the front of his suit. "Just trying to remind myself that this is real. I can't believe I'm about to be *on the Moon*. Have you heard of the reverse bungee jumping they have at the Taj? Where they tie you to a Moon rock and then shoot you into space?"

Drue just shrugged.

"It's cool, I guess. The first time is fun, but after that it's just OK because there's not really a lot for you to look at from that high. The Moon's actually kind of ugly up close."

"Whoa, whoa, whoa," Benny said, shaking his head and raising his hands in front of him. "You mean you've been up here before?"

"Sure. Last summer. I told them they should add jet packs to the bungee jumping if they really wanted to make it worth doing." Drue smirked. "The best part of the trip, though? I totally shook Elijah West's hand."

Benny narrowed his eyes. One of the few rules in the scholarship application was that the recipients should be kids aged eleven to thirteen who might not have the chance to visit the Moon otherwise (which, Benny understood, was a really nice way of saying that the EW-SCAB was charity and not for someone rich enough to actually visit the Lunar Taj with their own money).

Drue leaned back in the driver's seat and put his feet up on the locked steering yoke in front of him. "This time I want to go inside Elijah's private garage. I hear there are all sorts of Space Runner prototypes hidden away in here. I'm hoping he's got something more like a motorcycle with a hyperdrive. Super fast. Sleek. Now *that* I would get pumped about."

"I'm pretty into ATVs. Maybe he's got something like that."

Drue let out a snort. "If Moon buggies excite you, you're going to have the best time of your life." Drue's eyes lit up a little as a smile spread across his face. "You're lucky you got assigned to my car. Stick with me and I'll show you the good life. You'll have a great time! Trust me."

"Can't wait," Benny said, not sure if that was the best or worst choice he could make. It didn't matter, though. He was stuck in the Space Runner for the time being. Plus, there was something else on his mind. "So . . . what's Elijah West like?"

"He's seriously the most awesome guy in the universe," Drue said. He shook his head a few times, like he couldn't believe such a person really existed. "I mean, I only got to say a few words to him, but I feel like we made a connection. Did you know that after inventing the Space Runner, he took it out himself on a test run because he wanted to be able to say that he was the first person who drove a car into space, even though it was crazy dangerous? And when he was overseeing the building of the Lunar Taj, a bunch of businesses offered to give him a ton of money for a stake in it, but he spent his own fortune so he could have full control over the place? Also, did you know that he's trying to figure out how to turn the rings of Saturn into a race track? That dude is cooler than anyone alive. Or dead, probably." Drue let out a long breath and closed his eyes. "When I'm a trillionaire, I'm driving a different Space Runner every day."

Benny caught his own reflection in the shiny black dashboard and realised that a huge, goofy grin had taken over his face. He was so close to the Taj. Soon, he was going to be walking on the Moon.

"So, it's not weird being there, right?" he asked. "It just feels like Earth? Because *I* heard that one tiny hole in the Grand Dome around the Taj would mess up the pressure inside so badly that it could suck your brain out of your nose."

Drue's right eye cracked open, staring at Benny.

"Uh, not true. The artificial atmosphere isn't *that* strong. Plus, the whole resort is actually encased in a gravity force field. Who told you that?"

Benny shook his head. "Actually, that might be something I told one of my dumb brothers to scare them. I spent a lot of nights this week telling them about imaginary space wars to get them to stop complaining about me getting to go on this trip."

"You've got brothers?" Drue asked.

"Two, yeah. You?"

"None. I'm an only child."

Benny was not surprised. He'd only known Drue a few hours, but he didn't exactly seem like the sharing type.

"Probably pretty quiet around your house, then," he said. "Not like mine."

"Yeah," Drue said. "My parents like it that way. It's, you

know, the first thing they tell new nannies. Or tutors. Or whoever. They don't even like me to invite people over. If there were more Lincoln kids running around, we'd probably all end up at boarding school."

As Drue spoke, his smug smile drooped into what was almost a frown. Benny was trying to figure out what question to ask next – as well as wrap his head around the fact that Drue had nannies and tutors while he was the one who was basically in charge of his brothers most of the time now that his dad was gone – when Drue groaned and let his head fall against the thick glass that separated him from the cold expanse of space.

"This is so dumb. I can't believe my father made me leave all my gaming implants at home. What am I supposed to do for a whole *five-hour trip* to kill time?"

"I don't know." Benny offered, "Look at the stars?"

Drue rolled his eyes.

"I could do that at home. At least there I've got telescopes."

Benny really wished he had that holographic spider.

CHAPTER 2

As they neared hour five of their journey, Benny caught sight of a shining dot on the surface of the looming Moon: the Lunar Taj. His thumping heart might as well have been powered by a supercharged hyperdrive engine.

The Taj was not the only thing to blame for this. Benny was starting to worry that Drue might get them killed before they even landed.

"Maybe I can pry this loose and we can take this thing out for a real joyride," Drue said through clenched teeth as he tried to wrench the Space Runner's flight yoke out of its locked position.

"Uh . . ." Benny said. "Should you really be pulling on that?"

"Don't tell me you're scared." Drue's face was starting to turn red from exertion. "Trust me, I know what I'm doing. Don't you want to be the first person to carve your name into the surface of Mars or something?"

"How would we do that?" Benny asked, but it was obvious that Drue wasn't listening. He made a final desperate pull, only to end up losing his grip and crashing back into the pilot's seat.

There was a heaving sound from behind them.

Benny had almost forgotten the third member of their party. He and Drue turned, peeking over their headrests at the girl in the back seat. Her freckled skin had an almost greenish cast to it.

"Hey," Benny said. "Are you OK?"

"Negative, flyboy," the girl replied in a chirping, clipped tone. She put her hands on the back of her head, burying her fingers in the reddish-blond hair that was pulled off her forehead with what looked to Benny like a piece of twisted silver wire. "Girl down. Out of commish. Max sploitz."

Drue cocked his head to one side. "Are we sure that's English?"

"Sounds like she's talking in robot," Benny said.

"Newbz," the girl muttered.

Her suit said "Robinson", but her first name was Ramona. Or at least, Benny was pretty sure that was right. She'd been jabbering quite a bit before take-off, not to him or Drue but to the various electronics she'd brought with her. Benny *thought* her accent was British, but based on the gibberish she spouted he couldn't be sure. Since blast-off, though, Ramona had hardly said a word. As far as Benny could tell she'd spent most the flight with her head between her knees, braced for a crash landing.

There were only supposed to be a hundred EW-SCAB winners. Benny's invitation had said so. Yet when the transport dropped him off at the launch site earlier that morning and he saw the rows of fifty shining Space Runners for the first time, the adults in charge mentioned that there would actually be a hundred and one kids going to the Moon. Benny had been assigned to the vehicle with an extra kid in it. As he watched Ramona reach for a sick bag with shaking hands, he worried that his Space Runner assignment and the missing spider were bad omens for what the rest of his visit to the Moon was going to be like.

Drue leaned closer to Benny. "If she pukes, I'm flushing her out of the emergency airlock."

Benny chuckled until he heard Ramona groan while wrapping her arms around her stomach. Then, feeling a little bad for her, he turned back around in his seat. In front of them, the Moon was getting larger by the second. Drue tapped on a few of the dashboard displays. Benny watched his fingers fly over the screens, adjusting the cabin lights and air-conditioning. He seemed right at home in the Space Runner.

"No point in going back to sleep, I guess," Drue said. "We're only a few minutes from descent."

"Have you done sims for this or something?" Benny asked.

Drue shrugged.

"I have a few, but I never play them. My father has one of the first Space Runner models, so I've ridden around in it a little bit. They're pretty easy to handle once you get out of the atmosphere."

Benny's forehead scrunched up as he considered this, trying to figure out how someone whose family owned a Space Runner ended up winning an EW-SCAB. Perhaps Drue was just lying about his previous visit to the Taj and everything else. Or maybe he was a spoiled kid who lived in a shining tower in one of the luxury buildings for the richest of the rich that had sprung up when the cities began to be overrun with drought refugees.

"So, what was your application vid like?" Benny asked, thinking this might get him some answers. "Why do you think Elijah picked you?"

Drue shrugged. "I bet he saw some of himself in me.

An adventurer. Brave, smart – a young Elijah! What about you?"

"Well, some of it was of me pulling tricks in my dune buggy," Benny said, grinning. "I got my hands on a floating GoCam for a few days and it caught me doing all sorts of flips and stuff out in the desert. You should have seen the height I got on some of the jumps. It was insane. Then this kid got separated from our caravan, which was really sad and all but I—"

"Wait," Drue said, jutting his head forward, one eye narrowed and the other opened wide. "Did you say 'caravan'? Like, one of those groups of homeless people who live in what used to be California and Nevada and stuff out west?"

"Well, yeah," Benny said, the excitement fading from his voice. "But we're *not* homeless. We just . . . camp a lot."

Drue's expression twisted for a moment. Then he shook his head and opened his mouth a few times like he was going to say something, but only air escaped. Benny reflexively wiped his hands across his space suit, trying to knock any extra dirt off it. He felt his cheeks burn, and another, different heat rising inside him. Drue was again staring at him with a mixture of pity and disgust. Benny had seen that look countless times, sometimes even from members of the caravan – newcomers who had been driven out of the cities because they couldn't afford it any more, just like Benny's family had been when he was a little kid. They'd hated the canned food or how they weren't allowed to shower or take a bath because it wasted water, having to rely on old baby wipes instead. Mostly they complained about how boring caravan life was. Benny's dad had been quick to tell him to be patient with these new recruits. He'd said their attitudes were just to hide how scared they were and that with time they'd come around. Not all of them did.

His dad had always looked for the good in people. It was something Benny had always loved about him. He'd never even heard him say an unkind word about his mother, even though she'd walked out of their apartment one morning when they were still living in the city and never come back.

Though, now, Benny couldn't help but wonder if his dad maybe should have been more cautious around people. Then he might still be alive.

Benny glanced into the back seat to see if Ramona had anything to say about their conversation; she'd plugged her ears with wireless headphones and was sprawled out with one arm over her eyes. So he tried to follow his dad's advice and give Drue a chance. He kept talking.

"Anyway, this kid, right? He got separated from the caravan. He was little, five or six, and you don't survive out in the desert very long if you can't take care of yourself or don't have any water. I took an ATV out and found him. The GoCam caught all of it. Me picking him up in my buggy and everyone all excited when I got back and stuff. I think it made for a good vid. The aerial shots of us returning were pretty impressive."

"Wow," Drue said. "Lucky for you, I guess. Did they give you a medal or something?"

"No, it wasn't about . . ." Benny started. "In the caravan we all try to look out for each other. It's how we survive."

There was more in the application that Benny was leaving out – things like him helping others fix up their trucks and trailers, and teaching his younger brothers how to accelerate in the desert sand without digging themselves into a rut – but he didn't think Drue would be too impressed by all that. And there was another thing, too: the ending of the video, the last thing he filmed before sending it off to the EW-SCAB committee.

But that was personal.

Drue was quiet for a few seconds as he cracked his

knuckles. Finally, he weighed in. "No offence or anything, but living in an RV in the Drylands sounds terrible. No wonder you're so excited about space. Maybe you'll luck out and get to stay at the Taj and then you can kiss the Drylands bye-bye." He flashed a grin. "You can have a room next to mine. I'm going to be the newest member of Elijah's Pit Crew."

"Yeah," Benny said, trying to keep his cool in front of someone who'd just called his entire life *terrible*. "You and every other EW-SCABer thinks that. Right?" He motioned back to Ramona, who hiccupped – though he wasn't sure if this was a response or just a coincidence.

It was common knowledge that a few kids each year had been invited to stay at the Lunar Taj as permanent residents and pupils of Elijah West and his staff. Though no one really knew how these kids were chosen, it was rumoured that from the time you got into your Space Runner on Earth, you were being watched closely. And while a dozen EW-SCABers had stayed on the Moon since the scholarship was founded, only five were considered direct apprentices to Elijah himself: his elite Pit Crew. One person from each year had been given this honour – the exception being the previous year, when twins from Tokyo had accepted Elijah's invitation.

"Come on," Drue said. "Like you're not trying for a spot on the Crew, too?"

"Nah," Benny said. "What would I do when it's just super-rich people at the resort all the time? Besides, my family's back on Earth."

Drue let out on laugh. "You're nuts, man. But it's probably for the best. I've got a lock on that spot."

Benny leaned back in his seat, ignoring Drue. What would his family be doing without him, in their dirt-covered RV? His brothers were probably wrestling in one the bedroom in the back, that was barely big enough for a mattress, while his grandmother drove or worked on another of the multicoloured quilts she was always putting together in order to make their little home feel cosier. He hated to think of their cramped house on wheels while he was hurtling towards the most luxurious resort in the solar system, but he reminded himself for the hundredth time that day that he shouldn't feel bad about it. After all, when he returned to Earth in two weeks, things would be different for all of them. They'd stop scavenging for water and resources and move into an apartment. They'd have space. They could have their own *rooms*. Maybe he'd even have enough money for an entire house. Maybe a place with enough land that the dozens of vehicles that made up their caravan could camp on the lawn.

Drue pressed more buttons on the Space Runner's dash, changing the music. "This model does *not* have the upgraded sound package," he muttered. "Weak."

The Space Runner suddenly jerked and began to slow, causing a tingle to run from the top of Benny's spine down into his gut and Ramona to pop up in the back seat, bracing herself as best she could.

"Error, error," she murmured.

"What did you do?" Benny asked Drue.

"It's *so* your first time in one of these." Drue smirked. "We're just slowing down for the final descent. You nervous?"

"Not at all," Benny lied.

"It's only the Moon," Drue said, putting his hands behind his head. "Trust me: by the end of the second week you'll be hoping for an alien invasion to keep things interesting."

"Now *that* would be a story to take back to my brothers," Benny said. "Maybe the news is wrong and there *is* intelligent life out there."

It had been a decade since a deep space probe had found what scientists believed to be an abandoned alien outpost on Pluto. A few rock samples and tools were brought back to Earth by a collection bot, but it was widely believed by scientists that the place had been empty for millennia. Still, Benny reckoned that in the whole wide universe, there had to be other forms of life.

"Actually, I hope we're the only smart species," Drue said. "If not, then it's only a matter of time before all the aliens out there on sad planets figure out that the Taj is the nicest place in the galaxy. Then it'll be *really* hard to get into."

Benny snorted. "True. I'll be happy catching air in Moon buggies and exploring craters. And if I do somehow get bored, I'll just pull some pranks with the voice modulator I brought with me from home." At least his brothers hadn't swiped *that*, too.

"Voice modulator, huh? Old school. But I can see where it could be fun." Drue flashed a set of perfect white teeth. "Benny, I think you and I are going to get into a lot of trouble together."

CHAPTER 3

The Lunar Taj was a brilliant red palace adrift in a sea of grey. From space, the five-hundred-suite compound looked like a *W*, the top of which butted up to a dark section of the lunar surface that Benny had read was called the Sea of Tranquillity. A tower rose from the centre of the building – the middle peak of the *W*. Huge, scalloped sheets of gold topped it, all layered over one another, as if the building was crowned in a fireball frozen mid-explosion. It was a popular rumour that this was where Elijah West's private quarters were located because the man refused to sleep at a lower elevation than anybody else, though Benny wasn't sold on this particular story. He liked to think that Elijah was the same kind of person his father had been – just much, much richer. His father had slept on the floor of the RV or sometimes on the ground outside, letting his boys take the one big bed in the back and Benny's grandmother have the mattress in the alcove above the driver's seat. He was the kind of guy who wouldn't close his eyes for days if it meant that other people in the caravan could get some rest, and would chase the wildest leads in search of water, never giving up hope that tomorrow would be better. Always looking for an oasis in the desert.

Benny tried to live his life in the same way, believing that the future held great things for him and his family if they just worked hard enough. The EW-SCAB was kind of like their own unexpected oasis, he reckoned.

Inside the Space Runner, Drue pointed to a long chrome tunnel jutting out from one side of the transparent dome that was barely visible around the Taj.

"That's where we're headed," he said. "And there's another, smaller entry tunnel coming out of the garage – that building."

He motioned towards a shiny cube beside the Taj that looked like a full stop next to the W.

"You should maybe brace yourself," he continued. "This part can get kind of bumpy."

Benny glanced back at Ramona, who made a noise that was part gasp, part burp as she tightened her seat belt around her waist. He clenched his jaw and tried to put on a brave face, partly to make her feel less afraid and partly to trick himself into not being concerned about turbulence or what landing would be like. He was good at that. In his twelve years on Earth, he'd made sure that his little brothers had never seen him look frightened or worried, even once. Even when they were running short on water or having trouble finding a part to get their RV running again. He'd become pretty good at pretending everything was always OK. It was only after his family had gone to sleep that he'd let himself be afraid of anything.

Through his window, Benny watched as the fleet of Space Runners holding the other EW-SCAB winners began to drift towards one another. They were definitely the *shiniest* cars Benny had ever seen, the outside made of a silver metal so polished and reflective that it almost looked as though they were comets flying through space. They continued to slow in speed, until eventually they stopped moving completely about a mile above the Moon's surface.

"Ugh," Drue said, reclining. "This is the worst part."

Benny had just enough time to wonder if they'd stalled before all the vehicles were diving forward, heading towards the silvery tunnel. Benny gasped, goosebumps prickling all over his body as they sped towards the Moon's surface. It looked to him like they were going to plough right into the ground. Fortunately, the Space Runners were precision vehicles, and just when Benny was sure they'd crash, the cars all pulled up, changing flight patterns like a flock of silver birds, until they floated a mere metre above the rock below as they raced into the tunnel connecting them to the Lunar Taj.

From the outside, the entrance had looked like nothing more than a long, shining chrome hallway. Inside, however, the walls were awash with a rainbow of colour, casting a kaleidoscope of reflections all over the Space Runner and its interiors.

"This is incredible . . ." Benny murmured as he held out his hands and watched the colours run over them.

Suddenly Benny's gut felt like it was twisting into knots. He wrapped his arms around his stomach and leaned forward. That's when his ears popped, and the roar of the vehicles vibrated in his head, escalating until Benny thought he could actually *feel* the sound.

Ramona let out a worried gurgle from the back seat.

"We're entering the pressurised zone," Drue said, stretching his jaw. "Don't worry. We're almost through already."

Suddenly the colours and the roar were gone, and the Space Runners sped into the Taj's courtyard: the Grand Dome. One by one the cars circled in front of the resort, giving Benny his first real look at where he'd spend the next two weeks. His eyes darted about, trying, impossibly, to take in everything at once. The Lunar Taj had looked like a *W* from space, but up close it was something else entirely, a playground of light and colour and shiny surfaces. The building itself was built out of a dark, gleaming red metal. Gold stairs led up to the chrome front doors, which were three metres tall, at least. The windows, too, were outlined in glittering metals. In fact, it seemed to Benny as if everything was ablaze with light, from the tower roof with its blooming sheets of gold to the spotlights casting projections of star systems onto the sides of the building, as if the resort itself were a secret galaxy all its own. On the ground, plants of unnatural colours blossomed in bejewelled pots: palm trees with electric blue fronds, metallic roses, shrubs made of neon.

The sight of the Lunar Taj was enough to cause him to forget about the popping in his ears and spinning in his stomach. In the back seat, Ramona muttered a string of indecipherable exclamations as she stared out at the sparkling building.

"Impressive, right?" Drue asked as he watched Benny shove his face against the car's window. "I want a resort of my own like this one day. Built like a big *L*. No, no. All my initials. *DBL* spelled out across Jupiter."

"Isn't Jupiter mostly gas?" Benny whispered, not taking his eyes off the Taj.

"You know what I mean."

The Space Runners lined up in five neat rows in the centre of the courtyard, near a big chrome statue of a hand reaching out of a pool of water, its fingertips almost grazing a solar system of gemlike planets orbiting it. Benny's vehicle parked itself in the back corner. Once it had stopped and the doors unlocked, he took a second to catch his breath and then climbed out onto the inky black gravel. Ramona spilled out of the back seat, basically throwing herself onto the ground.

"Eagle has landed," she whispered. "Environment stabilised. Stand by for system diagnostics."

"Uhh . . ." Benny started, but she waved for him to leave her alone as she climbed into a sitting position, leaning against the side of the vehicle.

The other kids were exiting their Space Runners and gathering near the fountain in front of the resort. Benny hadn't really met any of them back on Earth. In fact, half the Space Runners had taken off from different parts of the world and joined his group once they were already in flight. The scholarship winners came from all over the globe, sporting everything from shaved heads to waist-length braids woven with metallic thread, but they were all united in their awe of the resort in front of them.

Except maybe Drue, who pushed his floating travel bag around to the passenger's side, stepped over Ramona's legs, and put his hands on his hips.

"All right, let's see what they've got lined up for us. I hope I'm on the top floor or else . . ."

His mouth hung open like he had something else to say, but no words came out.

"Drue, what are you—"

"Shhh, shh, shh, Benny," Drue said, shaking his head and nodding forward.

It was only then that Benny realised Drue was looking at two girls unloading their Space Runner a few metres away from them. One was petite, with black hair cut into a short bob. The other girl was hoisting an overstuffed piece of luggage out of the back seat. A mountain of blond curls fell over her shoulders and added a few centimetres to her already impressive height.

"It just seems really . . . *fragile*," the blonde said. "Like, I'm a little freaked out that some idiot is going to throw one of these rocks at it and then it's bye-bye life because I'm sucked out into space. "

"The glass is really a secondary defence against the

37

outside elements," the other girl said. "Mostly for show. It's not even *glass*, but a practically indestructible polymer created by Elijah and his researchers. Besides, if something did happen and the dome was breached, you'd need to be much more worried about all the *oxygen* getting sucked out, not *you*."

The blonde girl frowned. "You're not making me feel any better."

Drue poked Benny with his elbow. "I think we just met our first Moon friend."

"Let me guess," Benny said. "The girl with the bag that looks like it's about to explode?"

"Psh," Drue scoffed, heading towards the girls. "Dream bigger, Benny."

"Huh?"

But Drue was already several steps ahead of him. Benny followed, half because he didn't know what else to do, and half because he figured there was a high probability that Drue was about to embarrass himself, and *that* he kind of wanted to see.

"Hey, there," Drue said when he was just a couple of metres away from the girls. Both turned and stared back at him, confused. "I'm Drue Bob Lincoln."

"I'm Jas—" the shorter girl began.

"Jazz." He shoved his hand out. "That's a cool name."

She started to protest but he ignored her, turning to the blonde girl. "You?"

"Hot Dog," she said flatly, raising one eyebrow and pursing her lips. "And you interrupted my friend here."

The other girl glanced at Hot Dog as if surprised for a second, before turning back to Drue, her eyes penetrating, sizing him up.

"I didn't mean to!" Drue said, flashing a smile at her. "Please, tell me more. Where're you from?"

"My name is *Jasmine*," she said. "Jasmine Wu. And, I'm sorry, did you say 'Drue Bob Lincoln'? As in, the senator?"

Drue shrugged.

"Technically I'm Drue Bob Lincoln the third. The senator's my father."

Benny wasn't exactly surprised about this news. It at least explained a lot of what Drue had said in the car. Neither of the girls seemed impressed, though, and as Drue winked at Jasmine, Benny wondered if it would be best to just slink away and abandon his travel mate.

"I noticed your necklace," Drue continued, pointing to the gleaming silver charm around her neck, a stylised *W* breaking out of a triangle, with a small black diamond in the centre. It was the same design as the hood ornaments on the original Space Runners. "That . . ." Drue laughed a little, shaking his head. "What am I thinking? It's not real, right? Elijah only had one hundred of those made for the original Space Runner engineers. I've been trying to track one down for *years*."

Jasmine's hand went up to the necklace, gripping it as she stared at Drue. "A senator's son . . ." Her eyes narrowed a little. "You must be the reason there are a hundred and one of us and not a hundred," she said. The look she gave Drue wasn't a glare, exactly. More a combination of disappointment and disgust.

Drue straightened his back.

"I deserve to be up here just as much as you do," Drue said.

"Right." Hot Dog looked him up and down, nodding at his suit and floating luggage. "So you're some rich kid senator's son who decided he wanted a holiday. I hope you at least had to pay for your ride."

Drue's mouth hung open, but he didn't seem able to form any actual words. As much as Benny was enjoying this, he thought he should introduce himself and maybe save Drue some face.

"Uh, I'm Benny. I was in the same Space Runner as Drue." He pointed a thumb over his shoulder. "That's

Ramona on the ground. I think. She's . . . interesting. So, you're Jasmine and . . . Hot Dog? That can't be your real name, right?"

"Of course not," Hot Dog said.

"Where'd you get the nickname?"

She tossed her hair.

"Get me behind the wheel of a Space Runner and you'll find out for yourself."

"Uh," Jasmine said, gesturing behind Benny. "Guys?"

Benny turned to find a vehicle unlike any he'd ever seen shooting into the Grand Dome from the entrance tunnel. It was a deep, shiny crimson and had a body similar to that of the Space Runner he'd just been in, only thinner. There was something else weird about the car, too. None of the Space Runners Benny had ever seen used wheels. On Earth, they floated above the streets just as easily as they did through space. Since the hyper-drives inside altered gravity and provided propulsion, there was no reason to include tyres in the design, except those that stayed up inside the car's body and were deployed only in emergencies. But the Space Runner speeding out of the entrance tunnel had three black spheres on the bottom – two in the back, one in the front – rolling over the ground.

And it was rocketing straight towards them.

"Look out," Jasmine shouted, jumping back and almost knocking Benny down.

As fast as the car was going, there was very little chance they could get out of its way in time. Still, Benny moved on instinct. In one swift motion he had grabbed Jasmine and Hot Dog's arms and was pulling them away as Drue yelped for help.

Just as the vehicle was within a few metres of Benny and the others, it turned sharply and slid sideways. In the second before it should have crashed into them, there was a low thumping sound and a flash of light from underneath the car, and then it was in the air, rotating. Benny could swear he heard screaming from inside as it spun over his head.

The car flipped a few more times, clearing the lined-up Space Runners. It landed, twisted back to face its original direction, and then finally came to a complete stop directly in front of the steps leading up to the Lunar Taj.

"Dude!" Drue said, bolting towards the new arrival and leaving the others behind.

"You OK?" Benny asked the girls. He realised he was still holding their arms, and quickly let go, shoving his hands into the pockets of his space suit. Jasmine nodded warily. And Hot Dog just laughed for a second before darting off herself.

By the time Benny pushed through the crowds to get to the car, he found Drue wedged halfway underneath its bumper, scoping out the undercarriage. Hot Dog stood a couple of metres away from it, eyes full of admiration.

"This is the most beautiful thing I've ever seen," she said.

The passenger door opened, folding back and into the car as if the entire construction was an elaborate piece of metal origami.

"Ohmigosh," Hot Dog whispered beside Benny, the syllables stringing together into one word.

A woman stepped out, wearing what appeared to be hundreds of draped layers of gauzy white fabric that made her look as if she was enveloped in a cloud.

"No way! Is that really her?" Hot Dog asked. Then she gasped, covering her mouth with both hands and muffling her voice. "Her hair's *metallic*. And she's got antigravity hair clips in! Look at it float! It's like she's underwater!"

The woman looked very, very unhappy.

". . . drives like a maniac . . ." Benny heard her say as she stomped away from the car.

"Is she famous or something?" he asked.

"Uh, yeah." Hot Dog's eyes went wide. "She won the last season of *Heart-throb or Hologram?!*"

Benny looked back to the woman, who was now all smiles as she posed for pictures and holovids with some of the other kids who had definitely recognised her. In seconds, two fashionably dressed people darted out of the Taj's front doors and were corralling all the EW-SCAB winners into one big photo opportunity.

Hot Dog started forward to join them, but stopped after a few steps, turning her attention back to the car. Meanwhile, Drue crawled out from under the Space Runner and started to walk around it, letting his fingers smudge the thin layer of Moon dust that had settled on the vehicle.

"This must be some kind of prototype," he whispered in reverence. "Check out this paint job. I think those ghost flames are made of microscopic LED particles."

He didn't seem to notice the pilot's side door folding open, but Benny did. A man stepped out, the gold tips of his black cowboy boots glinting as gravel crunched beneath his feet. Benny instantly recognised the guy's trademark facial hair: a close-cut reddish-brown beard with three horizontal lines shaved into each side.

Elijah West.

CHAPTER 4

Elijah West was barely out of the car before two people in matching black coveralls were by his side. Both of them had long, slender noses that looked as though they'd been broken and reset at awkward angles. The man was nearly two metres tall – a bald mountain. The woman was shorter and built sturdily, the kind of person Benny would have liked to have with him when lugging around scrap. She definitely wasn't from the Drylands, though. The left side of her head was shaved, and the rest of her short, dyed-magenta hair was pushed to the right.

"She runs like a dream, but the acceleration's got a ways to go," Elijah said, taking off a pair of black driving gloves with gold studs on the knuckles. He tossed them and his keys to the big guy in coveralls. As he continued, the woman pulled out a HoloTek and made notes. "Let's punch up the horsepower. The new wheels are better, but we're going to need a different tread or more weight because I'm sliding all over the dust out there." He pulled off a fur-lined coat to reveal a dark red space suit covered in intricate stitching that pulsed with light. "And the brakes are too sensitive. The whole driving experience is just a little too . . . smooth. I want to feel like I'm behind the wheel of a muscle car, not a luxury SR."

"Maybe we should work on a motor and antigravity combo propulsion system?" the woman asked, not looking up from the screen.

Elijah smirked as he pushed a pair of aviator sunglasses to the top of his head to reveal big, hazel eyes.

"Now you're speaking my language, Ash."

"Bo and Ashley McGuyver," Hot Dog whispered. "The best mechanics in the universe."

Benny wasn't sure if she'd been talking to him or herself. He was still in a state of shock. He'd been on the Moon for all of five minutes and he'd already nearly been hit by a car *and* was standing within a few metres of Elijah West. Fortunately, the *Heart-throb or Hologram?* celebrity and her assistants were still taking photographs with their backs to the courtyard, meaning most of the kids hadn't realised Elijah was there.

"Good news," Ash continued. She motioned to the bigger guy. "Bo's finished retrofitting that Chevelle you had shipped up. She's ready for a spin outside the resort whenever you are."

A smile took over Elijah's face. "I'll take her out now."

"Oh, no you don't!" A woman's voice came from somewhere behind Benny.

Elijah frowned – just for a flash. Benny turned around in time for a woman wearing a tailored pink suit to walk through him.

The chill that went down his back was so strong he thought for a second his knees might give out.

"Whoa," Hot Dog said beside him. "Ghost woman on the Moon."

But it wasn't a ghost. Benny turned back around to get a better look at what he guessed was an incredibly realistic hologram, way more advanced than his spider back on Earth. There must have been a swarm of microscopic hover-mechs projecting her image from somewhere.

"Pinky," Elijah said, his smile coming back, "why do you sound so upset? Don't tell me Trevone's been trying to hack you again. You know it's only to look for flaws in your security."

"I do not have security problems, thank you very much. Of course, you'd never know if I did because *you had me muted.*"

"You kept trying to get me to do things I didn't want to." Elijah shrugged. "Besides, you do have the capability to unmute yourself."

Her hands curled into small, tight fists before motioning for Elijah to follow her away from the Taj and around one side of the fountain so they could talk more quietly – and so they wouldn't be in the background of all the photos still being taken at the entrance. Benny crept around the other side of the big metal hand, trying to figure out where Pinky's image was being projected from.

Pinky took a deep breath, tucked a strand of white-blond hair that had fallen out of her bun behind her ear, and continued. "I had to explain to three European royals, half a dozen internet TV egos, and the CEO of HoloTek Japan that they'd all have to leave in preparation for our scholarship arrivals without getting to talk to you in the flesh. Even though you'd *apparently* promised all of them that you'd see them off personally. If you had actually bothered to tell me you weren't going to be here . . ."

"Relax, Pinky," Elijah said. "I'll handle everything. And besides, you were the one who suggested I take that woman out for a tour."

"Yesterday," Pinky said. "You were scheduled to take her out *yesterday*. And don't think I didn't see that you went on a short joyride instead of out to the see the old Moon landing site like you were supposed to."

"Not short enough," Elijah said, glancing over his shoulder. "If I had to listen to her talk about her burgeoning singing career any more, I'd have walked out of the Space Runner without a helmet on. Speaking of which, will you make sure she and her handlers are on the transport back to Earth with the last of the guests and seasonal staff in an hour?"

"Impressive tech," Jasmine said from Benny's left. He hadn't even realised she'd come up beside him. The water in the fountain must have covered the noise of her footsteps.

"Yeah," he said. "Impressive, angry tech."

"At least the EW-SCABers got a few pics with her," Elijah continued.

"Please don't call them that," Pinky said. "It sounds so disgusting."

"What? I think it's funny."

"I don't know why I even bother making schedules if you're just going to ignore them." Pinky sighed.

Elijah smiled at her. "You're being dramatic."

"No. Not yet, but I'm about to be. There's something else. Take a look at the readings we've got from the deep

49

space probes. I found some anomalies that at first we thought were solar winds but now . . . well, I'm not sure what they are."

Elijah tapped once on a slim band wrapped around his right wrist, and a series of graphs appeared in front of him. They were made of light, but he swiped through them as if they were tangible.

"How is he doing that?" Benny whispered.

"Must be some kind of motion sensor," Jasmine surmised.

With each swipe, Elijah's eyebrows drew closer and closer together until finally they were almost touching. Benny watched the graphs pass by, but they might as well have been in a foreign language to him.

"You're sure there hasn't been an equipment malfunction?" Elijah asked. "These readings don't make any sense."

"All probes are functioning normally. I've triple-checked everything," Pinky said.

"What is that?" Jasmine asked. She put one foot up on the side of the fountain to lean forward and get a closer look at the projections, knocking a few rocks into the water as she did so.

Elijah glanced over his shoulder and did a double take, pushing the charts out of the way with one wave of his hand.

"Jasmine Wu," he said. He nodded to her necklace. "You got my gift. I'm glad."

She froze, staring up at him.

"Y-you know who I am?" she stammered.

"Your suggested changes to our manufacturing process for hyperdrive engines increased productivity by three percent," he said. "Of course I know who you are."

"Technically it was a little *less* than three percent," she murmured.

Elijah didn't smile, exactly – it was more of a look of approval, Benny thought.

Drue was suddenly pushing past Jasmine and extending his hand to Elijah.

"Mr West. It's an honour. You may remember meeting me last year. I just wanted you to know that—"

"I know who you are, though not because we've apparently met," he said. Then he turned away from Drue and nodded to Pinky. "Prepare a report for me on these charts. I'll review them before dinner."

"Elijah," she said, "there are guests waiting for you. The *charts*. Where are you—"

"They can wait, Pinky. Right now I've got a date with an American classic."

And then he was heading towards big frosted-glass doors

that led into the garage, Pinky and the McGuyvers trailing after him. Now, it was easy for Benny to see why he'd thought the building glowed from space: the exterior was covered in the same highly reflective metal as the Space Runners.

Benny looked at Drue, who was standing perfectly still, his hand held out even though Elijah was gone. Finally he let it drop, and his face softened a little. Benny saw something flash in his eyes. When he spoke again, he sounded friendlier. "So, Jazz, you really helped him overhaul his manufacturing?"

"It was nothing," Jasmine said as she shoved her necklace inside her space suit, avoiding looking any of them in the eyes.

"Really? Because it sounded pretty impressive."

"It was just a matter of having a specific outcome in mind and looking at all the possible ways I could get to it."

"Wait," Drue said. "Are you the person who suggested that they recycle the fission coolant to be used as secondary radiation shielding?"

Jasmine blinked, finally looking at him. "That's right."

"I'm glad they managed to find some people as smart as I am." Drue grinned. "So, listen, next time you talk to

Elijah, put in a good word for me, OK, Jazz? Tell him I've got a ton of great ideas."

Jasmine just stared back at him.

Hot Dog raised an eyebrow, leaning towards Benny. "You spent the entire flight from Earth with him?"

Benny shrugged. "He was asleep most the time."

By this time, the kids had all realised that Elijah was in the courtyard, and everyone was following him in a massive swarm, keeping a few metres of distance, as if they were afraid to get too close. He paused in front of the entrance to the garage, turning to the rest of the kids gathered behind him. Standing before Elijah in their matching space suits, Benny thought they looked kind of like a miniature army, ready to follow their beloved commander.

"Hello," Elijah said with a bulletproof smile. "Welcome to the future." His voice boomed through the courtyard, pumping out of hidden speakers. "I hope you're all ready for an exciting life up here on the Moon." And then his expression changed, for a moment looking somehow sad. "This year's scholarship winners represent the most impressive applicants I've ever had the pleasure of welcoming to the Taj. I have such high hopes for all of you."

He held out a hand, and the big man in coveralls gave

him back his black driving gloves. Then Elijah turned and walked through the garage doors.

Drue, Hot Dog and Jasmine immediately turned their attention back to the custom Space Runner. Benny's mind was still buzzing over the hologram technology he'd just seen. He'd known the Taj was full of electronic wonders, but to see them up close and in action was something he couldn't have prepared himself for. He wondered what kind of holograms he might be able to design if he had access to that sort of tech. The insane pranks he could pull. Intangible zombies rising out of the football field to attack opposing teams. Holographic monsters waiting under his brothers' bed. The stuff he had at home – the ramshackle machines and electronics that made up their caravan – might as well have been prehistoric in comparison.

Who needed spiders?

He tried to make a mental list of everything that had happened so far as he looked at the sky. Hundreds of thousands of miles away was Earth. His family. The Moon was sure to have all kinds of new experiences waiting for him, but part of the excitement was knowing he'd get to tell his brothers all about them when he got home. After all, they were the main reason he was up here in the first place – apart from the obvious excitement of going to the Moon. Their minds would be blown by the Space Runner trip alone, and he hadn't even set foot inside the resort.

As he stared at the planet above him, Benny promised himself that he'd get at least one good adventure out of his time at the Lunar Taj. Something to share when he got back home. Maybe he'd even figure out a way to bring some of the magic back to Earth with him. Not just money. And something more meaningful than Moon rocks or holovids.

CHAPTER 5

"**A** hem."

The sound of a throat being cleared filled the Grand Dome. It took Benny a moment of looking around before he realised a man was standing behind a chrome podium beside the front doors of the Taj.

"Hello?" His deep voice boomed. "If I could have your attention."

He snapped his fingers and his image was projected on either side of the Taj, nine metres high, at least. Even in the video Benny could tell that he was exceptionally tall and so thin that he wondered if the man simply floated away whenever he stepped out of the resort's artificial gravity field.

"Gather round," the man said, motioning for the kids scattered across the courtyard to come closer. He paused, looking up at his image on the side of the wall and taking a moment to smooth down the pointy beard on his chin, which was dyed the same minty green colour as his hair. "We'll have plenty of time for meet and greets later, but we've got a schedule to keep. My name is Max Étoile. Once, I was talent manager to the stars, but now . . . now I live among them!"

He flung his arm dramatically towards the sky and stayed that way, frozen, for a few seconds before continuing.

"Life on Earth was glamorous, but when Elijah West offers you a spot managing the Lunar Taj, you don't say no. Not that you're our *normal* clientele. Let's get you all accounted for so we can begin orientation. The first thing we're going to do is get you set up with a new state-of-the-art Lunar Taj HoloTek that will guide you through the rest of your stay *and* give you your room and group assignments. If you'll make your way inside in an orderly fashion, you can sign in at any of the guest check-in terminals using your biosignature and—"

The crowd of kids surged forward, pushing past Max and through the entry doors.

"An orderly fashion!" he said again, sighing into the microphone.

"Let's go!" Drue shouted back to Benny before running forward.

Jasmine and Hot Dog started after him. Benny was at

the tail end of the group, but he didn't mind – it meant that when he stopped, breathless, inside the doors to gape at the main lobby of the Lunar Taj, there was nobody to run him down.

The lobby was four storeys high, with walls that were at first metallic blue but then began to shift, until Benny realised that the entire room was made up of screens slowly cycling through the colour spectrum. The floors were black marble, speckled with just enough gold leaf to make it look like he was standing on the night sky. On one wall hung a portrait of Elijah in a silver tuxedo. It must have been five times Benny's height. Along another wall were framed paintings of speculative Lunar Taj designs and various blueprints. On the opposite end of the room, giant windows looked out onto the lunar landscape.

Benny walked up to one of the check-in terminals. A gold-framed sketch of what appeared to be a first-generation Space Runner hung above it. Elijah's signature was at the bottom right corner, dated almost ten years ago. Benny would have been two years old when Elijah was drawing this. It was shortly before his father lost his job and his mother had left. Right before they'd been forced to leave their home and join the caravan because they couldn't afford the rent any more.

A flash of light in front of him broke his train of thought. An outline of his body and heartbeat appeared on the wall, identifying him based on his unique biological signature.

"Check-in complete," Pinky's voice said. "Welcome, Benny Love, to the Lunar Taj. You're going to have a great time. Please take your complimentary HoloTek for further information."

A panel slid away on the wall, revealing a sleek rectangle that appeared to be made of glass or some kind of shiny plastic. The top left and bottom right corners of the device were edged in chrome. As he picked it up, the electronic screen powered on, and he realised that by pulling on the metal corners, the HoloTek could stretch instantly from a pocket-size gadget to a thirty-centimetre-wide tablet. It was the type of hyperfast computing equipment he'd always dreamed of owning but never could in real life.

Until now.

On the wall in front of him, he saw his heartbeat speed up before the image faded away.

"What room are you in?" Drue asked, coming up beside him. The boy was tapping away at his own HoloTek, hardly looking up at Benny.

"Huh?"

"Bottom right on your screen. What do you have?"

It was only then that Benny noticed a small red horse on his HoloTek. The numeral twenty-six was glowing on its side.

"Number twenty-six? A horse?"

"Horse here, too! But I'm number one." Drue grinned. "Let's go see what those girls got."

He grabbed Benny's sleeve and dragged him away from the wall, eyes scanning the crowds until he spotted his targets near the windows at the other end of the lobby.

"Hey, so what rooms are you girls in?" he asked as he approached. "This might shock you, but I got—"

"Drue, shut up," Hot Dog said. "Look at this view."

"Hey, I was just trying to—" Drue started.

"Whoa," Benny said, interrupting him. Beyond the four-storey floor-to-ceiling windows in front of him, a swatch of carbon-coloured land extended for miles to the horizon, eventually giving way to a starry sky. It was so utterly still that for a moment Benny was sure he was looking at a high-definition picture. But he wasn't. This was real.

"Mare Tranquillitatis," Jasmine said, her voice breathy, barely above a whisper. "Also known as the Sea of Tranquillity."

"It's where Apollo Eleven landed," Drue said. He pointed. "Look, you can almost make out the American flag, right by that glowing alien."

"What?" Hot Dog asked, pressing her face up against the window. "Where?"

Drue snorted.

"He's trying to be funny," Jasmine said, glaring at him for a second. "The landing site is on the other side."

Benny raised his hand to the glass, placing one finger on the point where the surface of the Moon and the sky met. The landscape seemed oddly familiar, not unlike that of the Drylands, just without wind blowing dust around everywhere. He wondered if he'd feel at home out there, too, racing across the grey plains.

"Barely into the first day and the resort is already getting gummed up by grubby little hands," Max said from behind them, tapping one shiny purple shoe on the floor.

They all took a step back from the window.

"Pinky, get them to their rooms and arrange to have these windows cleaned as soon as everyone's gone. Elijah may be treating this place like a sleepaway camp but it's *still* a luxury resort."

Pinky's voice was then everywhere, reverberating through the lobby. Her image appeared on one of the walls. This time she wore a pair of glasses with thick black frames.

"Please note your room assignments on the bottom right corner of your new HoloTeks. Because of the number of scholarship winners this year, we've broken you up into four randomly assigned groups that you'll stay in for the remainder of your visit. The teams will be led by members of Elijah's Pit Crew, and will be staying on separate floors. Throughout the next two weeks, your team will be your family, and you'll compete against the other groups in a variety of challenges. There may even be a special prize for the team who proves to be the most courageous, ambitious and brainiest."

"This is it," Drue said. "I bet this is how they'll pick who gets to stay."

"I'd better be on a good team," Hot Dog said.

Benny glanced at Jasmine and Hot Dog's HoloTeks. They both had horses as well. At least he'd already met a few other members of his group.

"Oh, man, I've gotta be on the Miyamura team. *Please* let me be on the Miyamura team," Drue whispered. "Those twins are the fastest racers in the universe behind Elijah. I need to know their speed secrets."

"I hope I'm with Trevone from the second EW-SCAB

year," Jasmine said. "He's so smart. I read his interview in *Lunar Wired* last month and he's just—" she blushed – "so *interesting*."

"On the first floor we'll have the Firebirds, led by Sahar Hakimi," Pinky said. Sahar's face appeared above the icon of a golden bird, tail feathers splayed out like flames. Her eyes were piercing, the same dark colour as the scarf wrapped around her neck and head.

"I tried to talk her into letting me drive her car when I visited the Taj last summer," Drue said. "I thought she was going to break my face."

"I hear she hardly says a word," Hot Dog said.

"She doesn't have to. Her eyes are very, uh, *expressive*. I could definitely tell what was going through her head that day."

Benny had read that Sahar was from the Middle East and came from a caravan similar to his. They'd tried to cross a desert, but something had gone wrong along the way. They'd run out of water, or maybe it was petrol – Benny'd seen several versions of the story, but Sahar herself had never gone on record. All he knew for sure was that in the end, only she had emerged from the desert, barely alive. The next year, she'd gone to the Moon.

"On the second floor," Pinky continued, "are the Chargers, led by Trevone Jordan."

A blue lightning bolt appeared below Trevor's photo.

"Of course," Jasmine said quietly. "It's his favourite colour."

"The Vipers will have joint leaders – the Tokyo twins, Kai and Kira Miyamura – on floor number three."

Drue looked back and forth between the red horse on the screen and the smaller one on his HoloTek.

"Crap," he muttered.

"That means—" Benny started, but he was cut off by Hot Dog's gasp.

"Finally, the Mustangs will be on the fourth floor, led by Ricardo Rocha," Pinky said.

"The beast from Brazil!" Hot Dog half shouted. There were practically hologram hearts in her eyes. "The only person from the first scholarship year to be invited to stay on the Moon. Did you know he was living in an abandoned building and leading a street gang in South America before he got invited to the Taj?"

"It wasn't a gang," Drue said. "It was an amateur football team that ran drills in the streets. I don't know how *he* was the one who got picked to stay up here. He's not even a very good pilot."

But Hot Dog either didn't notice Drue was talking or didn't care about what he had to say.

Pinky smiled. "Now, please make your way to the lifts at the back of the lobby and find your rooms. Simply place your hand on the door to unlock it – the room is already keyed to your unique biosignature. And once again, welcome to the Lunar Taj. I guarantee it's an experience you won't forget."

CHAPTER 6

Benny stopped half a metre inside his assigned room. The rucksack he had slung over one shoulder dropped, hitting the floor behind him. He'd been expecting the place to be nice, but hadn't really given a lot of thought as to what that might actually look like. And now he was here, standing in a suite that was at least ten times bigger than his RV on Earth. Everything was plush material and dark, polished metal, the walls a slate grey with thick red stripes shooting across the room. Huge pictures of distant planets and celestial bodies hung in metallic frames on all the walls except the furthest one, by the bed, which was just one big window looking out onto the Moon. There were multiple sofas, a small dining table, and—

There was a flicker of light a few metres away from him, and suddenly a woman with blond hair piled high on top of her head was standing beside a tufted chair.

"Hello there, Mr Love," she said.

Benny took a step back, nearly tripping over his bag as he let out a string of half-words.

The woman smirked. "Sorry, I probably should have warned you before I appeared. We haven't been *officially* introduced. I'm Pinky, the artificial intelligence who runs the Lunar Taj, and your personal concierge for the duration of your stay. We've found that our guests are much more comfortable being able to visualise the entity keeping their oxygen regulated and appointments in order instead of trusting a dismembered voice. And, as a privacy measure for our guests, my holographic form serves as a reminder that I'm not always watching or listening. I'm only present in your room when I'm *here*, if that makes sense. Do you understand, Mr Love?"

Benny stared back at her in silence.

"No one's ever called me Mr Love before."

"Would you prefer Benny?"

He nodded. Pinky smiled.

"All right, Benny. How about a quick tour?" She turned away from him, motioning to the kitchen at her left. "Against my nutritional recommendations, Elijah insisted that the pantries be stocked with all sorts of packaged snacks and pastries in addition to fruits and vegetables grown in our lower-level greenhouses."

Benny made a mental note to fill his rucksack with anything left over on the last day – free souvenirs for his brothers.

Pinky continued, leading him deeper into the room.

"This wardrobe is full of custom-fit space suits and some casual clothing for downtime. Of course, that's all yours to take with you in two weeks. This desk is equipped with a holosurface that can project three-dimensional images of the resort, your daily schedule, et cetera. Ah, and the entire wall across from your bed is a screen operated by your new HoloTek. You should find any sort of media you want streaming from our servers – music, videos, games. We have everything."

"Everything?" Benny asked. He'd rarely been able to pick up enough of a signal to watch clips of cartoons whenever they were deep in the Drylands, and now he had anything he wanted at his fingertips, presented in trillions of ultradef pixels.

Pinky nodded. "If we don't have it already, we'll get it for you. Just say the word. Now, a next-gen gaming system is built into the server. You'll find instructions on operating the holographic interface on your HoloTek, but there are a variety of controllers on the dresser should you prefer something a little more old-school. Apart from that, everything should be self-explanatory. Is there any way I can be of service now, before I go?" Pinky asked.

Benny could feel goosebumps prickling his arms underneath his space suit. He was pretty sure it wasn't from the sight of the room alone.

"It's kind of cold," he said.

"The suite is set at an optimal temperature of twenty-one degrees Celsius," Pinky said. Then she adjusted her glasses and bounced her head back and forth. "Of course, that's probably a little chilly for someone coming from the Drylands."

Benny felt warmer air blow across his face from a hidden vent.

Pinky continued. "This should be more comfortable, but if you'd like an adjustment, just let me know. All you have to do is say my name. Otherwise, please enjoy yourself." She grinned, and then she was gone, blinked out of existence in an instant.

Benny stood still for a few moments, unsure of what to do first. Eventually he started walking around slowly, looking at all the shiny surfaces and electronics. Everything was so *clean*. He was almost afraid to touch anything for fear of getting grime on it. Despite all the amenities, though, the thing that he ended up focusing on was the kitchen sink. He stood in front of it, just staring for a while, before turning on the tap and taking a step back. For someone who'd spent most of his life in the desert searching for clean water, seeing a seemingly endless supply shooting out of the tap was almost as exhilarating as the high-tech electronics or the fact that he was on the Moon at all. He splashed his face, and then drank deeply from the stream – huge gulps that hurt his throat – before suddenly feeling guilty and turning it off. The tap seemed almost wasteful, too indulgent, though he assumed the water would be recycled somehow and that the people who normally visited the Taj were probably far less concerned with such things.

It didn't take him long to unpack his stuff once he managed to stop gawking over his temporary accommodation. He didn't have many belongings on Earth to begin with, apart from a handful of gadgets he'd either salvaged or traded for, and knowing that the resort was going to provide space suits, he hadn't brought much in the way of clothes. He tossed a few ragged T-shirts in one corner and fished out the small voice modulator he'd packed and placed it on the bedside table. At least his little brothers hadn't taken *that*. He pulled his beaten-up old HoloTek from his rucksack, the screen cracked and clouded with dirt that had somehow become embedded in the datapad, and then tapped on his shiny new device to start a data transfer, importing all his old files. After a few seconds, the transfer was complete, and he scrolled through some videos to make sure everything seemed in order. Most of them were outtakes from his scholarship vid. There was one, though, that looked unfamiliar. He checked the file's info and found it had been created the day before. He tapped on it.

To his surprise, the video began to play not just on the HoloTek but on the wall across from him as well. His grandmother and two younger brothers sat inside their RV, threadbare curtains tacked up over the windows, dust motes floating in the shafts of light that poured through the many holes. Their faces were all smiles, blown up to huge proportions and illuminating Benny's room.

"Hi, Benny!" all three of them said at once, waving. He wondered when they could have recorded this – maybe while he was out saying goodbye to the rest of the caravan.

"We wanted to leave you a surprise," his grandmother said. "I hope you find this! Otherwise we messed up. Boys, tell your brother that you love him."

Both his brothers rolled their eyes, putting up a fight for a few seconds.

71

"Just don't forget about us," Alejandro, the youngest, said.

"Sure, and bring us back some cool stuff." Justin grinned.

"Oh, yeah, and we took your holospider out of your bag. If you want it back for your trip, tell us before you leave, OK?"

"And tell Elijah how cool I am. I'll be old enough to apply next year!"

His brothers started to bicker over which of them deserved to go to the Moon before the other. Benny sat on the bed, his knees feeling wobbly. It made no sense, given the extreme luck he'd had in winning the EW-SCAB, but suddenly he kind of wished he were back on Earth.

Eventually, his grandmother turned the camera so that it focused only on her. She was all smiles, her darkly tanned flesh crinkling like raisin skin around her eyes.

"Your father would be so proud," she said, tears threatening to fall at any moment. "You know that, right, Benicio?"

The video ended like that, with her frozen, staring into the camera, as if waiting for him to respond.

Benny set the HoloTek down and fished the last remaining item out of the bottom of his rucksack. A tarnished silver hood ornament in the abstract shape of a human. The figure appeared to be moving so quickly through the air that its body blurred, trailing behind it like wings or the tail of a comet. His father had pulled it off an old car he and Benny had found on a salvage trip one day when Benny was six or seven.

"See this?" his dad had asked. "This is like us. Always moving forward. We keep going, no matter what. We never give up."

Benny brushed a piece of lint off the statue and put it on the nightstand beside his bed. It looked shabby in the high-tech room. Benny could relate.

He wasn't surprised his brothers had taken the spider but left the hood ornament. The three of them might have spent a lot of their days pulling pranks on one another and fighting over toys or tech, but Justin and Alejandro both knew what that silver piece of metal meant to Benny. Each of them had mementos that the others knew were off-limits. Stuff from their father. Salvaged junk that meant the world to them. Now that their dad was gone, it was all they had of him other than their memories.

It hadn't even been a year since he'd led a small team out into the Drylands in search of water. Only two people had returned. Benny's father was not one of them. In the course of a day, the world as Benny knew it had ended.

Benny had already been filming for his EW-SCAB video when it happened – he had *always* planned to try for the scholarship. But he'd almost abandoned the application in the week following his father's death. Part of this was because of sheer exhaustion. He spent all his time making sure his brothers were OK, talking to them or trying to distract them when tears cut streaks down their dust-covered cheeks. He tried to turn himself into a rock, stone-faced, promising them he'd never leave – another reason he almost gave up on the EW-SCAB. It was only at night that he let himself really think about his father, when he'd climb up to the top of the RV after everyone else was asleep and wonder how in the world they were going to survive without him. One night, he'd taken the hood ornament up to the roof and realised that his dad would have wanted him to apply. Of *course* he would have. He'd want Benny to keep fighting, keep trying for everything he yearned for in life. Always moving forward. Never giving up. And what Benny wanted more than anything was to help his family.

So he went for it. He poured every ounce of his heart into his application materials.

And somehow that had been enough to get him this far.

Now, with the hood ornament on his bedside table, he

almost felt like his father had guided him there. And he knew that despite being away from his family right now, he'd be back soon. He'd take care of them. He'd be the kind of person his dad would have wanted him to be.

CHAPTER 7

A soft electronic ping sounded all around Benny's suite, and suddenly the frozen image of his family was gone from the screen.

Pinky's voice filled the room.

"Message received from Ricardo Rocha. Would you like to view it now?"

"Uh . . ." Benny said, jumping to his feet. "Yes?"

The Pit Crew member appeared on the wall, his chin held high, arms crossed across the chest of his dark red space suit.

"Greetings, Mustangs," he said in a deep, slightly accented voice. "It's an honour to have you on my team. Please join me in the common room at the end of the hallway near the lifts." He set his square jaw, eyes staring straight into Benny's. "Now."

Benny immediately started for the door. There was something commanding in Ricardo's voice – maybe because as the first Crew member he was almost five years older than Benny – that left no room for hesitation. The other Mustangs must have felt the same way, because by the time Benny got to the common room, they were almost all there, making small talk and comparing HoloTek apps as 3D images of red horses galloped or reared back silently along the walls. He spotted Hot Dog using her HoloTek's camera to see herself as she fixed her hair. Ramona, unsurprisingly, had her face close to a screen as she lounged in a chair against one wall. Jasmine was on the other side of the room, leaning against a corner with her hands in her pockets as she stared at the floor.

Drue was standing near the door, talking to a girl Benny hadn't met yet. He watched as she rolled her eyes and walked away from him, flicking two long dark braids behind her. Drue crossed his arms and made a face at her as she left, then scanned the room until he saw Benny. His eyes lit up as he waved him over.

Benny stood still for a second. There were a lot of other people he hadn't met yet, but there was something about how frantically Drue motioned to him that made him feel like Drue *needed* him by his side. And Benny had to admit, even though Drue was kind of full of himself, there was something exhilarating about his confidence and energy.

"Who was that?" Benny asked as he approached.

"Just some girl named Iyabo. No one interesting."

Benny guessed this really meant that it was no one interested in talking to Drue.

"I've been scoping out these losers and I'm pretty sure we're the team's best hope of coming out on top if we're pitted against the other groups," Drue continued. "As long as you really *do* have the kind of ATV driving skills you say you do. That'll come in handy if we do fight Moon buggy paintball wars or something."

"There's a big difference between being aware of your abilities and being full of yourself, Drue Bob Lincoln," a voice came from behind them. "The *C* in EW-SCAB stands for courage, not cockiness."

Benny turned to see Ricardo Rocha towering over them. He was at least two heads taller than everyone else in the room, and much broader, too. He looked like he could bench-press Benny if he wanted to.

Benny hoped that he didn't.

The room around them got quiet. Drue paused for only a moment before holding out his hand.

"It's a pleasure to meet you. I'm a huge fan. I guess you already know who I am."

"Benny Love," Ricardo said, ignoring Drue. His penetrating eyes were the same dark brown as his crew cut. It felt to Benny as though their leader was sizing him up as he continued. "I saw your video. Nice moves out on those desert dunes. I'm eager to see how those translate into low-gravity speed runs on the lunar surface. And saving that boy took some real bravery. I'm proud to have you in my group."

Ricardo thrust out a red gloved hand with such speed and precision that Benny tensed up and almost jumped. He shook it, murmuring thanks.

Ricardo glanced at Drue. "You didn't have a video, so we'll have to see if you live up to all that big talk."

Drue smiled, but Benny could see that he was gritting his teeth. He looked back at the rest of the room. All eyes were on them. Hot Dog had her hands clasped in front of her, a huge smile on her face as she stared at Ricardo.

"Attention," Ricardo said, walking past Benny and stepping up on a raised platform in front of one of the animated mustangs. "As you probably already know, I'm Ricardo Rocha, the first member of Elijah's Pit Crew. That makes me his right-hand man. Part apprentice, part assistant, part bodyguard."

"And complete idiot," Drue muttered, still smiling and clenching his jaw.

Ricardo continued. "While you're on the Moon, you're my responsibility, and anything you do reflects upon me as your leader. That means I expect nothing but the best from you for the next two weeks. *Elijah* expects nothing but the best. And I'm guessing you all want to impress him, right?"

The Mustangs erupted in shouts and cheers. Ricardo smiled.

"Good. Now, let's get to know each other. Remember, these are your teammates – it's in your best interest to get along with them and work together."

One by one, they introduced themselves. Many were from places Benny had never imagined he'd ever see. Iyabo, the girl Drue had been talking to, came from Cameroon. A skinny, pale boy with dark eyes and hair was from Greece. Jasmine had originally been born in China before coming to America. Despite their home countries, almost everyone seemed to speak passable English. Benny got a few weird looks when he introduced himself as being from the Drylands, but he figured that was to be expected. Unless you lived in a border town or out in the desert, you didn't exactly come across caravan members in your everyday life.

Ramona was the last to introduce herself. She didn't

say anything, only clicked her tongue and held up her left arm, which had a HoloTek strapped to it – an older model, not the one she'd been given when she checked in. As she tapped on the screen, purple numbers began to scroll across the room's walls, replacing the Mustang logos.

```
01011010 01110101 01110000 00111111 00100000
01001001 00100111 01101101 00100000 01010010
01100001 01101101 01101111 01101110 01100001
00100000 01100110 01110010 01101111 01101101
00100000 01010111 01100001 01101100 01100101
01111010 00101110 00100000 01011000 01000100
```

No one seemed sure what to make of this. Even Ricardo looked dumbfounded. Finally, Jasmine took a timid step forward.

"My binary is a little rusty," she said, "But you're . . . Ramona from . . . Wales?"

Ramona chuckled.

"Woot," she said. "Much leet, Jazz."

"OK," Drue whispered to Benny. "Maybe you were right. Maybe she *is* speaking robot."

A new series of numbers and what looked to Benny like gibberish strings of letters appeared. Jasmine's eyes chased after the lines of code, her face scrunched in concentration. Finally, she laughed a little, apparently getting some joke that was lost on the others.

"Excuse me." A woman's voice filled the room as Pinky's hologram walked out of the wall, causing a girl near her to scream. The screens scrambled, and were then replaced by the mustangs from before. "What exactly do you think you're doing messing with my projection systems?"

"It's OK, Pinky," Ricardo said. "It looks like we've got quite a programmer on our team."

Ramona let her reddish-blond curls fall back down into her face as she opened a can of fizzy drink, grinning at Pinky.

"Also," Ricardo said, "hasn't Max been on at you about popping up out of nowhere?"

"Humph." Pinky casually walked through the open doorway, blinking out of existence when she was a few steps into the hall.

The skinny boy from Greece raised a hand. "So, Pinky seems cool and everything, but can I get a talking dog or something as my room butler instead?"

"Elijah's pretty protective of the AI's form," Ricardo said.

"Why? It's just a hologram, right? It could be anything."

"Well . . ." Ricardo paused for a moment. "Pinky was

Elijah's personal assistant for years as a flesh-and-blood person. She was still here when I was an EW-SCABer. I got to meet her a few times."

"So, what happened to her?" Hot Dog asked.

"She didn't like it up here. She missed the ocean and the sunshine on Earth. Elijah was . . . *upset* when she said she was leaving. He kept himself busy in his quarters and made her spend her last week here with the newly designed artificial intelligence system. She basically uploaded her personality into it. I have to say, she's pretty similar to the original."

"I guess we know who the all-seeing eyes of the Taj are," Benny whispered to Drue.

"Seriously. Remind me not to say anything bad about the computer lady."

"OK, Mustangs," Ricardo said, straightening his posture like a soldier about to march. "Enough talk. Who wants to see the rest of the Taj?"

Excitement surged through Benny so quickly that he didn't even realise he was shouting until his voice was ringing out through the room. They were *all* yelling, ready to explore.

Ricardo led them through the halls, pointing out things of interest. A solid-gold replica of the first Space Runner encrusted with diamonds. Astroturf football fields out back, with goals floating three metres off the ground. A room made up entirely of grey rubber that Ricardo referred to simply as a "virtual gaming environment". Even the kitchen was a technological wonder. Jasmine gasped when she saw the state-of-the-art lasers used to chop vegetables and flash-cook food.

With each new marvel, Benny's understanding of what life could be like changed. He knew that wealthy people in the cities lived in a completely different way to those in the caravans – he'd had glimpses of this himself when he lived in an apartment as a kid – but the sort of luxury available at the Taj was mind-boggling. And as much as it filled him with excitement, he couldn't believe that some people lived like this all the time. What would that even be like?

He wondered if, just maybe, he *would* like to stay at the Taj. What would his family's life be like if they could all somehow live here?

"Why are we seeing all this without getting to *do* any of it?" Drue groaned. "That video-game room is new! Heck, I'd even be happy using one of those laser potato peelers right now. This is torture."

Benny noticed Ricardo looking back at Drue with disdain.

"Drue, Dude," Benny said, "you're going to drive everyone else *and yourself* insane with your complaining. You wouldn't last for five seconds in the Drylands."

"I could tough it out."

"Really? Because my caravan has taken on a few people who got forced out of a city before. They usually don't last for long."

Drue's eyes widened a little.

"You mean . . . you killed them?"

"What?" Benny asked. "No, are you crazy? They just ended up wandering off and getting lost in the desert because they were bored. Or left to try and hack it somewhere else. We don't *kill* people."

Drue shrugged. "You hear stories. The Drylands are supposed to be lawless. Full of roaming gangs and stuff."

Benny wondered if this was why he'd got some weird looks when he introduced himself to the rest of his team.

"Most of us are just trying to stay alive," he said. "The others . . . Well, the Drylands *are* dangerous, just not always in the way you expect them to be."

It was then that Ricardo stopped in front of a giant steel slab at the end of a hallway and turned to the group.

"You're about to enter one of the most exclusive places in the galaxy. Behind this door are the most sophisticated machines known to man. Personally, it's my favourite room in the Taj."

Somewhere towards the front, Hot Dog squealed.

"Welcome to the garage, Mustangs." Ricardo grinned, lifting his chin and looking down over the bridge of his nose at the group. "I hope you're prepared to prove you're worthy of the EW-SCAB."

CHAPTER 8

The inside of the garage was almost as bright as the outside, with steel walls and dark-stained concrete floors reflecting an entire ceiling made of light. Half the structure served as a work space and tinkering grounds for the McGuyvers, who were currently dismantling the front end of the crimson Space Runner Elijah had driven earlier. The other side of the garage was a sort of showroom. Space Runners in dozens of colours and models – types Benny had never seen before – lined the floor, alongside what looked like normal dune buggies and classic cars that had been retrofitted in order to function on the Moon.

Once inside, the Mustangs split up, running back and forth, trying to see everything at once. Jasmine observed the McGuyvers, keeping her distance from them. Benny climbed inside a two-seater buggy, bouncing in the driver's seat.

"The tyres on this thing are nuts," he murmured, imagining what a wild ride he could have racing it over the dunes of the Drylands, wondering what speeds it could reach.

"Dude, Benny, why are you bothering with that thing?" Drue called from across the garage. He ran his hands over a silvery Space Runner shaped like a long, thin rocket. "Look at this beauty! Oh, man, I gotta see what's under the hood."

Drue started pulling on the front of the car, his face turning red. When that didn't work, he banged his fist on the hood, as if that might cause it to spring open.

"Hey, hey, careful with that!" Ash McGuyver shouted, walking swiftly towards Drue while cleaning an oversized torque wrench on the front of her coveralls. "That's a prototype with a one-of-a-kind synthetic-mercury paint job."

"Synthetic mercury?" Drue asked. "What the what? OK, I've got to take a few buckets of that back with me. Can someone contact my dad? He can have his lawyers or whoever figure out how to get it down to Earth."

Ash turned to Ricardo, pointing a thumb over her shoulder and towards the exit. "I'm banning this kid from the garage."

"Give it a break, Lincoln," Hot Dog said, running her finger over the boot of the silver vehicle. "You can paint your daddy's Space Runner back home any colour you want, but this looks like too much car for you."

Benny watched Drue's face turn an even darker shade of red.

"I can hold my own in any Space Runner. Have you ever even been behind the wheel of one of these things? Today's automated flight doesn't count."

"I've logged over three hundred hours in SR flight simulators back home. For most of last year I was the top-ranked sim pilot in the world!" Her lips curved down into a frown. "Until I had to stop going to the arcades."

"There's a big difference between a sim and the real thing," Drue said. He cracked his knuckles. "If you crash in a sim, you can hit reset. In real life, you might *die*. These are machines, not toys."

Hot Dog narrowed her eyes. "What makes you think I'd crash?" she asked.

"All I'm saying is that I'm a dude who's got some *actual* experience behind the yoke of one of these things. I could totally beat you."

"Why not prove it?" Ricardo asked, stepping towards the two.

It was only then that Benny realised everyone was watching them. "Oh, boy," he murmured. He'd guessed that Drue's mouth would get him in trouble eventually, but he was kind of hoping it wouldn't be on the first day. Especially since so far Drue was the only person he'd really talked to all that much.

"What do you mean?" Drue asked.

Ricardo fixed his steely gaze on the boy. "Our first activity today was going to be testing the team's aptitude in the Space Runners. Why don't we start by pitting the two of you against each other to see who the better pilot is?"

"I'm game," Hot Dog said. She sneered at Drue, whose mouth was now hanging open. "What's the matter? Getting cold feet in that expensive space suit?"

Drue let out a snort. "Let's do it, but I call dibs on this silver one."

"Oh, no you don't," Ash said. She tapped on a HoloTek and suddenly the floor beneath several of the Space Runners on the other side of the room sank into the ground. There was a rumbling beneath them, and then another platform rose, a new line of cars replacing the old ones. "Here, you can take two of the SR trainers. At least that way if you lose control, Pinky'll save you."

"Ashley, will you get them strapped in and ready?" Ricardo asked. "The rest of you, outside. Let's see what your teammates can do."

Benny climbed out of the Moon buggy and followed the rest of the Mustangs. As he passed Hot Dog and Drue, they both looked over at him. He gave them a double thumbs-up, said "Good luck!" without specifying who he was talking to, and then continued out into the Grand Dome. There, the Mustangs were starting to clump into groups of three or four. He spotted Jasmine standing alone, inspecting one of the neon-blue palm trees. In fact, as he thought back to it, Jasmine had been alone most of the tour. One thing he'd learned in the caravan was that it was always best to have a partner, even if you were just going off over a dune to get away from the noise of the campsite. The Drylands were too dangerous to face alone – despite his *occasional* solo ATV rides – and while the Taj was certainly different, he thought the same principle applied.

"Who do you think is going to win?" he asked, stepping up behind her.

Jasmine tensed for a moment before letting out a breath and answering. "I have no idea what their abilities are." She paused. "But I'm really, *really* rooting for Hot Dog on this one."

"You know," Benny said, nodding, "I think I'm with you on that." Drue could definitely stand to be taken down a peg.

"If you'll turn your attention upward," Ricardo said once they were out on the dark gravel. "Pinky, load Möbius Track A-Seven."

In the open sky beyond the protection of the Grand Dome, a holographic course appeared, stretching well beyond the length of the Taj. It pulsed with a rainbow of colours. If Benny was seeing it right, after the first turn the Space Runners would actually be driving upside down for half a lap.

"The Taj is equipped with a number of pre-programmed courses," Ricardo explained. "Using antigravity tech, the Space Runners' hyperdrives lock on to the hologram, ensuring that they stay on track. Later in the week, you'll be designing your own courses."

"Whoa," Benny said, for what felt like the thousandth time that day.

"If you take out your new HoloTeks, you can follow along and see how your teammates are doing," Ricardo continued. "There they are now."

Two Space Runners alighted on the course's black-and-white chequered starting line. Benny patted his pockets before realising he'd left his HoloTek in his room. Jasmine noticed, raising both eyebrows.

"Forgot mine," Benny said sheepishly.

"I don't know how you could let something like that out of your sight," she said. "Here. We can share this one."

She pulled on the corners of her HoloTek until it was large enough that they both had to hold it. The screen was split into four quadrants – dash cam views of the track ahead of the drivers and of the drivers' faces themselves.

"No shame in backing out now, blondie." Drue's voice came from the HoloTek.

"I've been beating boys like you since I was in kinder-garten," Hot Dog sneered. "Always thinking I can't win video games or flight sims. I may even give you a head start just so I don't feel bad about taking you down."

"The first driver across the finish line at the end of the third lap wins," Ricardo said. His voice was coming out of the HoloTek now. Benny guessed he must have been tuned into the Space Runners. "Give it your best shot. If you take a look to your left, you'll see that you've got an audience."

He pointed to the top of the Taj's golden tower where a small window had opened. A figure stood there, silhou-etted by the light pouring out from behind him.

"Elijah," Benny whispered.

Back on the screen in front of him, he watched both drivers tighten their grips on the flight yokes.

"It's our first race of the 2085 EW-SCAB," Ricardo shouted. "Drue Lincoln versus Hot Dog Wilkinson."

He paused for a few seconds as the crowd cheered. Benny let out a whoop. Jasmine just smiled.

"On your marks," Ricardo continued. "Get set. Drive!"

Both Space Runners shot forward, going from zero to a hundred miles per hour in a matter of seconds according to the stats scrolling across Jasmine's screen. Drue let out a shout that devolved into laughter as his car accelerated, but Hot Dog stayed quiet, gritting her teeth and sitting up with a rigid posture as she focused on the course ahead of her.

The track was nothing but a blur of colour on the dash cams, a kaleidoscope of light that the vehicles raced over. Both Space Runners were neck and neck going into the first turn, but as they approached the curve, Drue jerked his flight yoke and twisted his car slightly, until it looked like he was about to careen into Hot Dog.

"Hey!" Hot Dog shouted, tapping her brakes to avoid a collision. "Are you nuts?"

"Eat my Moon dust!" Drue yelled as he pulled ahead

of her. He turned to the camera aimed at his face and stuck out his tongue. "See you guys at the finish line."

Benny watched as both Mustangs completed the curve and continued racing upside down, suspended on the bottom of the course thanks to their hyperdrive engines. He kept his eyes on the track ahead of them, trying to imagine what his moves would be.

He realised there was no way he'd stand a chance if he were the third Space Runner up there.

He looked over at Jasmine, whose forehead was creased with worry as she watched the race unfold on her HoloTek. She was obviously incredibly smart – even Elijah knew who she was. It seemed to Benny that all the EW-SCABers were incredible in some way. Even Ramona. They all had something in particular they excelled at.

Benny was good with ATVs, sure. But did that even matter, when Space Runners were the way of the future?

What did he have to offer his teammates?

Everyone around him in the Grand Dome was cheering. Back on the track, Hot Dog wasn't giving up on the race. She stayed on Drue's tail all through the next lap and a half, her face determined, eyes unblinking as Drue continued to heckle her.

95

"Why so slow?" he asked. "Checking your hair in the rearview mirror?"

Finally, as they were upside down and approaching the final turn, she spoke up. "You know what your problem is, Drue?" she asked.

"Please, tell me, Ms Dog."

She twisted her flight yoke sideways while hitting the instrument panels. Suddenly her car was swerving past Drue's – she'd tapped the Space Runner's gravity break at just the right time to send her car sliding at incredible speed through the last curve, shaving a few seconds off her lap.

She grinned. "You think that just because I have perfect hair and lip gloss, I can't kick your ass on the track."

Her Space Runner zoomed over the finish line. Benny watched Drue's mouth drop open.

"How . . ." was all that managed to escape his lips as the kids on the ground applauded and cheered even louder. Benny had only known Drue for half a day, but he felt pretty sure that this was probably one of the few times in his life he'd been beaten.

"Go ahead and take a few victory laps, Hot Dog," Ricardo said. "Pinky, bring Drue's Space Runner back down."

Drue's car entered the courtyard through the pressurization tunnel, coming to a stop in front of the fountain. Drue jumped out and stomped towards the Taj. Benny started after him to at least tell Drue that he'd put up a heck of a fight.

"Stupid upside-down turns," Drue seethed. "Pinky probably held my car back just to let *her* win."

"Hey," Benny said. "You all right?"

Drue stopped, glaring back at him. "What do you think?"

Benny was at a loss for words, trying to figure out what he could say. Drue just stood still, staring up at the window where Elijah's silhouette had been. Now there was nothing there.

"I've got to show him," he said quietly. "I deserve to be up here, too."

Before Benny could respond, Pinky's voice filled the Grand Dome, thunderous and echoing, louder than anything Benny had heard all day.

"Warning!" she shouted. "Everyone, get back into the Taj. My sensors have just picked up a—"

But Benny didn't hear what she said after that. All he could focus on was Hot Dog's Space Runner and the glowing comet that looked like it was headed straight for her.

"Look out!" he shouted, but it was no use. She couldn't hear him.

Fortunately she must have seen the piece of debris coming, because her Space Runner jerked to the side at the last second. The rock shot past her, landing somewhere outside the Taj's dome.

"Man, what was that? It almost hit her," Benny said. "She really *is* a good driver. No offence."

Drue let out a sigh. "That, or the Space Runner took its own emergency manoeuvres. They're programmed to do that—"

He shut up as a second rock slammed into the side of Hot Dog's car, sending it flying off the track and away from the Taj.

"Hot Dog!" Benny yelled.

Ricardo barked something about contacting Elijah into his HoloTek while the rest of the Mustangs erupted in panicked screams.

"Benny!" Jasmine ran to his side, holding her HoloTek out. On it, Hot Dog was a spinning, screaming blur. "The power went out, along with the artificial gravity. The backup battery just kicked in, but she's lost control!"

"Why isn't Pinky taking over?" Benny asked.

"Her systems must be damaged," Drue said, shoving himself between Jasmine and Benny.

"Um, Mayday?" Hot Dog's voice came through the device. "Anyone? My controls aren't responding."

"Here, I can adjust the video to spin with her so we can see what's happening," Jasmine said, tapping on the screen.

Hot Dog's image was stable, then, her hair flying all around her, body pushing against the restraints holding her in her seat.

Ricardo was trying to wrangle the Mustangs all around the dome, but no one wanted to go inside until they knew what had happened to the out-of-control Space Runner. To make matters worse, other teams had started spilling out into the Grand Dome from the Taj's front doors as the other Pit Crew members raced to Ricardo's side.

"Come on," Hot Dog yelled, reaching forward as best she could and slamming her fist against the dashboard. "Come back to life, stupid!"

There was a banging sound somewhere behind her, and a glittering flash of light around her head. Suddenly all her hair was smooshed up around her face, as though it were trapped in a bubble.

"Her space suit turned on its gravitational force-field

helmet," Jasmine said. "That means the cabin must be depressurising."

Hot Dog looked directly into the camera.

"I'm going to try deploying the emergency parachute," she said. "Ugh, I shouldn't have eaten so many of those sna—"

The connection cut out.

"Oh, no," Benny murmured.

"Hot Dog?" Jasmine tapped on the screen. "Hot Dog, come in!"

Benny looked to the sky, hoping to find her regaining control. Instead, he saw dozens of jagged boulders all shooting towards the Taj's dome.

CHAPTER 9

Glowing rocks rained down on the Grand Dome, exploding against the invisible bubble keeping the resort safe, bathing the courtyard in a split-second flash of blazing blue-and-orange light. With every impact, the Lunar Taj shook.

Chaos broke out in the courtyard as EW-SCABers ran in every direction, most trying desperately to get through the front doors and into the main building. The Pit Crew was shouting orders, but they were fighting to be heard over Pinky's warnings and alarms.

Benny had been in more than one freak dust storm in his lifetime. He knew the importance of finding shelter when things suddenly looked grim.

"Let's go!" he shouted over the roaring noise, pulling Drue and Jasmine's arms.

They followed Benny as he made for the closest struc-ture – the garage.

"We shouldn't be running," Jasmine said once they were inside. "We should duck and cover. Like in an earthquake."

"This is no earthquake," Benny said, though at that point another explosion sent tremors coursing through the resort.

"Hot Dog's out there in all this!"

"We can't do anything to help her if we're dead!"

Inside the garage, another blast caused Benny to stumble forward. He caught himself on the crimson Space Runner the McGuyvers had been disassembling. The mechanics were nowhere to be seen.

"Good idea!" Drue said, pulling open the Space Runner door and sliding into the driver's seat.

"What are you doing?" Benny asked. "This is no time to—"

"Are you kidding?" Drue flipped a few switches on the dashboard. Benny felt a buzz under his hands. "Space Runners have gravity shields. This is extra protection!"

Jasmine looked between Drue and Benny and then slid into the back seat. Benny followed her, just as another bang shook the garage.

"This is bad," Benny said once they were all inside. "Will the force fields hold up outside, Jasmine?"

"Why are you asking *me*?"

"Because you're the one who seems to know how everything works. And it looked like those rocks were *exploding*. Was that fire? How is that possible? There's not any oxygen outside, right?"

"I don't *know*." Jasmine blinked a few times, chewing her bottom lip.

"Hey," Drue said. "It's quiet now. Think it's over?"

The door connecting the garage to the Lunar Taj slid open. Elijah West bolted in, hologram stats and charts floating in front of him. Drue gasped. Pinky, Sahar and the Miyamura twins followed him, with Max and the McGuyvers making up the tail end of the group.

Pinky was speaking.

"Preliminary data shows that they're probably asteroids. I'll need a sample in order to be sure of their composition – that might help explain their incendiary nature."

"Elijah!" Drue whispered, reaching for the door handle.

"Shh!" Benny shot forward and stopped his hand. "They'll make us go to our rooms or something. Just listen for once. What are they saying?"

Max's face was pale, causing his minty hair to look even brighter. "They came out of nowhere."

"They came from *somewhere*," Elijah said, his voice on the verge of shouting.

"We should evacuate."

Drue gasped again. Jasmine started shaking her head so quickly Benny was sure the car was rocking. He leaned against the back seat window, trying to hear more.

"That would be unwise," Pinky said. "Space Runners are ill-equipped to deal with a large-scale asteroid assault. My sensors are also picking up foreign elements lurking miles above the Moon's surface, suggesting not all of the asteroids fell. The safest course of action is to stay inside the Lunar Taj's protective shield."

"What have you got on the Space Runner that went down?" Elijah asked.

"EW-SCAB winner Grace 'Hot Dog' Wilkinson was the pilot. The storm has interfered with our communications, though the last broadcast from her vehicle indicates that she was taking emergency measures and probably preparing for a crash landing."

"Holy crap!" Drue said. Benny clamped a hand over his mouth. No one outside the car seemed to have heard him, because Elijah continued, tapping one gold-tipped boot on the floor.

"Give me something I can use, Pinky," he said.

"I *have* triangulated the area where it is most likely that the craft crashed, but I'm afraid that given the minimal data I have to work with and her erratic flight patterns, the location isn't very precise."

"How big is the search area?"

"Eighty-seven square miles."

Elijah nodded. "All right. We'll find her."

"What? Elijah, be serious," Max said. "That search area's the size of a city. The girl could be anywhere. We don't even know if she's alive. What if there's another storm? You'd be trapped out there unprotected!"

Benny felt suddenly nauseous.

"That girl is my responsibility. I invited her up here." Elijah held out his hand. Bo pulled a pair of gold sunglasses out of one of his coverall pockets and handed them over. "Lucky for her, she's got the best driver in the galaxy looking for her." He turned to Ash. "The Vette."

Ash tapped on her HoloTek. A yellow car with wide black racing stripes powered on and drifted slowly to the centre of the garage.

"Man, *look* at that thing," Drue whispered. "I'm in love."

"Fine," Max said. "But don't come back pointing fingers at me about things going wrong. We should be in the off season as of this morning." His voice got quieter. "At least we got all the celebrities and CEOs out of here before this mess started."

"Kira, Kai, I want you in Space Runners searching the craters from above," Elijah said, pointing to a floating hologram map. The same maps appeared in front of the Pit Crew members, with Elijah's markings highlighted. "Sahar, we'll start on opposite ends of the search site and make our way towards the centre."

"*Hai*," the Miyamura twins said in near unison. Sahar nodded. Without being asked, Ash McGuyver tapped on her HoloTek and three Space Runners floated into the centre of the garage – two white, one green.

Elijah looked at the three of them for a moment and then shook his head. "I thought we had more time."

"More time for what?" Jasmine whispered.

"Pinky, where's the rest of my Crew?"

"Trevone is currently running analyses on the Taj's backup oxygen generators. Ricardo is carrying two EW-SCABers, who tripped in the panic, back to their rooms."

Elijah turned to Max and the McGuyvers.

"When Ricardo's done send him out to help with the search. Communications may be disrupted within the Taj, but we'll be able to broadcast to each other via shortwave out there." He marched towards the yellow Corvette, Sahar and the twins following. "Pinky, primary objectives: One: ensuring the safety of all of our guests. Two: warning any nearby space stations or ships about the possibility of further asteroids or debris. Three: get in contact with Earth."

"Directives confirmed," Pinky said. "But my readings show that due to satellite damage, our ability to communicate off-Moon has been substantially hindered. I can't get through to Earth."

"Then run a diagnostic. See what we need to get full communications back online. Get Trevone on it."

"Consider it done. And Elijah . . ." Pinky's electronic voice softened. "Be careful out there, you reckless fool."

Benny could see the flash of his white teeth.

"I always am, Pinky," the man said as he put on his sunglasses. "Open the auxiliary pressurization tunnel."

The Vette's door closed, and then the car was shooting through the garage tunnel, the Pit Crew following.

Max swore under his breath and waved at the McGuyvers. "I'll go find Ricardo. I'm surprised that kid isn't falling over himself to check on Elijah already."

As they walked towards the exit leading to the Grand Dome, Benny and the other two Mustangs hiding in the Space Runner ducked down, trying to not even breathe very loudly. They stayed like that for what felt like a long time. Benny started to sweat, thinking about everything he'd just heard and witnessed.

Finally Drue spoke, letting out a huge breath. "Well . . ." he said. "At least the asteroids stopped?"

"This is insane," Jasmine said, getting out of the car. Benny and Drue followed. "We should get back to our rooms. They're probably taking attendance and trying to make sure everybody's accounted for."

She started to move towards the exit, but Drue stepped in front of her.

"Wait, wait, wait," he said, a smile creeping across his face. "Think about this for a second. This could be kind of a lucky break. Our chance to get noticed. To make a name for ourselves."

"Our 'lucky break'?" Jasmine asked. "Are you nuts? Hot Dog is stranded out there somewhere!"

"Get that big brain working, Jazz."

"You're never going to learn my name, are you?"

"Come on," Drue continued. "If *we* were to go out looking for that missing Space Runner and found Hot Dog, we'd be heroes, right? Elijah would love us for that. We're *already* in the garage. We'd just have to hop into a car." He turned to Benny, raising his eyebrows. "Don't lie. You're totally itching to take one of these prototypes out for a spin." Drue leaned on the Space Runner beside him, stroking it with one hand.

"Well . . ." Benny had to admit that there was a certain

appeal to the idea. "Wait, you're just saying that because you're trying to figure out how to make up for losing the race."

Drue ignored him.

"Jazzzzzz," he said, drawing out her name. "Hot Dog's out there. She's our friend!"

"You just met her," Jasmine said. "So she's not really your friend. I actually don't think she likes you very much."

"Oh, come on. Aren't the odds of her getting rescued way better if there are more search parties? That's solid maths. And don't you want to impress Elijah with not only your brains but your bravery, too?"

"I don't do things like this," Jasmine said. "It's not who I am."

"Maybe not. But *this* is how you make a name for yourself. This is how you get invited to stay at the Taj when everyone else goes home in two weeks."

Jasmine thought about this for a few seconds, fiddling with the necklace she'd taken out of her space suit.

"Well, technically the odds would be better," she admitted.

"Look, if you don't want to go, that's fine, but at least don't tell on Benny and me."

"But I don't want to get in trouble."

"Neither do I!" Benny added.

"*Benny.*" Drue turned to him, jutting his hands out at his sides. "Come on, dude. Isn't saving lost people kind of your thing?"

Benny started to say no, but the words caught in his mouth. He thought of how happy the kid who he'd rescued out in the desert had been to see him. And then he imagined telling the story of how he saved a downed Space Runner pilot to his brothers when he got back to Earth. About how he'd faced an asteroid storm and the cold surface of the Moon to find her.

Plus, Drue had a point. Elijah would have to notice them if they succeeded. Benny wouldn't mind that.

"OK," he said. "I'm in."

"Do you even have any idea what to do if you get stranded out there?" Jasmine asked. "Or what kind of oxygen levels you need to make sure you stay conscious if your systems fail? We're not talking about an autopiloted trek from Earth to the Moon. Do you even know how to manually engage your space helmets if you have to?"

"Um . . ." Benny said. "I guess not?"

Jasmine shook her head. She raised her fingers and pinched the bridge of her nose. Finally, she let out a long sigh. "If you two are going to do something idiotic like this, I think I have to go along with you. Otherwise I'd feel guilty forever if you died."

"That's . . . good?" Benny asked.

"Jazz, you're not going to regret this," Drue said.

"I already do."

"Wait," Benny said. "How do we even get out of the tunnel?" He lowered his voice to a whisper. "Pinky controls it, right?"

"She's probably super-busy right now with everything that's going on," Drue said quietly. "Maybe we could sneak past her?"

Jasmine shook her head. "I think I know someone who could help us with that."

She pulled out her HoloTek and started tapping on it. Benny narrowed his eyes.

"What are you doing?" he asked.

"Sending a message to someone."

"That doesn't look like English? What is it, a code or something?"

"Technically, yes. It's binary."

Drue turned back to the Space Runner they'd hidden in. Only then did he seem to notice that half the car's parts were sitting beside the vehicle.

"Uh, so, I don't think this one's going to work," he said.

"We'll take something else," Benny said. He started towards one of the dune buggies when something else caught his eye – an electric green sports car with the word *Chevelle* spelled across the boot in shining chrome.

He thought of his father. He'd always wanted an old-school muscle car, but they were such petrol-guzzlers that they never made sense in the caravan. Still, some of Benny's best memories were of times when they'd come across a functioning classic and gone out into the desert to drag race against the backdrop of the setting sun, ignoring the wasted petrol and resources for just a few minutes while Benny sat wide-eyed and grinning in the passenger seat, fingers gripping around his seat belt as he wondered if at any moment the shaking, roaring vehicle might launch them into space.

Now he had the chance to sit behind the wheel of one himself. Wouldn't his father have loved to see that?

"Drue," Benny said with a grin, thinking back to all the cars, trucks, and RVs he'd worked on in the caravan. "You want to learn how to hot-wire a car?"

CHAPTER 10

It didn't take much convincing to get Ramona to hack into the garage's security systems and bypass Pinky's controls. In fact, from what Benny could tell, she'd have done it even if they weren't going out to try to find one of their missing teammates. After only a few minutes of tinkering on her old, custom HoloTek, the tunnel was open and Benny, Drue and Jasmine were in the borrowed Chevelle shooting towards parts of the Moon unprotected by the Lunar Taj's force field.

Since Benny was already in the driver's seat because he'd been hot-wiring the car, he took the wheel despite Drue's many, many objections. Drue might have had skills in a Space Runner, but they were driving on the ground, now, out over rocks and craters. This was the kind of thing Benny excelled at.

Besides, he was pretty sure they were all a lot safer with him calling the shots. If he was going to do this, he was going to make sure it was done right. Plus he got the feeling Elijah and Ricardo didn't have the best impressions of Drue, so if they *did* get in trouble, Benny didn't want Elijah to think he'd been talked into this by the senator's son . . . even if that was *kind* of true.

He stopped the car outside the Taj's dome once they were clear of the tunnel. It was hard to believe exploding rocks had just bombarded the place – except for some black marks, the dome looked untouched. The ground outside its protection, though, was dotted with deep, scorched pits in the Moon's crust.

"I'm kind of impressed that weirdo girl got past Pinky," Drue said as he stared out at the grey landscape.

"She's incredibly good with tech," Jasmine huffed. She tapped on her HoloTek in the back seat, pulling up maps and various calculations. "Just because she speaks in jargon doesn't mean she's weird."

"No, it means she's weird *and* smart. I'm guessing that's something you're a little familiar with."

Drue said this nonchalantly, but Benny saw Jasmine cringe in the rearview mirror. He was beginning to think maybe Drue wasn't actually trying to be annoying – he just didn't know any better. Still, Benny decided it would be best to change the subject.

"How'd you know she'd help us?" he asked.

Jasmine shrugged. "That second set of binary she had up in the common room was a joke about how a state-of-the-art AI would never beat someone with a brain. I figured she'd jump at the chance to get a better look at Pinky's operating systems, if she hadn't already." She glanced up from her HoloTek. A map was now illuminated on the screen installed in the Chevelle's dash. "All right I'm going to take us to the centre of the search area. Elijah and Sahar shouldn't have got there yet. You're going straight for about fifteen miles, and then we should come to a big crater. Got it?"

Benny just grinned. He was at home behind the wheel. He could almost imagine that his little brothers were strapped into the back seat, begging him to punch the throttle and send them flying over desert dunes.

Almost. There were plenty of modifications the McGuyvers had made that kept the car from feeling too familiar. Gravity stabilisers served the dual purpose of creating a force field around the passengers and keeping the vehicle horizontal – not to mention tethered to the ground. Still, there was more than enough power under the hood, and for the moment Benny forgot that he'd ever had reservations about taking the car out. Unlike the fairly quiet Space Runners, the Chevelle's engine purred, rattling the steering wheel, daring Benny to push its engine to the brink.

"Buckle up," Benny said, revving the engine. "Let's see how this thing handles on the open Moon."

Before the others could respond, Benny slammed his foot down on the accelerator, sending them roaring away from the Taj, kicking up a cloud of grey dust behind them.

"You're . . . not a bad driver," Drue said as Benny shot them across the lunar surface, dodging small craters and drifting through turns. He clung tightly to the roll bar at the top of the car.

"I'm good with things that have tyres," Benny said, kicking the car up into another gear. "It's space I'm not used to."

He glanced at the rearview mirror. Jasmine was in the middle of the back seat with both arms out, bracing herself. Her eyes were wide, and, as the Chevelle bounced over a dip in the ground, a high-pitched yelp escaped her lips.

"Jasmine, you still OK to navigate?" Benny asked.

"Yeah!" she said, fumbling for her HoloTek. "I preloaded the map and an accelerometer is gauging your speed so I think it's pretty accurate." She sat back in her seat again before adding quietly, "Hopefully we won't run into Elijah or the Crew. We'll get reprimanded *and* cut into their search time."

"The worst they can do is send us back to the Taj, right?" Drue asked, a smile growing across his face.

"No, the worst thing he can do is think we're a bunch of delinquents who never should have been invited to the Moon," Jasmine said. "I hate this. The only time I've ever been in trouble was when a foster family grounded me for baking dozens of batches of cookies. But that was for science! I was trying to figure out how different ingredients would affect the end result!"

"Lighten up, Jazz," Drue said, turning around in his seat to face her. "Remember that the *C* in EW-SCAB stands for *courage*? Live a little. Steal a car and go searching for your lost friend on the Moon."

But Benny knew Jasmine had brought up a good point. What if Elijah *did* regret giving them the scholarships? What if he decided to take back the cash prizes?

How could he face his family if he was kicked out of the EW-SCAB on day one?

He blinked and tightened his grip on the steering wheel, turning his attention to the terrain in front of him. Now was definitely *not* the time to lose focus.

"Hold on, guys," Benny said. "We've got a jump coming up."

"That's the big crater I mentioned," Jasmine said. "Maybe you should go around it instead of—"

But Benny had been over plenty of dunes before and was sure he knew what he was doing. They hit a hill and flew into the air, something he'd done a thousand times in his ATV back home. What he didn't take into account was that they were in lower gravity: the Chevelle didn't just drop back down to the surface but propelled up and forward at a remarkable speed, like it was going to launch into space.

"Uhhh," Benny groaned. "Oops."

"Hey look!" Drue said, pointing out of the window. "I think I see one of the Miyamuras, like, fifty miles away."

Jasmine closed her eyes and murmured to herself: "This will be OK. You aren't going to die with these two imbeciles in the cold vacuum of space."

But they didn't leave the Moon's gravity. Instead, they followed a long, high arc over the surface. When they finally *did* start to come down, the car nose-dived towards the ground.

"Oh, crap," Benny said.

"Fix it!" Drue shouted. "We're going to crash!"

"No, we're not!" Jasmine shouted. "Hit the manual gravity stabiliser! There has to be one!"

Benny looked at the panel of holograms and touch-screen controls that covered the Chevelle's dash. None of it looked familiar. He started pressing buttons at random. The air-conditioning kicked on, followed by the windshield wipers and some very loud classical music.

"Here!" Drue said, surging forward and slamming two fingers on the dash.

Suddenly, the car levelled out. Then it began to drop straight down.

All three of them screamed.

The Chevelle landed on its four wheels with a bounce. None of them said a word for a few seconds, until Drue turned off the music and Benny peeled his stiff fingers from around the steering wheel. He half expected the car to explode, but it didn't.

"OK," Drue said. "Benny . . . that . . . was . . . *awesome*! Let's do it again!"

Jasmine tapped on her neck. There was a slight glimmer in the air around her face as the space suit's helmet powered on, creating a force field around her head – a miniature Grand Dome.

"I've got to get out of here," she said, clawing at the door handle. "I think I'm going to be sick."

Before the door opened, the inside of the car depressurised, causing Drue and Benny's helmets to automatically power up as well. Soon, Jasmine was outside, taking a few wobbly steps away from them and coughing. The sound crackled out of a speaker in Benny's collar.

"Gross," he said. "What happens if she throws up in her helmet?"

Drue made gagging noises and shook his head. "Why do we always get stuck with girls who can't handle a little turbulence?"

"I can hear you," Jasmine shouted. "The comm systems in our suits automatically connect anyone within a certain . . ." She paused for a second, and then was yelling. "You guys! Get out here! I found Hot Dog's Space Runner!"

The boys looked at each other for half a second before they were both jumping out of the car.

The downed Space Runner was half embedded in the side of a hill fifty or so metres behind them. Jasmine stood a couple of metres away on the passenger's side. The windows were covered in so much dust that it was impossible to see through them.

Benny had seen some bad accidents out in the Drylands.

Cars that had gone over cliffs or simply spun out of control, rolling across the desert – the kinds of wrecks people didn't survive.

Like this one.

"I don't want to look," Jasmine said quietly as Benny and Drue approached. They stood on either side of her.

"Hot Dog?" Drue called.

There was no reply.

It took Benny a moment to realise that both Drue and Jasmine were staring at him. Drue's complexion was turning green, and Jasmine's head shook out of nervousness or fear or a combination of the two. So Benny did what he was good at: he put on a brave face, just like he would have back on Earth. He held his breath as he stepped around to the driver's side of the Space Runner, preparing for the worst.

But there was nothing. The pilot's seat was empty.

"She's not here," he said.

Drue let out a loud sigh as Jasmine pulled open the passenger door and climbed halfway into the vehicle. "Looks like the gravity-powered air bags did their jobs."

Benny stepped back and looked at the crushed body of the Space Runner. He was surprised anyone could have survived the crash – but then, Space Runners *were* filled with cutting-edge safety features. Still, the fact that Hot Dog walked away . . .

Walked away.

The thought triggered something in Benny's mind.

"There are footprints over here," he said, moving to the back of the car. "Not ours! We can follow them! She couldn't have gone that far."

"Hot Dog?" Drue yelled again as he looked at her trail.

"She must be too far away for our comms to connect," Jasmine said. "That, or . . ." She didn't finish her thought.

Benny searched the horizon, but all he could see was a grey landscape. Finally, he spotted a tiny silhouette in the distance.

"There she is!" he said, pointing. "Everyone back in the car."

"You go get her," Jasmine said, turning her eyes back to the wreckage. "I want to take a closer look at what brought down this Space Runner. Just make sure you come back for me."

The boys nodded, and piled back into the Chevelle. It handled differently after the fall, pulling to one side. A bent axle, probably – something Benny didn't look forward to explaining to Elijah when they got back.

Hot Dog looked over her shoulder once and saw their

approaching car, and then she turned her attention back in front of her. It wasn't until Drue and Benny were out of the Chevelle that she looked surprised to see them.

"Wait. *You* two?" she asked.

"Nice look," Drue said. Hot Dog's bountiful blond curls were all scrunched up against the inside of her force-field helmet, as if she had a mane crowning her head.

"My hair wasn't made for space travel," she said, adjusting the strap of a black bag hanging off one shoulder. "What are you doing out here?" Her face went white. "Oh, no, don't tell me he sent all the EW-SCABers out looking for me. That's so embarrassing."

"Actually, it's just us," Benny said. "We kinda . . . *borrowed* a car to come looking for you."

"It was my idea," Drue said, stepping forward.

A wave of surprise passed over Hot Dog's face before she let out a single laugh.

"You're kidding. You're dumber than I thought."

"We didn't want you to get stranded out here alone," Drue said. "Who knows what might have happened to you."

Plus, this way we look like heroes, Benny thought. That was the part Drue was leaving out.

"I can take care of myself," Hot Dog said with a little scowl.

"You say that," Drue grinned, "but you're headed in the wrong direction."

"I *know*." She shook her head, pointing to her right. "The Taj is that way."

"Then what are you doing over here?" Benny asked.

Hot Dog held up a small silver packet, squishing it in her hand. A label said H_2O in black letters.

"Thanks," Drue said. "I am a little thirsty."

"It didn't come from the Space Runner," Hot Dog said, turning back to the expanse of nothingness in front of her, where the surface of the Moon looked darker.

"What do you mean?" Benny asked. Drue had already pulled the straw off the side of the pouch, and was trying to figure out how to get it through the force field of his helmet.

"It was sitting outside the car when I came to." Hot Dog opened up the black bag to show them. "All of this was."

Inside were half a dozen pouches, some labelled as protein drinks and meal replacements, others marked as more packages of water.

"Wait, wait, wait," Drue said. "What?"

"I think someone left this for me." She paused, her eyebrows scrunching together.

Drue thought about this for a second. Then he gulped. "Are you telling me someone saw you crash, brought you a load of supplies, and then left you alone out here? Just disappeared?"

"I don't know. I was knocked out for a little while," Hot Dog said. "But there are some marks in the dust that could be from a hover-scooter. They head in this direction." She motioned towards a section of the Moon in the distance covered in shadow, an ocean of darkness. "But . . . I don't know where they would have come from. The Taj is the only building on the Moon, right? Unless it wasn't . . ." She didn't finish her sentence.

"Maybe you had an alien guardian angel," Benny said, trying to lighten the mood and wipe the concern out of Hot Dog's voice.

But she just shook her head. "You think that's a joke, but there's a *lot* of space out there we haven't reached yet. We *know* aliens existed at some point. Do you really think we're the only life in the whole universe?"

"The only intelligent life, yeah," Drue said. "Although, I don't know that I'd call—"

"Not now," Benny interrupted. "We can talk about this

back at the Taj. Please remember that we did *take* one of Elijah's cars."

"Relax, Benny, the Taj isn't going anywhere. We'll drive back when . . ." Drue trailed off for a second before his face lit up. "I'm driving this time! We'll pick up Jazz and speed back to the resort! I hope Elijah's got cameras filming the courtyard so he can see our heroic return."

And then he was off.

"Wait, you got *Jasmine* to come out here, too?" Hot Dog asked.

"Yeah," Benny said. "I get the feeling it's the first time she's ever broken a rule. I don't know how she's going to handle it."

"Seriously," she said. "Hey, thanks for coming to find me, by the way."

"No prob. But like you said, I'm sure you could have made it back without us."

Hot Dog bounced her head back and forth.

"Yeah, but it's a lot nicer to not have to walk. Although, if this *was* Drue's idea, I hope he doesn't think I owe him now."

Benny shook his head. "I can't figure out if he's my new best friend or worst enemy."

She laughed a little. Then her face turned serious as she started for the car.

"Hey," she shouted. "Shouldn't the *best* driver get to take the wheel?"

Back at the crash site they found Jasmine standing beside the wreckage, holding a fist-size piece of bright yellow rock. It was opaque, like some kind of dull gemstone.

"What's the story, Jazz?" Drue asked as they got out. "Collecting Moon rocks now?"

"Um . . . not exactly," Jasmine said. "I pulled this out of the hull of Hot Dog's Space Runner. I think it's what brought her down."

"Probably," Hot Dog said. "An asteroid or meteorite or something."

"The same stuff that exploded against the Taj," Benny said. Hot Dog looked his way, mouth agape. "Don't worry," he said. "The place is fine."

"It does *look* like some kind of mineral at first glance," Jasmine said, but her eyes were wide, staring at the other side of the rock. "Or maybe it was designed to look that way."

"Uh, Jazz . . . I mean, Jasmine?" Benny asked. "What are you talking about?"

She turned the piece of rock around to show off the other

side. At first Benny wasn't sure what the big deal was, but as it caught the light just right, he could see silvery patterns crisscrossing the rock. And sticking out of one section was what looked, impossibly, like several pieces of wire.

"Even the colour is strange. It looks like sulphur, but I'm pretty sure it's not," Jasmine said. "And with this metal sticking out of it . . . it looks like *circuitry*. I don't think this is a naturally occurring asteroid."

"Wait, what are you talking about?" Hot Dog asked.

"I think someone *made* whatever took down your Space Runner and fell on the Taj." She furrowed her eyebrows as she looked to Hot Dog.

"You mean, like, on purpose? You think this might have been an *attack*?"

The question hung there in the quiet expanse of the Moon as Benny looked back and forth between the other three. In that moment, he felt very far from home.

"We've got to get this back to the Taj," Jasmine said eventually. "We have to tell Elijah."

Benny swallowed hard, trying to make sense of what she was saying.

Drue just shook his head. "What? So someone's built an asteroid cannon or something? Who'd attack the Lunar Taj?"

Benny saw a flash out of the corner of his eye.

"Uh, guys," he said, pointing.

A glowing red blur was racing towards them from the sky. *Fast.*

"Maybe we're about to get our answer," Jasmine said.

The approaching Space Runner descended at a breakneck speed, slowing only when it was a few metres above the ground. The door folded open, and a boy jumped out.

Ricardo Rocha towered over them in his red space suit, eyes drifting from the wrecked Space Runner, to the stolen Chevelle, and then finally to Benny, who stood closest to him.

"Do you have any idea how much trouble you're in?" he asked.

Somewhere behind him, Benny heard Jasmine gulp.

CHAPTER 11

For most of the trip back to the Taj, no one spoke. Ricardo's custom Space Runner was too small for more than one passenger, but with a few taps on the Chevelle's dashboard he set the stolen car on an automated course back to the garage. The girls sat in its front seats, Jasmine shaking her head with her eyes closed. Her lips moved, but no sound came out. Hot Dog kept her gaze locked on the grey landscape ahead of them, taking deep breaths, a slight crease on her forehead. She held the black bag in her lap, Jasmine's rock sample inside. In the back seat, Drue let his head bang against the passenger window every few seconds while Benny mentally cursed himself for getting dragged along on this rescue mission. For ever thinking it was a good idea. He tried to prepare himself for a lecture or yelling or, worse, something he hated to even consider – that Elijah might kick all of them off the Moon for pulling a stunt like this.

If he *did* get sent home early, what would his family say? How could he explain this to his grandmother, to his brothers? What if, in one stupid move, he'd doomed everyone he cared about to stay in the Drylands?

They'd manage, of course. They'd get by as they always had, along with everyone else in the caravan. But how could he forgive himself?

There was another thought in his mind he couldn't shake. An image. His father's face, twisted in disappointment. His dad was a man who believed you could change the world if you set your mind to it. And what had Benny done when given the promise of real change? He'd thrown it all away. Drue's insistence back in the garage that Elijah would crown them as heroes if they found Hot Dog had seemed like solid logic at the time. Now, Benny just felt stupid.

He looked through the window, staring at the sliver of Earth visible above them as Drue broke the silence.

"Elijah will understand," he said, though it sounded to Benny as if Drue was trying to convince himself, not the rest of the car. "You guys'll see. He'll be proud of us. What we did was super courageous."

"And idiotic. I worked so hard to get here . . ." Jasmine muttered. She glanced in the rearview mirror. "I knew you were going to be trouble. I'm better than this. I've spent my whole life trying to find a real home. The Taj is it. All I've wanted is to be up here, and now . . ." She couldn't finish the thought.

Benny started to ask what she meant about finding a real home, but stopped. Instead, he tried to find a bright side.

"We *did* find Hot Dog," he offered.

"You stole one of his cars," Hot Dog said. "I mean, I'm happy you did, but—"

"What do you care?" Drue cut her off. "*You're* gonna make it out of this just fine."

"Hey, a little while ago I was shot out of the sky by an asteroid, OK? It's not like this was a good first day on the Moon for me, either."

And then they were all quiet until the Taj came into view.

"Do you . . ." Benny started quietly, not really wanting to ask the question. "Do you think he's going to send us home? After they figure out if there are going to be more asteroids, I mean."

"Hey, yeah, I almost forgot about that thing Jazz found," Drue said, his eyes lighting up. "We may have just saved the Taj if someone's really using asteroids as weapons.

Like, maybe we uncovered some kind of super-villain plot or something."

"You mean *alien* plot," Hot Dog said. "Those things came from space."

"Don't tell me you think ETs are throwing rocks at us."

"We don't know *what's* going on," Jasmine said. "Just that this could be important."

"I hope Elijah sees it that way, too," Benny said as their car slowed down, approaching the auxiliary tunnel into the dome.

Inside the garage, Ricardo jumped out of his Space Runner and pointed one finger towards the door leading into the Taj.

"Move," he said, his tone leaving no room for argument.

They didn't pass any other EW-SCABers in the hallways. Everyone must have been sent to their rooms for the time being. Benny would've given almost anything to be in his own suite, watching a wall of TV or raiding the snack pantry instead of marching towards some kind of inevitable punishment.

Ricardo led them to a meeting room, where chairs equipped with miniature hyperdrives floated around a circular holodesk so dark and shiny that it looked like a pool of ink. Ramona sat in one of the seats, spinning around, raising her fingers in a peace sign but not bothering to come to a stop as the others entered. Someone must have figured out she'd been the one who'd messed with Pinky's systems.

"Sit," Ricardo grunted.

Benny followed the instruction, as did the girls. Drue loitered near the entrance.

"Uh, maybe I should run up to my room," he muttered, starting for the door. "I've got a pretty good satellite phone in there that might help us contact Earth."

"Pinky?" Ricardo said.

"I'm on it." Her voice came from all around the room as she appeared in front of Drue, hands on her hips. He hesitated a second before darting through her, allowing just enough time for the door to slide shut. Trapped, he glanced back at Ramona.

"Don't even think about it," Pinky said. "We've confiscated her old HoloTek." Her voice got deeper. "Her programming skills are sloppy but effective."

Ramona grinned, still spinning, and made some sort of beeping noise with her mouth.

"Listen," Benny said to Ricardo, trying his best to keep his cool. "We had a good reason for going out." He turned to Jasmine. "I mean, tell him about the probabilities and statistics and stuff."

Jasmine's eyes went wide. "Don't blame this on me."

"Save it," Ricardo said, pulling out his HoloTek and tapping on it. "Elijah should be here any—"

The door slid open and Elijah blew through it like a cosmic wind, the rest of his Pit Crew trailing behind. He flung his sunglasses across the room where they crashed against one of the walls. He pointed at Hot Dog.

"Are you OK?" he asked.

"Me?" Hot Dog asked, startled. "Yeah, I'm fine."

"Pinky?"

"Scans show that she has no serious injuries," the holo gram said, "though she's likely to be very sore tomorrow."

Elijah nodded. His cheeks had turned a crimson colour, and one of his eyes twitched. He took a long, deep breath through his nose and then spoke quietly, looking back and forth between Drue, Jasmine and Benny.

"You took the Chevelle."

Benny nodded slightly. He didn't know if the others were reacting or not – he couldn't take his eyes off Elijah.

"You bypassed my AI's security, stole a re-engineered American classic that I hadn't even been able to test outside the dome yet and drove blindly out onto the Moon's surface."

Benny nodded again.

"Jazz mapped us, so technically we weren't . . ." Drue's voice got quieter as he spoke, before dying out. At least he was realising that talking was just making things worse this time.

Elijah closed his eyes, taking another deep breath. Benny noticed his fingers had curled into fists at his sides. Behind him, Sahar and Trevone had their arms crossed, while the Miyamura twins smirked at each other, as though they were enjoying the whole scene.

"Do you have any idea how stupid that was?" Elijah asked. His voice was measured, but Benny could tell he was on the verge of exploding, each consonant a staccato clip, every vowel threatening to transform into a yell. "You could have been killed. Or you could've got lost. Or . . . You thought, what, that since everything was in chaos here I wouldn't notice that you'd stolen a car and gone on a joyride?"

Benny and the others all started talking at once. Elijah held up a single gloved finger and everyone stopped. Even Drue.

"Trevone, take Ms Robinson with you and have her show you *exactly* what she did to Pinky. If she was able to break through her security that quickly, we must have overlooked a serious flaw in our systems." He motioned to his Pit Crew. "The rest of you, check in on your charges. They're likely scared out of their minds."

The older kids nodded, and Ramona followed them out, not looking the least bit concerned about being in trouble. As the door closed behind them, Hot Dog stood up.

"Mr West, they were trying to save me," she said, gesturing to the others. She glanced at Drue. "Even though it was a dumb thing to do."

Elijah tapped the gold-tipped toe of his right boot on the floor and raised an eyebrow.

"Is this true?"

Jasmine was staring at the floor, unable to meet Elijah's eye. Benny saw Drue take a few steps forward – but he wasn't exactly sure he wanted him to speak for the group.

"Of course," Benny said quickly. He swallowed hard, trying to calm the thundering in his chest. "There's no way I'd steal a car if we weren't worried someone was out there lost, maybe hurt." He shoved his hands into his pockets. "We were in the garage when you were talking to Pinky and heard how much ground you had to cover. We figured we could help."

"It was Drue's idea," Jasmine said. She looked surprised at her own words, raising one hand to cover her lips.

Drue turned to her with a look of shock on his face. "Traitor," he mouthed.

Elijah let his eyes roam over the kids' faces for a few moments before speaking again.

"Not unlike the boy you saved in the Drylands – am I right, Mr Love?"

Benny was taken aback for a moment. He didn't realise Elijah remembered his video out of the thousands he must have screened.

"Exactly."

Elijah seemed to relax, if only a little. "I handpick every EW-SCAB winner. My name's on the scholarship. I get the final say in who comes up here. And you were some of my brightest, most shining applicants. I had high hopes for you." He began to shake his head. "I'm not angry. I'm disappointed."

Benny's heart might as well have fallen out of his body. He almost wished that Elijah would start yelling, would get mad. *That* he could deal with.

"We'll make it up to you, Elijah!" Drue said, jumping to his feet.

"He's right for once," Jasmine said. "We'll do anything."

"Please don't send us home," Benny said, repeating the first word over and over again in his head.

Elijah raised a palm again, commanding silence.

"What you did today was reckless, *incredibly dangerous* . . ." He sighed. "That said, it was also quite brave." He tapped a gloved index finger against his lips a few times before continuing. "You can stay on the Moon, but on one condition: you *will* make it up to me. I want to see you at your best in the coming days. Show me that I didn't make a mistake bringing you up here."

"No problem," Drue practically shouted.

"Of course, sir," Benny said. He was so relieved he felt light-headed.

"My name is Elijah, not sir. Now, which one of you hot-wired and drove the Chevelle?"

"I did," Benny said. The words came out before he had time to decide if he should be scared or proud to admit this.

Elijah grinned, baring his teeth. "How'd she handle?"

A smile spread across Benny's face.

"Like a turbocharged dream." And then he remembered. "Um, I think I might have messed up an axle or something, though. But I can help fix it! If you just give me the tools—"

"Nonsense. I'll get Ash on it. We'll replace whatever bent with titanium reinforcements."

"There's something else," Jasmine said, getting to her feet. She grabbed Hot Dog's bag and took out the asteroid. "I pulled this from Hot Dog's Space Runner. I think it's what brought her down, and what hit the Grand Dome."

Elijah's mouth dropped open for an instant before he clenched his teeth and crossed the room in a few long strides. He snatched the craggy chunk from her hand, holding it up to the light.

"I've never seen anything like it before," Jasmine continued. "It's almost like some sort of rock-and-tech hybrid. It looks *engineered*."

"Fascinating," Elijah said, turning to Jasmine and smiling. "I'll run some scans on it just as soon as I've reviewed Pinky's readouts on the state of the Taj, our communications systems, the likelihood of another wave of asteroids, et cetera, et cetera." He looped his finger through the air a few times.

"There was other weird stuff," Hot Dog said. "Someone left supplies for me outside my Space Runner, but when I came to there was no one around. Who could have done that?"

"Came to?" he asked, stepping towards her and narrowing his eyes in curiosity. "Ms Wilkinson, it looks like there's a bruise starting to form at your hairline. You must have hit your head in the crash."

"Well, yeah, a little." She raised a hand to her temple and cringed as her fingers found a sore spot.

"Then of course you're confused. Visit the infirmary when we're through. Pinky will run tests to make sure you don't have a concussion. The Space Runner you were in had emergency supplies in the boot." He motioned to the bag on the ground. "You must have found them in a state of shock and then forgot."

"I guess that's possible."

"Um, back to the rocks," Benny said. Now that he knew he was staying at the Taj, he was starting to realise what else could be at stake. "If this is something that someone *made*, like Jasmine thinks, we could be under attack. *Earth* could be in danger."

Elijah slowly turned to face Benny. He pursed his lips for a second before letting one side of his mouth curl up in a half-smile.

"Benny, my boy, when you've lived a life like I have, you see a lot of crazy things, things that don't always make sense at first. You learn to value perspective." He tossed the rock sample in the air, and then caught it. "I assure you that this is nothing to be concerned about. Now, why don't you go back to your rooms and freshen up a bit? It's been a long day. Dinner's in half an hour, and Pinky's computerised kitchen makes vegetarian baby back ribs that are the most impressive delicacy in the solar system, trust me."

And then he turned on his heel and left, leaving the four of them behind trying to make sense of everything he'd said.

"That's it?" Drue asked. "I kinda hoped we were saving the world."

"Yeah," Jasmine said slowly.

"I don't know," Benny said, trying to put himself, impossibly, in Elijah's shoes. "There was something about the way he smiled before he left, like he *knew* how important this was. I think he just didn't want us to worry. Could be he's putting on a brave face. He's probably rushing back to his labs or whatever right now to look everything over."

Drue let out a loud breath. "Of *course* he is. You're right."

"Well, if you're still not sold," Hot Dog said, pulling a little hunk of rock out of the bottom of her bag and flicking a piece of wire sticking out of it. "Looks like we've got a piece of it we can run our own tests on."

She held the sample out to Jasmine, who eyed it for a moment before shoving it in her space-suit pocket.

CHAPTER 12

They retreated to their own suites as Elijah suggested. By the time Benny made it downstairs to the Taj's restaurant for dinner, most the tables were filled with kids, laughing and talking over one another. No one gave him a second glance as he walked in. They probably had no idea what he and the others had done.

The restaurant was dimly lit by golden constellations – probably holograms, Benny thought – floating overhead and reflecting in the dark marble floor. Unlike the sleek surfaces of the rest of the Taj, plush dark curtains hung on the walls, embroidered in swirling patterns that pulsed with light. Benny looked around, trying to find a place to sit in the crowded room. Finally, he spotted a ten-person table with only two people in a corner. He even recognised the kids at it – two other Mustangs.

"Can I sit here?" he asked as he approached.

"Sure thing," a girl with two long black-and-silver braids said. "You're the one from the caravan, right?"

"Yeah," Benny said, taking a seat and staring at the big, sweating jug of water on the table in front of him as he braced himself for the inevitable questions.

But they didn't come.

"I'm Iyabo," the girl said. She pointed to a thin boy across from her. "This is Herc."

The boy let out an exaggerated groan. "My name's *Alexi*," he said. "Iyabo apparently just started learning about mythology and I made the mistake of telling her I'm Greek." He turned back to Iyabo. "And it's *Heracles* in Greek myths. At least get your stories straight."

"Whatever," Iyabo said. "Did you see these tablecloths? They're threaded with *actual* gold."

Alexi rubbed his fingers over the cloth. "I could buy a small island if I took all these home."

"Sure, if you wanna spend weeks unravelling them and picking out all the gold," Drue said, coming up from behind Benny's chair. He rounded the table and sat beside Alexi. "I'm starving. I was afraid I'd miss the first course."

Iyabo eyed him up and down. "I just thought you were too embarrassed by getting your ass kicked on the track earlier today to come to dinner."

She smirked. Alexi giggled. Benny tried to hide his smile behind his hand. He'd forgotten that whatever Iyabo and Drue had talked about earlier in the day had ended with her walking away and rolling her eyes.

"I did not *get my ass kicked*." Drue said. "She got lucky and—"

"Speak of the devil," Iyabo said, cutting him off.

"Hey," Hot Dog said as she pulled out a chair next to Benny. Jasmine stood behind her.

"Couldn't keep away from us, huh?" Drue asked.

She silently pushed the chair back in and started to walk away.

"Wait," Benny said. "Come on, there aren't many seats around. Sit here." She paused for a second and then came back.

"Hey, are you OK?" Alexi asked Hot Dog as she and Jasmine took their seats. "You got owned by that asteroid. Where'd you end up landing?"

Hot Dog retold the story of the afternoon, leaving out the rock Jasmine found and the weird bag of supplies. Still, the story had Alexi and Iyabo speechless, until finally, when Hot Dog had finished, Iyabo looked back and forth between Drue and Benny.

"You two are the lamest heroes I've ever met."

"Thanks?" Benny said.

"Tell me more about this Chevelle," Alexi said. "What kinda mods did it have on it? And why do you even know how to hot-wire a car?"

Before Benny could say anything, half a dozen platters floating on mini hyperdrives landed on their table. They were piled high with crisps, chips and raw vegetables, all vibrant yellows, oranges, greens and purples. Slabs of cheese glistened in the light beside tiny loaves of bread. Bowls of unidentifiable sauces and dips dotted the spread.

Benny was pretty sure everyone in the restaurant must have heard his stomach growl. He'd never seen so much fresh food in one place in his life. The others at the table seemed just as impressed with the display. Even Drue. They all stared at the feast in front them, hardly breathing. And then, as if something had snapped in the air, they were digging in, ferocious, not realising how hungry they'd been.

"This is amazing," Benny said, biting into a purple carrot with a snap. "I don't know the last time I had a vegetable that wasn't half mush."

"Elijah and his researchers grow organic produce hyper-fast," Jasmine said, plunging a radish into a chunky pink spread. "One of his biggest goals when building the Taj was to make it as self-sufficient as possible. They've made all kinds of advances in gardening."

"You guys aren't doing this right," Drue said as he stacked a mountain of cheese onto a wedge of buttered bread. He dunked all of it into a thick white sauce before shoving the whole thing in his mouth. "This is the life."

"Wait, so what do you eat in the caravan?" Hot Dog asked, ignoring Drue.

"Usually canned food or fortified meal bars," Benny said. "We scavenge whatever we can. A lot of our food comes from houses. We find a neighbourhood and pick it over."

"Like, stealing?" Drue asked through a mouth full of bread.

"Like, *surviving*," Hot Dog said.

"Yeah," Benny continued with a thankful nod towards Hot Dog. "I mean, almost everywhere's been abandoned. Half the time the houses have been swallowed up by the sand, so we have to dig them out. Then we pool whatever we find together and the leaders divide everything equally. There are maybe a hundred of us, depending on who's coming and going, so we have to ration. It's not so bad when we're close to the edges of the cities, because we can stock up on sustenance squares at relief stations. But those things taste like dust and farts. We've been lucky. Some caravans starve out there."

"That's crazy," Drue murmured.

"It sounds like a smart system," Jasmine said.

"All that camping doesn't sound so bad," Alexi said. "That's how I live. On the water. We have the most beautiful beaches in Greece."

"Oh, now *that* I'll fight you about," Iyabo said. "You've obviously never been to Cameroon."

The two of them began a heated argument about which of their countries had better coasts. Meanwhile, Hot Dog turned to Drue.

"I don't suppose *you've* ever had to eat a sustenance square."

"I'm not going to feel bad about living in a city and having real food, if that's what you're trying to get at." He shoved more cheese into his mouth.

"You're a pig," Hot Dog said.

"Whatever. Where are you from, huh? You don't seem like the caravan type. All that sand would get stuck in your lip gloss."

Hot Dog made a face at him. "I'm from Texas."

"Eesh. I'm sorry."

She tightened her hold on the fork in her hand. Jasmine stepped in before she could retort.

"I was in Texas for a little while. You could see the sky for miles around in some places."

"Yeah, but the state is in anarchy half the time because they're scared the Drylands are getting closer," Hot Dog said. "Or that desert refugees are going to take over all our towns. I've heard it's harder to cross the border into Texas than it is most countries. Why were you there?"

"A family adopted me." Jasmine hesitated. "Well, they gave me a trial run. It didn't last."

"Oh," Hot Dog said quietly. "Sorry."

"It's OK. I'm used to it."

"Didn't you say you were from China?" Benny asked.

"Technically. My parents were killed in the big Sichuan earthquake of 2075. I barely remember them. Or China, really. A lot of us kids were shipped to orphanages across the world. I ended up in Florida. Since then, I've bounced back and forth between foster homes and adoptive parents. I think a lot of people are looking for kids who want to sit and watch cartoons all day, while I was more interested in doing science experiments. People . . . got weird about that."

"They let you do chemistry at home?" Drue asked.

"Not all science involves test tubes and Bunsen burners."
She smiled. "Baking is a perfectly respectable form of
scientific experimentation."

"That doesn't count."

"You've obviously never tried to cook a soufflé."

"So, don't take this the wrong way," Drue continued,
"but how are you so smart if you've been moving around
orphanages and stuff so much? It's not like you could go
to one school for very long. Much less have a good tutor."

"*Drue*," Hot Dog said.

"What? I'm trying to get to know her!"

Benny dropped a handful of crisps onto his plate. "Trust
me, you can learn plenty on your own without actual
school."

"He's right," Jasmine said. "I always liked solving problems. Finding the most efficient answer. Science and
numbers are based on fact, not opinion or emotions. It's
not like the rest of life where there are so many variables.
Fears, expectations, potential adopters looking for
someone taller or whiter or more 'normal'. I think a lot
of people just had a hard time with the idea of having
a daughter who was smarter than them in ways they
didn't understand."

"Adults are the worst," Hot Dog muttered.

"Except Elijah," Drue said.

"Dude, we all think Elijah is cool, but you are seriously one step away from stalker-level obsession."

"Not all adults are bad," Benny said. "My dad was the best."

"I dunno," Drue said. "My father's a senator, remember? He's, like, super powerful."

"Being powerful isn't the same as being good," Jasmine said, filling a leaf of lettuce with roasted vegetables.

Hot Dog hadn't taken her eyes off Benny. "Tell us about him."

"Well . . ." He didn't know where to begin at first, and then the words flooded out. "He was amazing. The whole caravan could be depressed and he'd cheer us all up somehow, find some way. The worst possible catastrophes could happen, and he'd find some good in them." He slowed down. "But then water was getting short, and we kept hearing rumours about some untapped aquifer out in Death Valley. There was supposedly enough water that we could settle down there for good and stop moving. He led a scouting party out there but . . ." Benny stared down at the abundance of food in front of him and the beads of moisture on the side of the water jug. "Those stories you hear about the gangs roaming the Drylands? A lot of them are probably fake. But not all of them. Death Valley was a trap."

He went quiet, along with the rest of the table. A few moments passed before he looked up at everyone else. They were still staring at him.

"Whoa, hey," he said. "I didn't mean to—"

"No," Hot Dog said. "I'm glad you told us."

"What about . . ." Jasmine started.

"Your mum." Drue finished her thought for her.

Benny shook his head. "I don't really remember her that much. Most of what I do is probably stuff I made up anyway. I have two little brothers, though. And a grandmother. She's great. Takes really good care of us." He took a deep breath. "And when I'm back, I'll be able to take care of all of them."

Across from him, Jasmine smiled, but the others stayed quiet.

"*Anyway* . . . What's your all-powerful senator dad like? And your mum?" Benny asked, ready to focus the conversation on anyone else and guessing Drue would have plenty to say.

"Being a Lincoln is great," Drue said. "An honour. My ancestors helped found America and fund, like, the revolution or something. I've got a lot to live up to."

"You didn't really answer his question," Jasmine said.

"Oh. Right. Well . . . Being a senator means you're really busy. And my mum's on the board of the biggest non-profits in DC, so she's got a lot of responsibility, too. I think she even does stuff for desert refugees."

"Oh, I get it," Hot Dog said. "Your parents got tired of having you around so much, so they bribed Elijah to make you the hundred and first EW-SCABer."

Drue squirmed in his chair across the table before piling more food onto his plate, muttering something about the pesto being too salty. Hot Dog chewed on her bottom lip, her eyebrows furrowed together.

"Oh," she murmured, looking down at the napkin in her lap. "Sorry."

Suddenly the trays lifted off the table, floating toward the kitchen.

"Oof," Benny said, trying to get everyone's spirits back up, or at least distract them. "I'm stuffed."

"*Stuffed?*" Iyabo asked, finally breaking off her argument with Alexi. "You know that was only the appetiser, right?"

By the time Benny had made it through the subsequent selection of exotic fruits, vegetarian baby back ribs and a chocolate tart with essence of elderberry that had been wafted through a candy floss mist, he could barely speak, let alone move. Almost everyone must have felt this way, because by the end of the meal the only person who was talking was Iyabo, who recounted an urban legend about a group of Taj builders who'd gone insane and now stalked the dark side, kept alive by some sort of cosmic radiation. On especially dark nights, she said, their skeletal forms would roam the outside of the Grand Dome, clawing at it, trying to get back in – the tattered remains of their space suits floating in decaying strips behind them.

Benny hung on her every word, looking forward to terrifying his brothers with the story when he got back to Earth. By the time Iyabo had finished, dinner was over. Benny's full belly, combined with everything he'd been through that day, caused him to basically collapse on the bed when he returned to his suite.

The mattress beneath him might as well have been a cloud, far softer than anything he'd ever felt. He slept deeply, dreamlessly, still dressed in his space suit and lying on top of the covers. He might have stayed that way all night, facedown, if the bed hadn't started to vibrate.

He stretched, trying to shake off sleep. As he sat up, dim accent lights powered on at the bottom of the walls, casting a faint glow in the room around him. The clock by his bed said it was after three in the morning. His body seemed to be trying to pull him back into sleep.

Then he remembered the asteroid storm from earlier, and leaped from the bed, darting over to the window.

But there were no rocks crashing against the Grand Dome. Everything outside was quiet, unmoving, peaceful.

He could *still* feel a slight vibration through the plush carpet, though. He was about to chalk it up to some kind of weird by-product of being on the Moon, or a fancy sleep aid, when suddenly there was a stronger shaking for a split second.

Something felt wrong.

Not knowing what else to do, he darted out into the hallway, half expecting to see Ricardo yelling at everyone to evacuate to the lower levels.

But there was only Hot Dog.

She stood in front of one of the wide hallway windows dressed in pyjamas and a shiny pink robe, her blond hair slightly dishevelled.

"Hey," he said.

She jumped, letting out a yelp, and then twisted around, arms raised like she might smack him. Once she saw it was just Benny she relaxed a little.

"You scared the crap outta me," she said, glaring.

"Sorry." He rubbed his eyes.

She let out a long sigh. "It's cool. I just thought I was the only one up."

"No. Wait, why *are* you awake?"

"I'm more of a power-napper than a real sleeper," she said. "I've been playing flight sims on the giant screen in my room for the past few hours. Then my eyes started to burn, so I thought I'd take a break."

"So the shaking didn't wake you up?" He was only now starting to think clearly, and began to second-guess why he was out in the hallway to begin with.

"Oh, *that*?" She pursed her lips in curiosity. "To be honest, I thought I was still feeling aftershocks from my last virtual run. This place has killer 5D immersion environments."

"No," Benny said. "It's real. I think."

"Meh," Hot Dog said, shrugging. "Probably a generator or something. Who knows what kind of stuff Elijah's got down in the basements."

"I guess . . ." he murmured. Maybe the vibrations had been coming from the room next door, someone playing video games late into the night. "You're probably right."

Hot Dog turned back to the window.

"I can't believe any of you can sleep. We're on *the Moon*, Benny."

"Turns out travelling through space is kind of tiring," Benny said.

Hot Dog looked at him. "The Drylands must be worse. Hot. Dusty. Too much sun. And that's coming from someone who really likes to be outside on a summer day in Texas."

"You get used to it, though it's nice to wake up without sand in my pockets." Benny shrugged. "What's Texas like?"

"Pretty lame. Crowded. At least where I am in Dallas."

"Whoa, so you're in a legit city."

"Yeah," she said. "I know what you're probably thinking, but the cities aren't all shiny skyscrapers and clean streets. There are plenty of gross parts."

"You spend a lot of time at the arcades, though, right? That's how you know the sims so well?"

"I spend a lot of time anywhere that's not home," she said, a hard edge to her words. "There were some free science museums I used to go to a lot. One had a great sim arcade. That's where I learned to fly. Then people started complaining I was always there and I got asked really nicely to not come back so much."

"That's dumb." Benny wasn't sure what else to say. "You

don't have any systems at home, I bet, huh? I mean, I'm lucky I had a crappy HoloTek."

She let out single laugh. "No. No systems. My parents . . ." Her voice got quiet. "They're not like your dad was. They spend most their time yelling at each other about how there's no money. Or how if all the people from California and the other states wrecked by the drought hadn't moved to the cities, they'd be able to afford to live in a nicer place. About anything, really. They assume I can take care of myself, which is kind of funny since it's not like *they* can find jobs. So I stay outside or sneak into movies or hang out with friends. I don't think they notice much."

Benny nodded slowly. "You're hoping you get to stay up here, huh?"

She let out a laugh.

"Aren't we all? After hearing everyone talk at dinner, it sounds like having bad or missing parents is almost a requirement for winning the EW-SCAB."

"Except for Drue."

"No, I think he's included in that." She twisted her lips to one side as she nodded to herself. "The way he was talking . . . Let's just say I understand what it's like to try and make excuses for your mum and dad. I used to do the same thing."

Benny thought about this for a second. Before he could respond, an unexpected yawn took over.

"Jeez, didn't mean to bore you, Benny," Hot Dog said.

"No, it's not that," he managed to say. "I just—"

But Hot Dog was already heading back towards her room, laughing a little and waving a hand to dismiss him. "Go back to bed, Love. I've got a fleet of enemy pilots to shoot down, anyway."

Too tired to put up a fight, Benny did as he was told. Back in his room, he noticed a glimmer beside his bed. The hood ornament had fallen to the floor. He picked it up and set it back on the nightstand. He was just starting to wonder what kind of gaming environment could cause so much shaking when sleep conquered him once again.

CHAPTER 13

Benny's suite came to life with lights, music and a simulated sunrise on the wall the next morning, signalling that it was time to get out of bed and meet up with his group. He quickly discovered that a hot shower was perhaps the greatest pleasure in life he'd been missing out on in the Drylands. Afterwards, he threw on a new space suit – fresh clothes being yet another unthinkable luxury – and made his way to the Mustangs' common room. After breakfast, they spent the morning designing custom Space Runners on their HoloTeks based on never-before-produced prototype models and getting their first taste of weightlessness in a zero-gravity chamber on the first floor.

It wasn't until lunch – loads of pizza – that Benny had time to think about what had happened yesterday. And all over again, he was worried. What did the asteroid they'd discovered mean for the Taj? For Earth?

When he found himself behind Jasmine in the pizza line, he was quick to bring up the strange rocks.

"I can't stop thinking about them," she said, lips drawn down in a frown. "I still want to get the sample we have analysed. There's something . . . I'm sure Elijah is on top of this, but I'd like to know for sure what these things are."

"Yeah." Benny piled food onto his plate, trying to remind himself that the smartest man In the galaxy had this under control. "Well, if we ever get a break from all our scheduled stuff, we'll figure it out, OK?"

Jasmine smiled and nodded. "Deal."

She sat with Iyabo and a few other Mustangs. Benny was going to join them, but then he saw Drue sitting by himself and plopped down next to him instead.

Drue grinned. "Honestly, I could eat this for lunch every day for the next two weeks and be just fine."

"I'm totally with you on that," Benny said.

A few minutes later, Hot Dog came over.

"Hey," she said. Benny watched as she glanced over at Jasmine, who sat across the room. The girl nodded to her, eyebrows raised, like she was encouraging her to continue. Hot Dog smiled nervously at Drue. "I just wanted to thank you for coming out to get me yesterday. And to say . . . you know . . . I'm sorry about what I said last night."

Drue stared back at her, unmoving for a few seconds.

"Said about what?" he finally asked. Then he took a massive bite of pizza. "Have a seat. This cheese is super good. I bet they make it here."

Hot Dog sat down with them, and that was the end of that.

Eventually Ricardo took to the little stage in the common room again, a glint in his eye.

"I hope you're fuelled up," he said, "because we're about to go to war."

Before any of them could ask what he was talking about, their leader was out of the door. Benny and the rest of his teammates tried to keep up as they jogged through the halls of the Taj.

He led them to the place he had referred to as the "virtual gaming room" the day before, which Benny guessed was the size of a football field – maybe a little bigger. Grey rubber lined the floor, walls and ceiling, and the whole environment had the faint, acrid smell of electronics.

Ricardo spoke again.

"This afternoon you'll have the chance to prove you not only that you have what it takes to be here, but that you're the most capable of the four groups on the Moon. This is where we see what you are made of. I won't accept anything less than your best." He leaned against one of the walls. "Your space suits have microscopic antigravity units sewn into them – the same technology that makes a Space Runner fly. When combined with the state-of-the-art holographic environment systems in this room, the suits create simulated pressure points. An easier way of looking at it is like this: If a hologram of a ladder appears before you, you'll be able to climb it thanks to the suit's ability to affect the gravity around you."

"And if you're hit with a holographic bat, you'll feel it," Jasmine said.

"Exactly," Ricardo said.

"How can I get some trainers with this tech built in?" Drue asked as he inspected the seams of his space suit. "Now I see why Pinky said I had to wear this today."

Several of the rubber tiles slid out of the wall, revealing a rack holding dozens of shiny silver gloves. A murmur of awe-filled confusion filtered through the EW-SCABers.

"What you see before you are multipurpose gaming manipulation units," Ricardo continued. "Outside of this room they're useless, but inside they're capable of punching through boulders in one simulation and shooting lasers in the next. For this game, they'll be gravity gloves." He grabbed one and slid it onto his right hand. A blue band lit up across the knuckles. "Point one at an object and press the side button, and you'll be able to move your target in any direction. Observe."

A holographic duplicate of his red Space Runner appeared a few metres away. Still looking at the group before him, he held out a palm and made a big show of making a fist, smashing his thumb against his index finger. When he lifted his arm, the car began to rise, then move side to side and back and forth, following his motions. Eventually he let his thumb off the button, and the Space Runner fell fast, crashing against the floor and turning into a cloud of light particles.

"Any questions?" Ricardo asked.

A few seconds passed before everyone started talking at once.

"I want a pair!"

"What are we doing with them?"

"Do they come in other colours?"

"These are *awesome*," Drue said to Benny. His eyes were big and shining. Benny recognised the expression – it was the same look his little brothers had any time he or his dad had brought home something new for them from a scouting trip.

After explaining the finer points of using the gloves and how to adjust the direction of the gravitational force, Ricardo began passing them out, one per person. Benny slid his on. When the knuckle band lit up, he couldn't help but grin. All around him, the group buzzed with excitement, several Mustangs throwing quick punches into the air.

"Your objective today is simple," Ricardo said as he armed his group. "In a few moments, you'll find yourself on a planet far, far away where hostile robotic life-forms have taken over. In order to win, you'll have to protect yourselves and your teammates from all the enemies seeking to destroy you. Take *them* down instead."

Three glowing red hearts appeared over each of their heads.

"Whoa," Benny said, reaching up and running his hand through the holograms.

"Your enemies are armed and don't like you on their turf," Ricardo continued. "Get hit three times and your glove dies. You're a ghost. Out of the game."

Ramona took out her EW-SCAB HoloTek and started tapping on it.

"Don't even think about it," Ricardo said to her. "I assure you that if you try to cheat in this game, Pinky will power down every electronic device within your reach before you can say 'woot'."

Ramona sucked her teeth. "Uber lame."

"Let's do this," Hot Dog said, pulling a pink band from her pocket and tying her hair back into a high ponytail. She flashed a smile at their leader. "Are you gonna be joining us?"

Ricardo shook his head. "No. You're on your own, but I'll be watching. Don't make me look bad. I'll start the simulation in fifteen seconds." He tapped a HoloTek and then was floating in the air above them, taking a high observation point.

Jasmine glanced around at her team. Everyone stared at one another, unsure of what to do. She took a wary look at her gloved hand before inhaling deeply and nodding.

"We should spread out," she said, motioning to the Mustangs. "We're too big a target grouped together like this, and, for all we know, there will be robots dropping bombs on us in a few seconds."

The EW-SCABers all stared at her.

"You heard her," Benny said. He looked up at Ricardo, who seemed to approve. Then he turned back to the group. "But stay in teams of two so no one ends up alone. Come on, guys. Go!"

They started to scatter. Benny gave Drue a thumbs-up. "Let's watch each other's backs, yeah?" he said.

Drue nodded and crouched, like he was ready to leap out from a hiding spot and ambush some unseen enemy.

Benny didn't know quite what to do, so he just spun around a few times, looking for signs of the room changing. Then he blinked, and when his eyes opened again, he was in another world.

Quartz-like boulders dotted the landscape around him in a rainbow of colours, jutting out of the grassy earth. They were twice his height, some taller. The sky was streaked with thin white clouds and lit by three small orange suns. Everything was so bright, so *vivid*. He felt as though he'd just been transported into some sort of painting or cartoon.

There was a strange sound, too. Something he couldn't quite place until he climbed up the tall embankment beside him and froze, his brain unable to fully comprehend what he was seeing.

Water. A surging river thirty metres wide at least, cutting through the landscape, disappearing over the horizon in what must be a magnificent waterfall.

For a moment Benny forgot that everything he was seeing was fake, the river nothing more than a computer program. All he could think was that this was more water than he'd seen in his entire life. That his caravan could live on land like this forever. It was the kind of thing his father always dreamed about, and now it was there, in front of him, so real-looking that he was sure he'd drown if he stepped into it.

"Get down!" Hot Dog shouted somewhere off to his side.

A flash of light shot out of the dense forest lining the other side of the river, and the ground near Benny's feet exploded in a shower of dirt and debris, causing him to tumble backward down the embankment. He jumped to his feet and dusted himself off as soon as he stopped rolling.

Fifteen metres away Hot Dog shook her head. "You've obviously never played a first-person shooter before."

"We didn't exactly have arcades in the Drylands," Benny muttered. Above him, one of the hearts blinked out. "Aw, man. Already?"

Nearby, Drue was pointing his fist at the ground, causing chunks of dirt and grass to fly into the air. He tried to lift one of the giant quartz pieces beside him but it didn't budge. Still, he didn't seem put off. He just flexed his fingers as he locked eyes with Benny.

"Let's go mess up some robots."

The two of them carefully climbed back up the embankment and took cover behind another outcrop of the gemlike rock near the river, where the grass gave way to black sand. Further up the bank, the rest of the Mustangs were making their way to the water with cautious steps. Hot Dog and Jasmine stayed close together, within Benny's earshot.

"OK," he said, peeking around the corner of the rock. "So who tried to explode me?"

As if on cue, a dozen metallic beasts flew out of the trees. Benny could only stare wide-eyed as he watched creatures of silver, gold and bronze shoot across the water, leaving faint chem trails behind them. Their bodies were segmented, like insects, but their faces were closer to human skulls. Five sharp-looking appendages opened and closed like claws as they darted through the air. In the trees, larger robots seemed to be patrolling at ground level, shaking the underbrush.

Benny wasn't sure what he'd been expecting, but it definitely wasn't anything as creepy as this.

One of the flying enemies paused partway across the river, catching sight of Benny and Drue. Its grinning jaw unhinged and some kind of neon-yellow energy shot out, bouncing off the side of the quartz they hid behind.

"Whoa!" Benny shouted. "Laser-shooting psycho bee bots!"

"They don't stand a chance against Drue Bob Lincoln." Drue paused. "Against *us*."

Benny nodded, and swung back around to face the oncoming hordes.

Several of the flying robots appeared to have already been affected by the gravity gloves, crashing into the water or onto the riverbanks. The Mustangs were proving themselves a force to be reckoned with. Benny tried his best to lock on to one of the bronze beasts flying his way, but it was too fast, too agile for him to catch.

So instead, he improvised. As the robot he'd been trying to take down dived close to the river, he targeted not the metallic insect but its surroundings. A jet of water shot up when he smashed the button on the side of his finger, knocking the robot off course and sending it spiralling through the air, landing somewhere behind him and Drue.

"Nice trick," Drue said. "We are totally space heroes."

"Mustang marines," Benny said.

"Elijah's secret squad."

"The Moon platoon!"

"Oh, that's got a nice—"

There was a high-pitched electronic whine, a flash of light, and then Drue went down, swearing. Benny spun around to find that the robot he'd downed hadn't been destroyed – though it was having a hard time getting back in the air.

He got the robot in his sights and shoved his fist forward again, using the antigravity to send his enemy soaring into the sky and then back down, crushing it against the ground.

This time it wasn't getting back up.

"That *hurt*," Drue said, getting to his feet and watching as one of the hearts above him disappeared. "I mean, not *bad*, but still. These suits aren't messing around."

Benny turned his attention back to the battleground, but it looked like the robots were retreating. The Mustangs were actually *winning*, though he could see that several of his other teammates up the river had also taken damage.

"Is that it?" Drue asked. "That was nothing."

"I don't think so," Jasmine said as she darted to join the boys behind the quartz, Hot Dog covering her. "They're just retreating to regroup. If we want to defeat them, we're going to have to go on the offensive."

"No problem," Hot Dog said. "Let's kick some metal butt."

"Uh, *big* problem," Drue said. "There's a raging river between us. I'm a good swimmer, but even I couldn't make it across this thing." He twisted his lips in confusion. "Also, I don't really know how holographic water works."

"OK, so let's build a makeshift raft or something."

Benny glanced around, but there wasn't much in the way of raft-building material on their side of the river. They'd have to be resourceful and work together, but the only thing they had was . . .

He stared down at his glove for a moment before looking back up at Drue.

"I've got a better idea," he said, a smile spreading across his face. "I'm going to punch you."

CHAPTER 14

"I'm sorry, what?" Drue asked.

"Just trust me," Benny said. "I think this will work."

"Wait, let's talk about—"

Benny balled up his fist and shoved it forward, coming within a few inches his teammate's stomach. He smashed the button on the side of the glove and Drue flew back, shouting as he sailed over the water, flailing his arms and legs.

"Oh crap! Oh crap, oh crap, oh . . ." He came to a stop as Benny pulled his fist back. Drue looked around and patted his arms and legs, the fear in his eyes starting to fade. Slowly, he placed his hands on his hips as though he were some kind of superhero floating in mid-air. "Actually, this is kind of cool." He twisted himself around, face scrunching in determination as he pointed across the river. "Get me over there!"

As Benny navigated Drue through the air, he shouted to Jasmine and Hot Dog.

"Look! It's working. We can get our team to the other side."

Jasmine looked at Hot Dog, hesitant.

"Um, I don't want to hurt you, but—"

"Can it, Jasmine, and just shoot me already," Hot Dog said. "I'm not letting him beat my kill count."

And then there were a dozen kids flying through the air, following Benny's lead. Some of them brought their teammates over once they were on the enemy's side, but then the robots started firing again and the airspace over the water became too dangerous to try and pass through.

"OK," Benny said to Jasmine as they crouched behind the quartz, "so what do we do now? We're useless over here."

"Not at all," she said. "We have a better line of sight and can cover the rest of the Mustangs this way. It's actually the best plan, I think."

"Sure," Benny said. If he trusted anyone to devise a strategy, it was going to be Jasmine, based on her track record so far – though he was pretty sure part of the reason she was saying this was because she didn't want to be slung through the air while all the fighting was going on. Not that he could blame her.

For the most part, things seemed to go well. The Mustangs were getting better at using their gloves and managed to drive the robots back into the trees, racing in after them. Benny was able to take down a few more robots that darted out of cover, saving the hearts of several teammates. He couldn't tell what was going on past the trees, exactly, but he hoped things were OK.

Still, he didn't like being out of the action for too long.

He was just starting to get impatient, and was about to ask Jasmine to send him over, when he spotted Drue running out of the trees, chased by three flying robots. Drue managed to knock one into the other, causing them both to go down in a shower of sparks, but the third got the better of him, and landed a shot directly in the boy's stomach.

Drue fell backward, rolling across the beach. His second heart blinked out as the robot swooped down, attacking him with the claw on the bottom of its body. No, not attacking – the robot snatched Drue's gravity glove, leaving him defenceless. Drue scrambled across the sandy bank, yelling something Benny couldn't make out over the sound of the water. Then he disappeared behind one of the quartz pieces, outside Benny's line of fire.

"No!" Benny shouted. "I can't get you out of there if I can't see you!"

But it was no use – Drue couldn't hear him, either. Benny turned to Jasmine, but an errant shot from across the battlefield had knocked her down the hill. She was just now getting to her feet.

More flying robots began to spill out of the trees. One made a beeline for Drue's hiding spot, but Benny managed to catch it in mid-air, sending it flying off course. The enemy exploded against a tree.

There was no way Drue was going to survive on his own, unarmed.

Benny took a deep breath. The way he saw it, there was only one choice – only one way of saving the boy who, despite sometimes being a pain, was probably the closest thing to a friend he had on the Moon so far. He turned his back to the river and shoved his right fist into the centre of own chest.

"This is a bad idea," he muttered as he pressed the button on the side of the glove.

He shot into the sky, involuntarily shouting in a mixture of excitement and fear. At first he wasn't even sure which direction he was going, but after letting go of the button and retriggering the antigravity a few times, he managed to get his bearings and set himself upright. Then, after taking a moment to congratulate himself on not immediately crashing and burning, he flew forward, the river churning six metres below him.

"Don't fall, don't fall, don't fall," he repeated to himself as he jetted over the water.

And he didn't. At least, not until he was hovering over the sand on the opposite bank from where he'd started. He even managed a pretty soft landing, all things considered.

He found Drue leaning against a rock, breathing heavily.

"It's too dangerous over here," Benny said. "We need to get you back to the other side."

"Stupid robot," Drue spat. "Where'd that thief go?"

There was a crashing sound behind him as a metal behemoth on three spiked legs burst out of the dense forest, splintering two trees. Its skull-like face turned to the two boys, sizing them up in a split second. Then it raised a cannon-like arm in their direction.

"What the—?" Benny said.

"Crap!" Drue shouted. "Those things are tough! Watch out!"

They didn't have time to get out of the way, but Benny could do *something*. Without a second thought, he

177

pushed Drue aside and twisted his body, shielding his friend from the blast. Benny's space suit only simulated the pressure of whatever weapon the robot was using, but it still caused momentary pain to course through him. He fell hard, the breath knocked out of him, leaving him gasping for air on the sand as Drue tried to get to his feet. Above him, one of his hearts flickered and disappeared.

The robot moved forward, its metallic limbs clicking, cannon recharging. Benny struggled to aim his glove, but it was hard to steady himself when he was still trying to breathe. Drue was on the other side of the quartz, staying out of sight.

Benny was pretty sure this was the end.

That was when a big tree limb crashed against the robot's head. The branch rose again, then came back down, over and over until the metal monster crumpled in on itself and fell over in a shower of sparks.

Hot Dog stood behind the mangled machine, smiling, her fist aimed at the floating log.

"That's another one for me," she said.

"Benny, my man," Drue said cautiously, peeking around the side of the rock. "Did you just . . . lose one of your hearts for me?"

"We said we'd watch each other's backs, didn't we?" Benny asked.

Drue looked confused for a second, and then smiled meekly. It looked different from the grin he usually had plastered on his face.

"Thanks," Drue said. "Seriously."

"No problem."

"Now . . . how about you let me use your glove?"

"In your dreams," Benny said, getting to his feet.

The leaves around them rustled as more Mustangs streamed out of the forest, some chased by robots, others shouting into the open air that they'd almost won – that most of their enemies had been destroyed. Not everyone looked happy, though. A few teammates like Alexi and Ramona had lost all of their hearts and were now practically see-through. Benny realised there were holograms projected onto them to make them look like ghosts walking around the simulation, but still, it was a little spooky.

"Let's finish this up!" Benny shouted, catching a flying enemy in the air with his gravity glove and sending it diving straight into the river.

That's when the rumbling began.

It started off soft, like the slight vibration Benny had felt beneath his feet the night before, but soon the entire world around him seemed to be shaking, as though the ground might open up and swallow the Mustangs.

"What's going on?" Hot Dog yelled.

The answer came in the form of a clawed metal hand that reached up over the edge of the horizon where the river turned into a waterfall. It was skeletal, huge – big enough to scoop up two Space Runners in a single swipe. Veins running through it pulsed with blue light. A second hand appeared on the other side of the riverbank, and then a head popped up over the centre of the river, shaped like some kind of inhuman skull with an elongated, protruding jaw and two black horns sticking out of the back. There was only one socket for an eye in the centre of its forehead, and inside a floating blue orb pulsed with energy as the enormous robot hoisted itself up further, until its full metal torso rose above the horizon.

"What the heck is that?" Benny asked.

"Haven't you *ever* played a video game?" Hot Dog asked. "This is the final boss. We take it down, and we've won this thing."

She pointed her fist at the metal giant and pushed the trigger button a few times.

"Perfect," she said. "These things are useless against it. I don't suppose anyone found a rocket launcher in the trees?"

The gargantuan monster lurched forward again, and suddenly its jaw split open, exposing more of the orb. A wave of blue energy shot out, coating the opposite side of the riverbank and taking out the hearts of any Mustangs in its path.

"Jasmine!" Hot Dog shouted. She spotted the other girl and used her glove to float Jasmine over before she was caught up in the blast. Jasmine screamed and thrashed her arms and legs, though Benny wasn't sure if this was because of the giant that had appeared or the fact that Hot Dog had plucked her off the riverbank with no warning.

Benny tried smacking the robot's face with a felled tree trunk, but it didn't even make a dent in the thing. Drue ran around, trying to find something to fight with, while the rest of the Mustangs attempted – and failed – to use their gloves against the beast. When Jasmine was finally on the ground again, Hot Dog grabbed her by the shoulders.

"OK, you're the smart one," she said. "What do we do now?"

"I don't know!" Jasmine shouted. "Why would *I* know?!"

"Well, then *guess*."

"Um, the eye maybe!" Jasmine said. "In the centre of his head? If that's a power source, maybe we can corrupt it."

"Yes!" Hot Dog said. "Every boss has a weak spot. That's so obvious – why didn't I think of it?"

"Yeah, but we need something to hit it with," Drue said as he jogged over to the robot Hot Dog had taken down. "We need one of those robo-cannons."

"Why don't we just throw a big rock at it?" Benny asked.

He focused on one of the big purple shards of quartz sticking out of the ground. It was at least two metres tall and twice as wide as Benny. He pointed his knuckles at it and held down the glove's side button, but the thing didn't budge.

"I've tried that," Drue said. His voice was strained as he tried to wrench the weapon from the downed robot's grip. "They're too heavy."

"Maybe for one person," Benny said. "Let's see what a few of these gloves can do."

Jasmine and Hot Dog nodded and ran over to his side, targeting the rock themselves. It began to shake.

There were other Mustangs skulking through the trees, coming back out into the open to see what was causing the earth to tremble.

"Hey! Guys!" Benny yelled. "Help us out over here! I've got an idea!"

In a flash there were almost a dozen gloves trained on

the rock. It began to rise, slowly at first, and then quickly as it was pulled from the ground. Meanwhile, flying robots continued to buzz around them.

"Someone cover us!" Jasmine shouted. "Watch our flanks!"

"I've got you!" Drue said. He crouched in the sand beside them and fired the weapon he'd pried from the downed robot, completely obliterating one of the enemies.

"We've got this," Benny yelled. "Aim for the big glowing thing. Go, go!"

The crystal shot forward like a Space Runner, sailing through the air. It hit the giant's chest, scratched it and then fell into the river.

"Oops," Drue said.

But Benny was already rallying. "OK. We might have a better shot if we split up." He pointed at Iyabo, who stood beside him. Based on the way she commanded conversation at dinner the night before, he figured she'd have no problem getting people to follow her. "Take five Mustangs and head upriver. Do the same thing again. Everyone else, with me!"

Iyabo's team got to a piece of quartz first. The purple mineral was sailing through the air as Benny's group was just getting their piece out of the ground.

It shot past the robot, missing it completely.

"There's no way of controlling it once it gets that far away!" Iyabo shouted.

"So we get closer," Hot Dog suggested.

Benny nodded as their yellow rock floated in the air. "Let's go."

The six of them ran alongside the riverbank, Benny taking the lead and guiding the point of their big, floating weapon. The closer they got, the more he had to clench his jaw to keep from shaking as the huge metal skeleton gnashed its teeth.

When they were just outside the thing's reach, they stopped.

"Now!" Benny shouted.

He punched his fist into the air, trying his best to keep the quartz on track. It shot through the sky, a yellow missile.

And by some miracle, it hit its target almost dead centre, sailing through the eye socket and crashing into the blue orb just as the giant was getting ready to unleash another wave of energy aimed at their side of the river. A low, bass-heavy electronic sound filled the air, and for a moment the giant robot was perfectly still. Then the entire front of its face exploded, showering the water with flaming shards of metal as Benny and his fellow Mustangs ran back towards safety. Its arms jerked forward, fingers clawing into the sand as it struggled to stay upright before collapsing face first into the water, where it appeared to power down. All around them, the remaining robots fell out of the sky.

"Wahoo!" someone shouted, and then they were all yelling, Benny included.

"We destroyed a giant robot," Benny said to himself, wondering how in the galaxy he'd reached a point in his life where this statement was true.

As they celebrated, a bridge appeared across the river, and the Mustangs regrouped in the centre of it, the ghosts coming back into full view as the team caught their breath, trying to figure out what would happen next.

The sound of clapping filled the sky.

Benny turned to see the giant robot smacking its claw-like hands together, only they were beginning to disintegrate now. The hologram fell apart, along with the rest of the artificial environment, until they were once again standing in the big grey room.

The sound continued, though, as Elijah West made his way towards them. Applauding.

"Impressive work, Mustangs," he said. "The groups who went through this exercise this morning failed to defeat my robotic cyclops. The team remaining will have your performance as the standard to which they are compared."

"He was here," Drue said. "Watching. That monster was *him*!"

"Do you think he's annoyed that we shoved a giant rock into his eye?" Benny murmured.

"It wasn't luck that made you successful," Elijah continued as he got closer to them. "You were able to do something the other groups couldn't: you worked as a team."

"Mostly," Ricardo said from above. Benny had all but forgotten about their leader, who was now floating back down to their level.

"Yes," Elijah said. "I watched this match closely. Many of you acted like heroes today. You showed wisdom, talent and bravery. One of you more so than the others."

He turned his gaze to Benny, who suddenly forgot how to breathe.

"Benny Love," Elijah continued, "you showed not only resourcefulness and ingenuity today – you also put your teammates before yourself. I think my friend here would agree."

Ricardo nodded.

Elijah smiled. "Hold out your hand."

Benny did as he was told. Elijah stepped forward and dropped a silver band into his palm.

"An advanced holographics bracelet. Something I've been working on lately. If I'm remembering correctly, you mentioned that you're a big fan of this sort of technology in your application video. Something to do with spiders, I believe it was."

"This is . . ." Benny started, but he was at a loss for words.

"*Yours*," Elijah said. "Enjoy it. You earned it. You should be proud of yourself. *I'm* certainly proud of the work you did."

Benny saw Drue tense up at his side, but he ignored him. Elijah smiled, and there was something about it that made Benny's chest feel like it was full of fizzy pop. It wasn't just that he'd somehow managed to impress *the* Elijah West, or that he'd apparently been the best kid on the battlefield – it wasn't even because of the insane tech he'd just been given, a gift that he couldn't wait to test out.

It was another reason entirely: there was something about Elijah's expression that reminded Benny of the way his father used to look at him when he'd done something good.

"Try syncing it with your HoloTek. I guarantee you'll

get a kick out of it," Elijah said. "Now, I've had Pinky on mute for a while and should really check in before she ends up locking me in my office or something." He grinned and winked at the Mustangs, and then he was gone.

The rest of the kids congratulated Benny, a few patting him on the back, but everything seemed like a blur to him. Even after leaving the video-game room, Benny felt as though he were still floating. He'd always looked up to Elijah West – who *wouldn't*? – but he hadn't exactly come to the Moon for the purpose of impressing the man. But now he wanted to cling to the feeling he had when Elijah was happy with his performance, to hold on to it as long as he could. Benny was beginning to understand the sort of drive he'd seen in Drue – a ferocious desire to make Elijah proud.

It was a feeling Benny recognised. He'd felt the same way about his father, always wanting to do his best so that he could in some way try to live up to the standard his dad set. Benny had assumed he'd never meet another person who he'd want to prove himself to outside his family.

But maybe he'd been wrong.

Back in his room, Benny stood in the kitchen area and stared down at the band Elijah had given him. With one tap, the top layer of the bracelet fell apart, drifting up into the air like a puff of smoke. Then, in the blink of an eye, there was another Benny standing in front of him, staring down at his own wrist.

Benny yelped and jumped back. His clone did the same thing. If it weren't for a slight sheen of light around the other him, it would have been a perfect twin.

"This thing is incredible," Benny whispered.

The mist of metal must have been nanotech hologram projectors, he guessed. Incredibly advanced. He reached out. His hand met his mirror's but passed through it. Unlike the special constructs in the video game room, this was a normal hologram. Still, it was a billion times cooler than anything he'd ever seen back on Earth.

He pulled out his HoloTek and, with a few taps, Benny was able to control the hologram's projections using pictures he had saved on the datapad. One second it was another Benny in front of him, the next it was his brother Alejandro, then Justin and then his grandmother. But there was something slightly off about the vacant stares in their eyes that made him feel at once both homesick and a little creeped out.

He tapped his new bracelet again and the mist of nano-projectors flew back, the hologram disappearing. He plopped down on the sofa, staring at the metal around his wrist.

His brothers – the whole *caravan* – were going to flip out when he showed this to them and told them that Elijah West had singled him out. That he'd done his family proud.

CHAPTER 15

Thanks to the lingering threat of asteroids still floating above the Moon, all FW-SCAB flight training outside the Grand Dome was temporarily cancelled. Ricardo assured his Mustangs that they'd still get plenty of time behind a flight yoke, only it would be concentrated in the second week of their stay.

To make up for this, the scholarship kids were gathered in the courtyard following another lavish dinner that night. Dozens of dessert trays floated around the Grand Dome. Benny stood in front of one, eating some kind of candy floss that turned into ice cream when he put it in his mouth. Beside him, Ramona was alternating sips between a rainbow-coloured milkshake and a canned energy drink. Benny was wondering if now would be a good time to test his bracelet and completely freak out Drue and the others when a girl he'd never met before came up to him.

"Are you Benny?" she asked.

He looked up at her, surprised. There were two boys behind her, both staring at him expectantly.

"Uh, yeah," he said.

"I'm Kavita," the girl said. "We're with the Chargers. I was just wondering . . . I heard you guys stole one of Elijah's cars and saved that girl who crashed . . . Is that true?"

Benny blinked.

"Who told you that?" he asked.

"Um," she said, looking around the courtyard. "Oh, him!"

Benny followed her gaze and saw Drue, surrounded by people from other groups, motioning wildly as he talked. Some of the EW-SCABers eyed him sceptically, but others seemed to be hanging on his every word.

"Of course," Benny muttered. "Uh, excuse me."

He started across the courtyard at a clip, passing Jasmine – who was biting into a brownie the size of her face – along the way.

"Hey!" she called to him through a mouthful of fudge. "Is everything OK?"

"Our friend over there is telling everyone about the Chevelle."

"*Drue*," Jasmine groaned, following him.

Drue was mid-story when they got close enough to hear him.

"That's when Elijah said, 'Drue, what you guys did today was *so* brave,' and – oh, hey! Here's Benny and Jazz now!"

The eight or nine people in front of him all turned to look at them.

"Did Elijah really offer to give you guys his Chevelle as a reward for saving her?" one of them asked.

"What was it like to puke on the Moon, Jazz!" another chimed in.

"What?" Jasmine frowned at Drue.

"Can we have a second alone with him?" Benny asked.

Reluctantly, the crowd walked away.

"Told you he was full of it," someone said.

"What's the deal?" Drue asked. "I'm just telling stories of our heroics. You should be thanking me. We're practically famous up here now!"

"Why does this story involve me throwing up?" Jasmine asked.

Benny shook his head. "Did you ever think that *maybe* it doesn't look good if everyone here is talking about how we stole one of Elijah's cars? And hacked his security? He probably doesn't want that getting around, and personally

I don't like people thinking I'm some kind of thief." He'd already attracted enough weird looks when he'd mentioned he was from a caravan.

Drue frowned. "Oh. You might have a point there."

"Of course he does," Jasmine said. "And why do I get the feeling *you're* the hero of this story?"

"I gave credit to everyone!"

"That's actually true," Benny said. "A girl just asked me about it."

"See? You're welcome."

"Did you tell them about the asteroids?" Jasmine asked.

"No, I left *that* part out."

She nodded and scrunched her brows together in thought. "Probably for the best. I wonder if Elijah's found anything out."

"You're still thinking about it, too, huh?" Benny asked.

"Elijah'll take care of whatever it is," Drue said. "Look around you. The man can handle a few space rocks."

"Still," Jasmine said, her gaze drifting across the courtyard. "It would be nice to know what was going on."

Her eyes settled on Ricardo, who stood talking to Trevone and Sahar near the garage door.

"We could go and ask," Benny suggested. "See if they'll talk to Elijah for us."

"I can't talk to Trevone," she said, turning her attention to the ground. "He's just so *smart*."

"Oh, I see what's going on here," Drue said. He motioned to Benny's bracelet, frowning a little. "You go and talk to them. Ricardo *likes* you."

"Sure," Benny said. After all, he wanted answers, too. What if there'd been more to the rock than Elijah had initially thought?

He left Drue and Jasmine behind and made his way to the front of the garage. As he approached, he caught the end of the Pit Crew's conversation.

"Wasn't it a little early to have them squaring off against each other?" Trevone asked Ricardo.

"He's much more compliant after his loss."

Trevone nodded, the goggle-like glasses sitting on top of his short, curly black hair bobbing a little. "Not a bad move, I guess. Especially putting him up against Hot Dog. She was bound to win."

"That was the plan, but for a moment there I thought I was going to have to have Pinky step in and slow him down."

"Still, your group's got a lot of spirit. That could be . . . problematic."

"Elijah estimates we still have almost a week before—"

Sahar cleared her throat, nodding her head.

"Benny," Ricardo said as he noticed the Mustang. He raised one eyebrow.

"So this is Mr Love," Trevone said. He crossed his arms over the front of his dark blue space suit. "I've been hearing your name a lot lately."

"You have?" Benny asked warily.

"Word travels fast around the resort. Once my group heard about your winning the robot simulation *and* that little rescue mission . . . well, let's just say I'm having to keep an extra eye on my Chargers every time we go into the garage."

"Do you have a question?" Ricardo asked.

"Actually, I was wondering if you could ask Elijah something for me," Benny said. "When we were out on the Moon, we found a rock that hit Hot Dog's Space Runner and—"

"Oh!" Ricardo interrupted him. "Right. I forgot. Elijah wanted me to let you know that he tested the rock himself and that it appeared to be a completely normal asteroid."

"Huh?" Benny asked, confused. "But there was a weird pattern on it and wire sticking out."

Sahar's lips curved down a little, her dark eyes penetrating.

"Ah, that," Trevone said. "Probably just part of the Space Runner that got embedded on impact. Do you know how quickly asteroids travel?"

Benny shrugged. "I mean, not really . . ."

"Well, I've read reports of hurricanes back on Earth driving straws through telephone poles. You can imagine what a falling celestial body can do."

"I guess."

Pinky walked out of the garage. "Crew members. We're going to be behind schedule."

"If you'll excuse us," Ricardo said. "We're tonight's entertainment."

And before Benny could figure out if he'd got any answers, the three of them disappeared into the building.

Hot Dog had joined Drue and Jasmine by the time Benny returned and shared what Ricardo said.

"I guess that's that," Drue said.

"Yeah," Jasmine said, though it sounded to Benny like she wasn't sure. But if Elijah said the rock was normal, it had to be. Right?

"Well, if you still want, we can—" he started.

That's when all the lights around the Lunar Taj went out, and the sky turned black, cloaking the Grand Dome in utter darkness.

Hot Dog screamed.

At least, Benny *thought* it was Hot Dog. He couldn't see a thing, and it was impossible to tell where the sound had come from. And anyway, after that first scream, a roar surrounded him as the other EW-SCABers began to freak out. Benny's heart kicked into a higher gear, pounding in his chest. He had never been someone who was afraid of the dark. But then, the night sky had never completely disappeared before. One nice thing about living in the Drylands was that he usually had an unobstructed view of the stars, as long as smog hadn't rolled too far inland from the coast.

Just as his eyes started to get used to the darkness, there was light. Not from the Taj or the sky, but from neon rings appearing in the air throughout the Grand Dome. Fifty of them, at least, Benny guessed. The closest one to him was only a few metres overhead. If he tried hard enough, he might be able to jump up and touch it.

"More holograms," he murmured to himself.

"They're . . . kinda beautiful," Hot Dog said, her face lit by the glow of an aquamarine circle.

Beside her, Drue was breathing heavily and looking around, his eyes wide.

"You OK?" Benny asked.

Drue nodded like the nodding dog Benny's father had found on a supply run and stuck to the dashboard of their RV. "It was just, like . . . *really* dark there for a second."

Around them the other EW-SCABers were trying to figure out what was going on, heads all tilted up to get a better look at the floating rings.

"The entire dome must double as some kind of electronic screen," Jasmine said, her eyes wide with excitement. "I wonder if the polymer is filled with micro—"

"Holy crap, Jasmine, look," Hot Dog said, cutting her off.

She pointed to the garage, where part of the wall was sliding away. It was dark inside except for five pairs of headlights. Before Benny had time to blink, vehicles shot out into the Grand Dome. They were smaller than the Space Runner he'd been in on his trip to the Taj – big enough only for a driver and maybe one passenger – and were trimmed in glowing neon that left tracers of light behind each car. They flew across the courtyard and then began racing around the inside of the dome itself.

"The Pit Crew in action!" Drue said. "Now this is what I'm talking about."

"The flames coming out of the back must just be for

show," Jasmine said. "Elijah would never create something that uses combustible fuel."

"Their Space Runners match the colours of their space suits," Hot Dog murmured once they were gone. "I think I'm in love."

It was true. Each of the Pit Crew's cars matched not only their clothes but the colours assigned to each team. Benny watched as the two white cars driven by the Miyamura twins broke away from the rest of the squad and flew higher, towards the top of the dome. They were barely more than blurs of light as they began to swerve past each other, looking to Benny as though they were coming within inches of crashing into each other at every pass. Their movements got even tighter the closer they got to the dome's peak, where there was no room for error.

"They must be in perfect sync," Benny said breathlessly. "One screw-up and . . ."

Drue made exploding noises with his mouth.

The other three cars darted through the air, looping through the holographic rings. Each time a Space Runner went through one, the circle exploded like a firework, showering the gobsmacked EW-SCAB winners with glittering particles of light. Further up, both the white cars twisted at the same time, and in a move that seemed impossible to Benny, the Miyamura twins drove bumper to bumper at insane speeds right at the top of the dome, a cyclone of metal and white fire.

"How are they doing that?" Drue asked. "Man, I *so* should have been in their group."

After a few minutes all the rings were gone and the five cars shot down towards the ground of the courtyard, landing in front of the entrance, the EW-SCABers backing away to give them room.

As the cars descended, Benny couldn't help but wonder what colour his Space Runner might be if he were part of the Pit Crew.

CHAPTER 16

The days at the Taj continued to be packed with activities, each one holding more unexpected wonders. Benny explored craters in automated Space Runners, was shot three hundred metres into the air via reverse bungee jumping, and ate what felt like more food than he'd had in his entire life. Between activities, he played around with his new hologram bracelet and showed it off to Drue, which meant that pretty soon *everyone* knew about it.

At night he slept deeply, soundly. If there were more vibrations in the early morning hours, he didn't feel them. If anything, he felt like he could use more sleep.

It was a few days after the giant robot fight that he finally got some downtime.

"Today was supposed to be our group's turn to observe Elijah as he demonstrated his driving abilities," Ricardo said to the Mustangs gathered in the common room. "But unfortunately he's unavailable at the moment. Something important came up that he must attend to."

A wave of disappointed sighs swept over the room.

Ricardo raised his hands in the air. "Don't *worry*. I promise you'll get the chance to see Elijah in action in the upcoming days. For now, take the morning off. We'll reconvene at lunch. Enjoy the entertainment in your rooms. Watch for shooting stars in the Grand Dome. Nap if you like. If you need anything, just ask Pinky."

Most of the kids followed Ricardo out, but Jasmine motioned for Benny and Hot Dog to stay behind. Naturally, Drue stuck to their side.

"So," Jasmine said once the other Mustangs had left the room, "I was wondering . . . We've been so busy these last few days, and I know Elijah said he was handling this but . . ." She trailed off as she reached into her pocket and pulled out the asteroid sample that had been left in the bottom of Hot Dog's bag. "I still want to get this analysed. Just to see what it's made of."

"Uh, yeah," Hot Dog said. "Let's figure out what almost blew me up."

Benny had actually kind of forgotten about the strange rock since asking Ricardo about it. He'd been so pre-occupied, and had been considering testing out his holographic bracelet's capabilities a little more during their unexpected free morning. But Jasmine was right. This *was* the perfect time to push this whole asteroid thing out of his mind once and for all. Afterwards, none of them would have to give it a second thought.

Besides, he had told her they'd figure this out.

"I'd be down with that," he said.

Drue sighed. "Guys, we could be doing literally anything else on the Moon other than playing space detectives."

"You *don't* have to come with us," Hot Dog said.

Drue scrunched his face. "Are you kidding? I'm not gonna get left out if this actually ends up being interesting." He shrugged, warming to the idea. "Plus, we're going to have to find a lab or something, right? I bet there's all kinds of cool equipment."

"Right," Jasmine said. "I know there are some research departments around here somewhere. I'll check the map on my HoloTek and—"

"Yo, Pinky!" Drue shouted. "Are there any labs or science geek stations we can tour?"

After a few seconds, Pinky appeared in the corner, filing her intangible nails.

"You're welcome to inspect the science facilities in

the basement level; though without an official escort, you won't be able to use most of the equipment yourself."

"Maybe we should find Ricardo," Hot Dog suggested. Her cheeks flushed. "See if he'd like to take us on a private tour?"

Drue held his hands out at his sides and sighed in exasperation. "Oh, come *on*. Are you still hung up on that Brazilian bonehead?" He quietened down, speaking in little more than a whisper. "We'll figure something out on our own."

The basement halls hadn't been included on their initial tour, and were more sparsely decorated than the rest of the Taj. Most of the walls were a plain, dull metal. Knowing they were underground, Benny couldn't help but feel a bit claustrophobic. Even in his tin can of an RV, there were plenty of windows. This just felt . . . unnatural. Jasmine led them, her HoloTek map open, until she stopped in front of a door at the end of a long hallway. A placard beside it read *Biological and Mineral Research and Development*.

"This must be it," she said, reaching out to press a button. The door slid open with a *whoosh*, and they stepped inside.

The lab was a giant space filled with rows of work-benches and tool chests. The sides of the room were lined with counters holding all kinds of gadgets and instruments that Benny had no idea how to use – strange-looking drills, centrifuges and boxes that looked like incredibly complicated microwaves. One wall was lined with glass cabinets holding mineral samples and vials of glowing liquids. In a corner across the room, a miniature Tesla coil connected electric currents to several pots holding metallic flowers.

To Benny, it looked like a mad scientist's lab full of stuff he probably shouldn't touch. Drue and Jasmine apparently saw things differently. They darted past him and Hot Dog, both their faces lighting up with glee as they made their way through the space, pointing out things.

"A thermodynamic calibrator!"

"Dude, that's a Tetroscope Nine Thousand!"

"There might be more rare earth metals here than on Earth itself."

"Lasers! *So many* lasers!"

Benny walked over to a nearby counter and picked up a long thin tube with a shining gemlike bulb on the end.

"What do you think this is?" Benny asked.

"Hmmm," Hot Dog said. "Some kind of magic wand, maybe?"

Benny laughed and swung the thing around. As he

did, the end of the instrument lit up in a neon-yellow flash, temporarily blinding him and causing Hot Dog to squeal.

"Oh, great, I didn't need to see today," she said.

"Guys, I found, like, a DNA library," Drue said. Benny was seeing spots, but could make out Drue tapping on a screen beside what looked like a giant freezer door. "Elijah's got samples of practically every plant and animal on Earth up here."

"Hey!" Jasmine called from the back of the lab. "We can use this. It's perfect!"

Benny and the others found her standing in front of a shiny white square that was raised two centimetres off a metal counter.

"Uh, what is that?" Benny asked.

"A matter spectrometer," Jasmine said, awe filling her voice. "I've only ever read about them. I can't believe he has one. Well, I *can* . . . I just can't believe I'm *looking* at one in real life."

"So, what does it do?" Hot Dog asked.

"It's a high-tech ingredient counter," Drue said. He was standing nearby, trying in vain to turn on a giant laser cutter.

Jasmine grinned, larger than Benny had seen her smile

in the last few days. She looked around a bit and then pointed to a ring on Hot Dog's finger.

"Can I see that?" she asked.

"You're not gonna melt it, right?" Hot Dog asked.

"Of course not."

She handed over the piece of jewellery. Jasmine set it in the square and tapped twice on the instrument, causing the area around the ring to light up. Letters and numbers began to appear in one corner.

"Aha!" Jasmine said. "See? It measures the composition of whatever you put on it and tells you the elements that make up the object. This ring, for instance, is ninety-one percent silver, one percent palladium and eight percent copper."

"What?!" Hot Dog shouted, snatching the ring back. "The guy I bought this from said it was *platinum*."

"I think you got scammed," Benny said.

"OK, so let's scan the asteroid piece," Drue said, coming to their side. "Unless we want to take turns putting our hands on it to see what *we're* made of."

"Mostly oxygen, carbon and hydrogen," Jasmine said, fishing around in her pocket.

"I could think of a few other things in your case," Hot Dog said, glancing at Drue.

"Unfortunately science has yet to add awesomeness to the periodic table." He flashed her a smile. Hot Dog rolled her eyes.

Jasmine pulled the yellow rock out, carefully placing it on the square.

"Asteroids are usually made up of mostly carbon, iron or silicate minerals. Based on the way this one looks, I'm guessing it falls into the last category."

The four of them stood in silence as they stared at the matter spectrometer, waiting for the percentages to appear. Light pulsed beneath the sample, but otherwise the square remained dark.

"Maybe it's broken," Hot Dog said.

"It's a possibility . . ." Jasmine replied, but it didn't sound to Benny like she actually believed it.

"This isn't normal, right?" Benny asked.

"Your guess is as good as mine. I've never used one of these, remember?"

Then, the numbers appeared.

"Small amounts of promethium and thulium, and fifteen percent platinum," Jasmine said. "That could be the metal circuitry and wire we noticed. And look, trace amounts of cesium."

"Ce— what?" Benny asked.

"It's an alkali metal."

"Yeah, one that goes *boom* really easily," Drue said. Everyone turned to look at him. "What? Jazz isn't the only smart one here, you know. I've had great tutors."

"So . . ." Benny started, trying to work things out in his head. "That might be why those asteroids exploded against the Grand Dome?"

"Maybe," Jasmine said. "If there was enough of it."

Suddenly the edges of the square lit up in red.

"That can't be good," Drue muttered.

New words began to appear: *unknown elements – 71%.* Beneath it, the unidentifiable substances were broken into further increments, four separate mystery elements in all.

"No way," Jasmine said.

"Does that mean what I think it does?" Benny asked.

"You can read, Benny," Drue said. "I think we just discovered druedium, bennium, jazzite, and . . ." He turned a questioning face to Hot Dog, who shook her head and looked to Jasmine.

"Are they really new elements?" she asked.

"Um . . . Well . . . I . . ." Jasmine stammered. "That's what the machine says."

"What does that even mean?" Benny asked.

Jasmine shook her head. "Maybe these asteroids came

from deep space, somewhere beyond human reach. Who knows what's out there?"

"And the circuitry and metal stuff?" Benny asked. "What about that? Trevone said it was from the Space Runner."

"Space Runners do *not* have platinum wiring."

"Guys, *elements named after us*," Drue butted in. "I think you're all missing the bigger picture here."

"At this point," Jasmine said slowly, "I have no idea what this thing is, where it came from, or if it's naturally occurring or not. The possibilities are endless."

"So, back outside the dome you said it looked like someone *made* these," Hot Dog said. "Do you still think that could be true?"

"Yes."

"But who'd make something like this?" Benny asked.

"Or what," Hot Dog replied, twisting her lips to one side.

"Here comes the alien conspiracy again," Drue said. "I thought they *helped* you after your crash."

"I'm just trying to keep an open mind."

"Well, whether they were shot at us on purpose or not, at least we know we're safe here at the Taj," Drue said.

"Yeah," Benny started. "But—"

Just then, the door to the lab slid open. Trevone walked in, face buried in a HoloTek.

"We don't have time to go scouring the dark side trying to find him, not if these new projections are accurate and—"

He froze when he saw Benny and the others. For a moment, none of them spoke.

"What are you doing in here?" Trevone finally asked, tapping once on his HoloTek, ending whatever call he was on or message he was recording.

"Just playing with some of these sweet toys," Drue said. He put on his usual big grin, but spoke softly through his teeth so only Benny and the others could hear: "We should keep the sample, right? It's *our* discovery."

"Uh-huh!" Hot Dog said, smiling right alongside the boy.

"But—" Jasmine started.

Benny's instincts took over as he looked down at the square. Back on Earth he and the rest of the caravan members shared everything they could. Tools, scavenged goods – whatever they could mine from the abandoned, half-buried cities and towns in the Drylands. But he also knew the importance of not letting on to the fact that they had something good before they were ready to trade it, especially when there *were* gangs roaming the dunes, ready to raid any caravan they suspected of having treasure stashed away. And so, in one swift move, Benny grabbed Hot Dog's hand, slipped the silver ring from her finger and placed his hand over the electronic square, palming the rock and leaving the piece of jewellery behind.

"Yeah," he said with a forced smile of his own. He glanced back down at the spectrometer, which was once again showing the ring's readout. "Turns out Hot Dog got ripped off by a dodgy jeweller."

Benny turned to Hot Dog, raising his eyebrows, goading her on.

"Oh, yeah," she said. "Last time I trust a dude on the street telling me he'll give me a special price because he's in a good mood. Although, now that I say all that out loud, I guess I shouldn't be surprised."

Trevone pursed his lips. "Maybe you four should head back up to your rooms. There's a lot of fragile equipment down here."

"You're probably right," Benny said, pushing Drue forward.

"Uh, yeah," he agreed.

"Wait," Jasmine said.

Benny turned to see her staring at Trevone with wide eyes.

"In your research, have you ever come across anything with an unusual atomic make-up? Perhaps—"

"*Jazz*, let's go!" Drue said, giving her a wide-eyed look. "Tre's obviously got more important stuff to deal with."

"It's Trevone," the Crew member corrected. As the four-some neared the door, he continued. "Pinky?"

The AI's voice filled the room. "At your service."

"The research labs are off-limits to EW-SCABers from now on."

He kept his eyes on the kids as they exited, not looking away as the door slid shut behind them. Outside in the hallway, Jasmine turned to the others with her hands out at her sides.

"What was that?" she whispered. "He's one of the Pit Crew. He could have helped us."

"If we turn this over to any of them, it should be Ricardo, right?" Hot Dog asked.

"Uh, I was more concerned about someone else not stealing our credit for discovering this stuff," Drue said.

They looked at Benny, whose mind was racing. On one hand, it was his instinct to protect whatever resources or valuables they might have discovered. On the other, there was no one better to look into this matter than Elijah West.

But then, they'd already given him a big sample.

"This is a *huge* scientific breakthrough," Jasmine said. "Four new elements!"

"*Our* elements," Drue added.

"Possibly *engineered* elements," Benny said. "Elijah must already be researching whatever this stuff is, right? If Jasmine noticed it was weird right off the bat, he would, too."

Jasmine nodded. "We should ask him to share his findings with us. We could be helping him."

"He's the busiest person in the galaxy," Hot Dog said. "He cancelled our whole morning because something 'important' came up, remember?"

"Maybe *this* is that important thing," Benny said. "Maybe he's found out more."

"Also, don't forget that he didn't seem too keen on talking about any of this," Jasmine added. She scrunched up her nose. "Actually, he didn't even seem very surprised by the sample in the first place."

Hot Dog clicked her tongue on the roof of her mouth. "Wait – do you think he knew about this stuff before I got shot out of the sky? Because I am so not cool with that."

"He probably just didn't want us to worry," Drue suggested. "Like you said, Benny."

"Worry about *what*, though?" Benny frowned, wishing they were back up in the main part of the Taj so he could look out of the window and see the bright blue-and-green ball he called home.

"What's wrong?" Hot Dog asked.

"What if this *was* an attack of some kind?" he said. "We might be fine here, but there's no dome around the Earth. What if . . ." He trailed off, not wanting to finish the thought.

"Well," Drue said, drawing out the word, "we could always try to find out what was going on ourselves. Maybe peek into Elijah's files? I bet he's got all kinds of crazy Space Runner designs no one's ever even imagined before."

Jasmine shrugged slowly. "Like I said, I think we could really be of use researching this. With our combined brain-power, maybe we could help figure out exactly where these asteroids came from. Even if Elijah didn't technically ask for our assistance."

She turned to Benny, who couldn't get the idea of his family being in danger out of his mind. He wasn't sure what was going on exactly, but he knew one thing for certain: he wasn't going to just sit around on the Moon *hoping* that everything was OK. That Earth was safe. He had to do something.

"Come on," he said finally, heading back to the lift. "I think we should see what Ramona's up to."

CHAPTER 17

They found Ramona in her suite. After answering the door, she turned away, head buried in her Taj-provided HoloTek, not offering so much as a hello.

"Uh, hey," Benny said, as he stepped inside her room. He wasn't really sure how to ask such a favour. "We were just wondering if, uh, you'd help us with . . ."

Drue snapped his fingers and motioned around the room.

Of course. Pinky. It definitely wasn't a good idea to say her name and risk her walking out of a wall.

Hot Dog took control of the situation, leaning in close to Ramona, relaying what the four had talked about quietly in the lift on the way up to their floor: the fact that if anyone could poke around the Taj's files and see what Elijah had discovered, it was the girl who acted like she could speak to computers.

Benny told himself this wasn't *really* stealing or spying. Well, OK, it *was*. But he needed to put his mind at rest with the knowledge that whatever these strange rocks were, there weren't more of them coming that might endanger his family. That trumped everything else. Even Elijah's approval.

Ramona listened, not taking her eyes off her HoloTek. But she did smirk, which Benny took as a good sign.

"You don't *have* to," Benny said, speaking in a hushed voice. "Just say no and we're out of the door. I totally understand if you don't want to get in trouble."

Ramona tapped on her HoloTek, and in a split second purple numbers were scrolling across one of the walls.

Benny looked to Jasmine.

"She's telling you to chill out," she said.

Ramona finally looked up at them. "Don't worry about Pinky. I mapped her eyes and ears. Max spyware, but blind here. Deaf. We're in a four-oh-four blackout zone."

Drue stared back at her. "I don't understand you at all, you strange, strange girl. But . . . you'll help us, right?"

She grinned. "What're your info needs?"

They explained to her as best they could what they were looking for. Ramona either wasn't shocked, or did a good job of hiding it as she focused on her screen.

"We don't want you to get caught, though," Benny said. "Be careful."

"Ha," Ramona scoffed as she plugged a portable drive the size of a fingernail into her HoloTek.

Something flashed on Ramona's screen. Her eyes narrowed to slivers.

"Does not compute. Max encryption. Total firewall."

"So . . . that's bad, right?" Hot Dog asked.

Ramona extended her HoloTek and turned it around to the others. There were blueprints on the screen.

"It's basement level," Jasmine said. "That hallway's around the corner from where we were earlier."

"Servers inside," Ramona continued. A door illuminated as she tapped on the screen. "No systems connecting in or out. Likely to be a cache of secret files. We're talking legendary loot drop."

"You mean it's something we can't get to," Benny said. *Great.*

"No," Drue said, stroking his chin. "It's just that we have to be there in person to access the files, right, robo-girl?"

Ramona clicked her tongue. "Bingo, troll."

She tapped on the screen a few more times, and suddenly several video feeds of the basement showed up. It was clear to Benny what they were supposed to be focusing on: right by the highlighted door was what appeared to be the Pit Crew's common room. Ricardo and Trevone stood inside, having what looked like a very intense conversation.

"Analogue security," Ramona said. "Unhackable."

"Analogue security?" Jasmine asked. "You mean, *people*."

Ramona shrugged.

"No way we're getting past those two," Drue said. "Not if they're in that room. Is there, like, a fire alarm we can pull?"

"Oh, yeah, that won't cause everyone to completely freak out," Hot Dog scoffed.

The rest of the group continued to brainstorm ideas, but Benny stayed quiet, thinking, trying to come up with something, anything that might help them.

He crossed his arms. A glint of metal caught his eye.

Maybe there *was* an easy way to distract the Pit Crew down in the basement.

"Ramona," he said, "if we went down there, could you unlock the door and scramble Pinky's security cams so she couldn't see us in the hallway?"

"For sure," she replied. "Feedback loop. Haxxor one-oh-one. Child's play."

"What are you thinking?" Hot Dog asked.

Benny's fingers grazed the loop on his left wrist.

"I think we create a little distraction for our fearless Mustang leader."

He tapped on his wrist, and suddenly there was another him standing in the room.

"Ugh. This thing is so creepy," Hot Dog said, waving a hand through the fake Benny.

"I just need to find the perfect diversion," he said, pulling out his HoloTek. He started scrolling through old saved photos, changing the hologram. One minute a mirror image of himself was standing in front of him, the next a super-villain from a cartoon he'd liked and then finally Elijah West himself.

"Ricardo will totally see through that one," Hot Dog said. "He's Elijah's right-hand man. Plus, we'd need to mimic his voice and stuff, too."

"Hey, didn't you say you had a voice modulator?" Drue asked.

"Please. There's a difference between sounding like Elijah and acting like him."

"I could pull it off!"

Benny played around with it a little more, and suddenly a giant tarantula was standing between them.

"Nope!" Drue said, covering his eyes and turning

away. "Anything but that. Do something a little less . . . spidery."

With a little more searching, Benny found a perfect candidate for their ploy. An image he'd used in the past to scare his little brothers while telling stories late at night.

"OK," Benny said. "I think I've got this."

After a quick stop in Benny's room, they made their way back to the lower level of the Taj, making as little noise as possible. Ramona stayed behind, working her technological magic and keeping a live feed of the security cams streaming to Jasmine's HoloTek. Ricardo and Trevone were still in the common room between them and the door to the locked-down server.

"Ramona's got a feedback loop running," Jasmine whispered. "Pinky's temporarily blind to the basement level." She looked up. "We're going to be in so much trouble if anyone finds out about this."

"*Ramona's* going to be in trouble," Drue said.

"We're not hanging her out to dry on her own," Benny muttered. "Look around. We need a place to hide."

As if in response, the door to the room they were passing slid open. All of them jumped except Jasmine.

"Oh, sorry," she said. "That was Ramona's doing. She

says it's clear inside." She paused for a second, looking at Benny. "You're *sure* this is the best idea?"

Benny let out a long sigh. "I think so. You want to know what's really going on with those rocks, right?"

She nodded slowly.

"We'll follow your lead," Hot Dog said.

Benny motioned for the others to hide in the newly opened room and then tapped on his bracelet. The tiny particles of the band flew into the air, and a two-and-half-metre-tall monster made of projected lights began to take shape in front of him. Two hollow nostrils appeared on what might have been called the creature's brow. It looked at Benny and grinned over two rows of long, pointy teeth. The three eyes floating around its head – connected to its neck by wisps of tendon – blinked at him.

Benny shivered, and then ran his finger over the bracelet, commanding his conjured terror. It floated across the hallway, the strips of soiled rags that hung from its body like seaweed sliding over the smooth cement. Finally, it came to a stop in front of the common room and opened its massive jaw.

Benny raised the voice modulator he'd grabbed from his suite to his lips and screamed as loud as he could, until his throat felt coarse and raw. The device changed his shout into a deafening roar that reverberated through the corridor. He ran his finger over his bracelet, and the holographic monster sprinted down the hallway towards him as he jumped inside the room where the others were hiding, the door sliding shut behind him.

"They're following it!" Jasmine whispered as Benny got to her side, watching the Pit Crew members chase his creation. He controlled it as best he could using the band. Somewhere behind him, Hot Dog was talking.

"Oh my God, you guys. Do you know where we are? This is *Ricardo's* room. This is . . . this is the dream of every girl I know in Dallas."

On the feeds, Benny watched the door to the lab they'd been in earlier slide open. His monster darted in, then he tapped his wrist twice and it disappeared, the tiny nanoprojectors flying back out into the hallway to return home to the bracelet. Ricardo and Trevone rushed into the lab. The door slammed shut behind them, locking them inside.

"Wow," Drue said, watching over Jasmine's shoulder. "Ramona *is* good."

"We need to move," Benny said. "Who knows how long it'll be before Pinky takes control again, or Trevone finds a way for them to break out."

"Can't we stay just a little longer?" Hot Dog asked.

Benny turned to see her reaching out to touch a dirty football on Ricardo's bookshelf.

"*Now*," he said.

They darted down the hallway towards the server room door. Two seconds passed before it opened, allowing them to slip inside.

"OK," Jasmine said, pulling a tiny flash drive out of her pocket. "We just have to get this connected to the server and then—"

She stopped talking when she got a good look at the room. The floors and walls were all cement, polished to such a shine that it looked as though they were standing on dark, still water. A large metal loading door was inset against one wall, but other than that the only thing in the room was a huge black box, at least three metres tall and twice as long across.

"Uh, so, I'm guessing that's it," Hot Dog said.

"Find a way in," Benny said. "We don't have much time and—"

He turned to Hot Dog and saw that she was wearing a red football shirt. *Rocha* was spelled out across the back in white letters.

"Seriously?" he asked.

"No time, remember?" she said, dismissing him with one hand as she started around the box.

They found a door on one side. Benny tried the handle, but a thick black padlock kept him from getting in.

"That's mechanical," Jasmine said. "Ramona can't help us. There's no overriding it."

"Benny, you're our hot-wiring expert," Drue said. "Can you do anything with this?"

"You can't hot-wire a lock," Hot Dog said.

"I know that, but if he can hot-wire a car *maybe* he can pick a lock."

Benny eyed the thing. He'd seen his father get past a few doors or locked tool cases before, but this was something else entirely.

"Sorry," he said. "This is way beyond me."

Jasmine knocked on door. "This is *thick*. We'd need a laser cutter to get through."

"We should have grabbed one from the research lab."

"Let's look around," Hot Dog said. "Maybe the key's here somewhere. My neighbour kept a spare to her place taped underneath a flowerpot on her porch."

"I doubt Elijah's hiding it in a shrub somewhere," Drue said.

"It won't hurt to *look*."

The two of them kept talking as Benny stepped away. Something else had his attention: there was a strange noise coming from the loading door at the other end of the room. He walked over to it and placed his hands on the metal. It was vibrating just slightly, the same way the Taj had a few nights before.

Why?

He glanced back, but the others were still fiddling with the lock. Curious, he pressed a button beside the door, and the metal rolled up.

"Uh, guys?" he said.

Before him was a staircase that looked as though it was carved into the crust of the Moon itself, smooth stone steps spiralling down, surrounded by smooth grey rock. A banister along one side glowed with a cool blue light. The stairway curved so sharply that Benny couldn't see where it led.

The others ran over, staring down the new passage.

"There's not supposed to be a sub-basement level," Jasmine said. "It wasn't on the blueprints Ramona pulled up."

"She's right," Drue said. "I've done my research on the Taj, too. This is . . . new."

"Secret staircase in a room full of secret files," Hot Dog said. "Nothing weird about that."

In the hallway outside the server room they heard foot-steps and the sound of Ricardo and Trevone shouting.

"Uh, looks like they got out of the lab," Drue said. He glanced at Benny. "Should we try another hologram?"

"No, no," Jasmine said, her voice panicked. "We're definitely getting kicked off the Moon this time. This was no rescue mission. We were trying to *steal* Elijah's research! And we don't even have anything to show for it!" She started pacing back and forth, feeling through her space suit for the necklace Elijah had given her. "I blew it. I'll have to go back to the group home."

"We're not doomed yet," Hot Dog said calmly. Then she turned to Benny. "What do we do?"

But Benny didn't answer. Instead, he did the only thing that might get them out of there without getting caught.

He started down the stairs.

CHAPTER 18

"**Y**eah, this isn't creepy at all," Hot Dog said as they hurried down the stairs.

"Would you rather they find us?" Drue asked. "Because we don't exactly have a great excuse for breaking Taj rules this time other than 'We were curious.'"

"The pursuit of knowledge is an admirable . . ." Jasmine started. Then she swallowed loudly. "OK, so technically we were trying to hack into Elijah's files."

"We'll find a place to hide, then double back when we get a chance," Benny said. "Maybe there's another way into the Taj from . . . wherever it is this leads."

"You think we'll be OK?" Hot Dog asked, a hint of worry in her voice.

"Sure. We've had to lie low on scouting missions from the caravan. You can usually get away with anything if you stay quiet and out of sight long enough."

"These aren't stupid Drylands gang members," Drue said.

"Watch out," Benny said flatly. "Spiders."

Drue gasped and stopped on the stairs. Benny grinned back at him.

"That's *not* funny."

As confident as Benny sounded, inside, his heart was running in overdrive. His palms were sweaty. They might have closed the door to the stairwell behind them, but it was the only way out of the locked server room. If Ricardo or Trevone or even Elijah were afraid someone had been in there, it was possible they'd investigate further.

They descended in silence for what felt like a long time, the staircase continuing to corkscrew down, giving them no idea when it might end. The banister glowed beneath Benny's white-knuckled grip. He could feel the shaking through his shoes. The further down they went, the dizzier he got and the more intense the vibrations all around them were.

"At least there's plenty of light," he muttered.

"Why would you say that?" Drue asked. His voice shook a little. "You're basically asking for a blackout."

"Hey, relax," Hot Dog said, the harsh edge usually accompanying her voice when she talked to Drue completely absent. "We've got our HoloTeks. We pull them out and we've got instant torches."

There was a slight distortion and sheen of light in the air around Benny's head as his space suit's protective helmet automatically powered on. He glanced back at the others, who looked as surprised as he was to see their own appear.

"Must be losing oxygen down here," Benny said.

"But our suits can supply enough breathing air for days, right?" Hot Dog asked.

"Right," Jasmine murmured, distracted. "Guys, these walls are so smooth. It's such precise work. How was this place excavated?"

"And why?" Benny whispered.

A few steps later, they had an answer to the first question, at least.

The staircase ended abruptly, opening up to a large, flat slab of smooth grey stone suspended in the air. In front of them was a cavern so big Benny couldn't see the other end of it. The walls were mostly craggy, but in some places the rock was more refined. In fact, it looked to Benny like it had been carved into familiar shapes. There were makeshift doorways and windows in the walls. Some of them even had glass panes and wooden doors, complete with stone balconies that had been chiselled out of the rock itself.

It looked like some kind of underground city in the process of being built.

"Holy whoa," Benny said after a few moments of forgetting to breathe. "What is this place?"

Dozens of platforms floated in the air around them, powered by hyperdrives. Big glowing lamps bobbed among them like miniature stars. A giant screen – it *must* have been a screen – on one wall displayed a beach view, the surf rolling in slowly. As one of the platforms dipped lower, Benny could see row after row of vibrant green plants, water misting around them from nozzles coming out of the ground. He couldn't help but think of the floating trays that brought food to the tables back up in the Taj's restaurant. Was this where their dinner had come from?

"Look. There are tunnels heading deeper into the walls," Hot Dog said.

"Are we in some kind of secret camp in the core of the Moon?" Benny asked.

"No way," Drue said. "We weren't on the staircase *that* long."

"Plus the Moon's core is made of iron," Jasmine said as she looked around. Her voice was soft, distracted – repeating facts without actually thinking about them. "At least, that's what scientists on Earth believe. Maybe Elijah knows more than we do."

"Why do I feel like that's becoming more and more of a thing the longer we're up here?" Hot Dog asked.

There was motion above them, and Benny watched as four floating balls of metal shot lasers into one of the walls. A rumbling filled the cavern as the rock was cut away, falling into freight containers waiting in the air below.

"This is what's been causing all the shaking," Benny said. "It's not earthquakes. It's someone carving into the Moon!"

"Not *someone*," Drue said. "This tech is obviously Elijah's design. I'd recognise it anywhere."

Jasmine nodded her head slowly. "It must be fully automated. I don't see anyone else down here, and it doesn't seem like there are any environmental fields activated except for those surrounding the gardens." She took a long breath. "This is . . . this is *incredible*."

"I dunno," Hot Dog said. "It's cool and all, but if he wanted to expand the Taj, couldn't he have just done it above ground?"

Benny spotted two silver doors in the side of the wall at the other end of the platform they stood on.

"There!" he said. "Those look like lifts, right? Maybe they go back up to the resort."

They ran to them. As Benny searched for a call button, Jasmine stared up at the ceiling so far above them that it was hardly visible.

"I'm not totally sure," she said, "but I think these might be connected to the main lift shafts that go through the lobby."

"I definitely didn't see a button for 'creepy cave town' in the lift," Hot Dog said.

"Pinky's probably programmed it to only let certain people down here." Jasmine's eyes lit up as she pulled out her HoloTek and tapped on it. Then her face fell. "I'm not on the Taj's connection any more. I can't contact Ramona."

"And I don't see a way to call a lift," Benny said.

"So, we're still stuck," Drue said.

"Guys," Hot Dog said. She started to jog away from them. "Maybe there's another way up."

She was heading towards three carts lining the edge of the rock platform. Benny and the others followed her, and the closer they got, the easier it was to see what Hot Dog had in mind. Each cart had waist-high railings and looked big enough to hold six or seven standing people. Two short metal arms were perched on the front of each machine, angled towards each other. And attached to the bottoms . . .

"Hyperdrives," Benny whispered as he watched Hot Dog climb over one of the railings. "These things can fly!"

"There's a screen here," she said, tapping on something Benny couldn't see. A holographic interface appeared, hovering over the front of the cart. "Wow. OK. This is new."

"What kind of controls are those?" Drue asked, his voice full of wonder. "It looks programmable, but I don't see a flight yoke or steering wheel."

"Can you fly this thing?" Benny asked.

"I can fly *anything*," Hot Dog said. Then she scowled a little as she turned back to the controls. "I mean, eventually. This might take a little bit of getting used to."

"We could always just wait and go back up through the server room," Jasmine said. There was hesitancy in her voice. "We could try to get past that padlock again and then sneak by everyone. At least then we'd get the information we came for."

"Yeah, 'cause that climb back up sounds like a lot of fun," Drue said. He hopped into the cart. "I could always pilot if—"

"Dream on, Lincoln," Hot Dog interrupted as she continued to study the lights in front of her.

Benny turned back to Jasmine. "They've got to be taking

all the rock they're digging *somewhere*, right? There has to be another way out. A way to the surface. Even if we end up outside the Grand Dome, Ramona can get us back inside."

"What do you think?" Hot Dog asked, turning back to them. "Wanna explore a bit?"

Jasmine thought about this for a few seconds before nodding, climbing into the cart. Benny followed her.

"You're *sure* you can handle this?" he asked.

"Yeah," Hot Dog said, squinting at the holograms in front of her. "I think the layout is similar to a Space Runner control board, just with a few extra buttons." She looked back at the others. "But, uh, I'd hold on if I were you, just in case."

Benny gripped the side of the cart. "OK. Let's go slow."

"Sure." She reached out a finger, letting it hover over a holographic button floating at chest level. "This should turn on the hyperdrive."

All four of them screamed as the cart suddenly shot straight up at such a speed that Benny fell, pinned to the metal floor.

"Too fast!" Jasmine shouted.

"We're gonna hit the ceiling!" Drue said.

Benny looked up at the grey rock overhead getting closer with every second.

"Do something!" he yelled.

"OK, OK," Hot Dog said. She reached out, pressing another button. A holographic flight yoke appeared in front of her. "Yes!" She grabbed it, pushing hard. The cart instantly changed directions, flying forward and causing Jasmine to stumble back. Drue caught her before she hit the side of the cart. She mumbled thanks as Benny struggled to get to his feet. He glanced over the railing and gulped at the blur of platforms beneath them and the complete blackness even further down.

"Hit the brakes!" Jasmine said.

"What brakes?" Hot Dog shouted over her shoulder. "The button I thought would slow us down just turned the headlights on."

The cart continued to zoom through the cavern as Hot Dog was forced to take evasive manoeuvres, swerving to avoid floating lights and platforms, throwing her passengers around inside the cart.

"Try this one!" Drue said.

He reached out and hit one of the holograms. The two metal arms at the front of the cart began to glow, and then yellow neon shot out of them – lasers. The two streams met and formed one thick beam shooting into the side of the cavern, sending chunks of rock falling into the darkness.

"Nice work!" Hot Dog said through clenched teeth.

Drue was trying to turn the thing off when a joystick-like hologram appeared in front of him. He grabbed it and pulled back, but that just moved the laser beam up, causing it to slice through the corner of a platform above them and destroy part of the ceiling.

"Oops," he said.

Hot Dog hit a button and the laser turned off, but debris was falling all around them.

"Hang on!" she yelled, pulling a hard right on the holographic yoke.

They shot around one of the floating lights, narrowly missing a falling chunk of ceiling. But this sent them careening towards a solid wall. At such a high speed, there was no time for them to turn around: the only way to avoid crashing was for Hot Dog to rocket them into a dark tunnel carved out of the cavern's side.

"No, no, no," Drue said over and over again as they continued through the narrow opening, hardly wider than the cart itself. Dim yellow lights lining the walls powered on. After a few seconds the tunnel broke into multiple paths, forcing Hot Dog to choose one at random. Then there was another split, and another. Drue yelped with every new route. Benny and Jasmine were crouched in the back of the cart, clinging on to the sides. All the while, Hot Dog kept hitting the button she'd pushed to start the machine, but it wasn't responding.

"Pinky?" she called out in a last-ditch effort. "Are you there? Can you stop this thing?"

There was no response.

"Look out!" Drue shouted.

Ahead of them the tunnel dead-ended in a large sheet of metal.

"Door button?!" Hot Dog shouted. "Anyone?"

They were seconds away from splattering against the wall.

"We're going to die!" Drue yelled, his voice high-pitched and cracking.

Jasmine grabbed Benny's shoulder. "Which button turned on the laser?"

"This one," Benny said. He lunged forward, slamming his palm onto the controls. The beam shot forward again, and he twisted the holographic joystick around, carving crisscrossed slashes into the metal.

The door was still there, but damaged. Weakened. He hoped that was enough – and that on the other side there was open space and not a solid rock wall.

"Get down!" he yelled, and then they were all on the cold metal floor of the cart together, trying to brace themselves for impact.

There was a terrible wrenching sound as they broke through the metal, the mounted lasers exploding in a shower of sparks. But the cart held together as they spun. Benny could make out tiny pinpricks of light overhead, which he barely registered as stars.

The controls blinked on and off a few times before something on the underside of the cart – probably the hyperdrive – seemed to blow out. Their makeshift vehicle crashed onto the ground below, sending them skidding across the surface of the Moon.

Finally, they came to a stop. No one moved. Their heavy breathing was the only sound as seconds ticked by.

"Are we dead?" Drue finally asked.

"I don't think so," Benny said.

"OK." Hot Dog let out a long, ragged breath. "Maybe that wasn't as good an idea as I thought it would be." She got to her feet carefully, staring at the broken display screen and the mangled lasers on the front of the cart. "Do you think this thing will still fly?"

"Oh, no, no," Jasmine said, climbing over the side. "I'm not riding on that any more."

"Well, we can't just walk back the way we came. I have no idea what tunnels I took back there."

Benny got out, too, thankful to have something stable and immobile beneath his feet again. Hot Dog and Drue followed, trying to catch their breath. The surface of the Moon around them was dark, even considering the fact that they were in a large crater. Huge mounds of rock were piled up at one side.

"Looks like this is where they were taking some of the stuff they excavated," Jasmine said, starting to sound like herself again.

Drue darted over to one of the piles and climbed to the top, taking a look around.

"Uh, so, I don't see the Taj anywhere." He jumped back off, floating down to the crater floor.

Something behind him caught Benny's eye. Fifty or so metres away, buried in a craggy wall, was a large, smooth rectangle coloured a dull greenish-yellow.

"Uh, hey," Benny said, "this is going to sound crazy but . . . doesn't that kind of look like a door?"

CHAPTER 19

The sickly-coloured stone was three times as tall as any of them. If it *was* a door, it must have weighed a ton.

"This is not normal, right?" Hot Dog asked, keeping her distance.

"Definitely not," Drue said.

"Maybe it's a back door into the dig site," Benny said.

"Or a way back to the Taj. That runaway cart was fun and everything, but I don't see it getting us back to the resort any time soon. Especially if we're not sure where we are."

"The dark side of the Moon," Hot Dog said.

"She's right," Jasmine added. "I can tell by the stars." She stepped forward, placing a palm on the smooth stone. "This rock doesn't look like any of the layers we saw underground. I wonder what it's made of."

"You can come back with a chisel," Drue said as he picked up a thick metal rod lying on the crater floor. "*Someone's* been out here." He waved it around a little, gauging its weight before wedging it into the space between the door and the craggy rocks surrounding it.

"What are you doing?" Hot Dog asked.

"What does it look like? There are scratch marks and chunks missing from this side. Someone's pried the door open before, which means we can, too." He leaned on the rod, straining, before calling over his shoulder, "Um, a little help here?"

Hot Dog grabbed the end of the makeshift crowbar and pushed with him. After a moment, the entire panel began to shift, sliding away without any more effort.

"OK, that wasn't all me and Hot Dog," Drue said.

"There must be a kind of counterweight or pneumatic system inside," Jasmine suggested.

The slab tucked itself into the side of the crater, leaving nothing but a rectangle of pitch-blackness in front of them.

"Anyone see a light switch?" Benny asked.

"I don't think we're that lucky," Hot Dog said, her voice wavering a little. "So . . . who wants to go inside the scary tunnel first?"

"Uh, I don't really *do* the dark," Drue said.

For a second, Benny was reminded of the bloodcurdling scream when all the lights went out in the Grand Dome. Maybe it hadn't been Hot Dog after all.

"We probably should have brought some torches or something," he murmured.

Jasmine reached out and touched a spot on his space suit's collar. A ring of glowing light formed around his neck, illuminating the cave for a couple of metres in front of him.

"Oh," Benny said. "Thanks."

"You should really read the safety regulations that came preloaded on your HoloTek," Jasmine said, turning on her own light.

"I didn't even know there *were* safety regulations," Drue muttered.

Jasmine sighed and stepped forward into the tunnel. "We're not going to find out where this leads if we don't actually go inside."

Benny took a deep breath and followed her, noticing that the floor and walls around them were made of the same stone as the door.

"I've got a bad feeling about this," Hot Dog said, coming up to Benny's side.

Drue shushed her.

"What?" she asked. "I do."

"OK, but shouldn't we be quiet?" Drue asked.

"Why?" Benny asked.

"Because talking somehow makes this a lot worse."

"Sounds like someone's about to wet his space suit," Hot Dog said with a huge grin on her face. Then she flinched as she bumped into Jasmine's arm.

They forged on in silence. Eventually the tunnel opened out to some kind of room, but Benny could only make out the vague, shadowy shapes inside.

"I'm beginning to think maybe this isn't the way back to the underground cavern," Jasmine said, taking a step out of the tunnel.

As soon as her foot touched the floor, the room seemed to power up, like someone had flipped an on-switch.

Dim lights glowed in what looked like computer terminals against the far wall, though they were certainly like no electronics Benny had ever seen. They seemed to have grown out of the floor, which pulsed with little rivers of light. Above them, the smooth walls turned into jagged rock, eventually giving way to thick, opaque stalactites hanging from the high ceilings. They glowed a pale green. Tables piled high with dust and unfamiliar machinery filled most of the room, which was big enough that half the caravan could have parked inside. On the right end of the room, a few circular nooks had been carved into the walls.

"What in the name of Saturn's rings are we looking at here?" Benny asked.

"It's kinda like . . . a weird cave apartment?" Hot Dog offered.

"More like a workshop," Drue said, taking a few more steps inside. "Jazz, what do you think?"

But Jasmine didn't answer. Instead, she stood with her mouth agape, her eyes wide.

Benny walked along one of the walls, dragging his fingers along a tabletop and clearing away a line of accumulated Moon dust. The surface beneath was some kind of polished red rock.

"I don't think anyone's been here for a while," he said.

"Jackpot!" Drue shouted, racing to a corner where two thin slivers of green light floated at chest level. They were thirty centimetres tall, and the space between them had a sparkling sheen to it that distorted the air.

"The last time you touched something you weren't supposed to, it turned on lasers!" Jasmine called to him. "We have no idea what any of this—"

But Drue was already reaching out, poking the air between the two beams of light. Within seconds there was a *whoosh* as all the rocks overhead dimmed. If it weren't for the lights on their collars, Benny would have barely been able to tell where the others were.

"Oh, that's perfect," Hot Dog said. "Let me guess: you were *trying* to do that."

Drue looked around, his body tense, until he was sure the lights weren't going out completely. Then he shrugged. "I see a button, I push it. I see floating lights, I touch them. That's just who I am."

"Something's happening," Jasmine said.

The slivers of light grew into rods a few metres long and flew to the middle of the room. There, they spun once, and then exploded into a shower of light particles, causing all four of them to gasp. The bits of light began to move, slowly at first, and then rapidly, until they were spreading throughout the entire area. Benny jumped back as the energy expanded, ramming into the wall behind him, afraid that Drue had accidentally set off some kind of booby trap.

But he hadn't. The lights started to form shapes Benny recognised.

"Is that . . . ?" he asked.

"Our solar system," Jasmine said.

"It's some kind of advanced hologram system."

Strings of light began to flow around them, like glowing

pieces of ribbon knotting up and looping every few inches, in constant motion. Some sections formed complete tapestries writhing through the air, weaving themselves together for a few moments before unravelling again.

Jasmine's eyebrows crinkled together. "It looks like these are patterns."

"You mean, it means something?" Benny asked.

"Maybe. I'm just guessing."

"We should have brought Ramona," Drue said. "I bet she reads space writing or whatever this is."

Benny stepped forward, focused on a pulsing green blob a couple of metres in front of his nose and set well apart from Earth's solar system, but connected to it by a silver line. He raised his hand tentatively. "What's this thing?" he whispered.

His finger touched the light, and suddenly it was expanding, minimising everything else and pushing their own solar system to the sidelines. In front of him was a new cluster of orbs, revolving around a trio of brightly blazing stars.

"What the heck is that?" Drue asked.

"I don't know," Benny said. "I don't recognise it."

"It's not any system I've ever seen before," Jasmine said.

"Uh . . . you guys," Hot Dogs interjected. "Am I crazy, or does this stuff look a little *too* familiar?"

She had her back to the holographic star maps. The sleeve of her space suit was caked with dust from where she'd cleaned a pane of clear, thick glass on the front of a cabinet that was moulded into one of the walls. Benny could just barely make out a row of sulphur-coloured rocks embedded with glinting circuitry sitting on the shelves inside.

"These are like the asteroids that took down my Space Runner," she said. "How is that possible?"

"How is anything in here possible?" Jasmine asked, crossing the room in a few swift strides to get a closer look at the cabinet.

Hot Dog took a few steps back. "These things aren't going to explode, right?"

Jasmine continued. "Maybe these are gathered samples. This could be where Elijah is testing them, or . . ." She trailed off for a moment before shaking her head. "No, that doesn't make sense. Look at the state of this place." She glanced at the dusty floor. "All these footprints are ours. These rocks must have been here a while."

"Wait, wait," Drue said. "So there could be some kind of connection between the asteroids and this workshop?"

"This doesn't make sense," Benny said. "If the asteroids were made by someone – if they were an *attack* – then, what, did they come from here? Who did this? Who built this place?"

Jasmine looked around. "Everything here is so . . . odd. Like these maps. They're of systems I've never seen in any online textbook. It's information we just don't have."

"Maybe not normal people," Drue said. "But Elijah might know. Or even the government. My dad's sat in on some top secret meetings before. There's probably a lot more going on in space than we realise."

"He told you that?" Hot Dog asked.

"Well . . . not exactly." Drue turned his attention to one of the dust-covered tables before muttering, "He kind of has a habit of . . . well, falling asleep at his desk. Or at the dining-room table. Mostly in the big chair by the bar in his office. Sometimes I sneak in to make sure he's OK. And maybe I take a look at whatever files are up in front of him when I do. Ever since they found that alien site on Pluto, there have been a lot of top-secret meetings about alien life. But they haven't *found* anything from what I've seen. I think they're just listening to too many crackpot scientists."

"OK, I'm just going to be the one to say it," Hot Dog said. "None of this stuff looks like it came from Earth."

For a few moments, no one said anything, but Benny's thoughts were exploding like miniature supernovas. What Hot Dog was saying sounded crazy, but if it could possibly be true . . .

Drue let out a single laugh. "You're serious?"

She threw out her arms in exasperation. "Dude, look around you. Does any of this look familiar? Seen any of it back home, or even at the Taj? You've been in Elijah's labs and the garage and they definitely don't look like this. So, what, you think some humans built a secret hideout on the dark side of the Moon and then created, these . . . these . . ." She gestured to the rocks.

"Unknown elements," Jasmine offered.

"These *unknown elements*?"

"I'm saying it's possible," Drue said, though he didn't sound nearly as sure of himself as he usually did. "Don't blame me for not wanting to believe in creepy spider aliens or something like that."

"This place does kind of look like the one in the photos from Pluto," Benny said. He and his brothers had spent hours poring over them. He was surprised he hadn't noticed the similarities before, but now they were everywhere. The smooth rock walls. The stalactite chandeliers.

Benny turned his attention back to the holograms. His mind was whirring, trying to sort things out. Despite the strangeness of the place and the connection to the asteroids, he was most concerned about something else.

"OK, so, let's just imagine Hot Dog's right . . ." He pointed to the map. "Then what's this line connecting Earth to another solar system?"

"Maybe some kind of flight plan?" Hot Dog asked.

"That might be a best-case scenario," Jasmine said.

Benny nodded. He knew what she was thinking. "It could be where the 'asteroids' came from."

"And following that logic . . ."

"The aliens are *definitely* not coming in peace." Hot Dog said.

Benny gulped. The impressive star map looked downright terrifying to him. "Let's hope we're wrong."

Drue pulled out his HoloTek and held it up at eye level.

"Please don't tell me you're taking holoselfies at a time like this," Jasmine said.

"I'm recording these maps. Whatever's going on, we need to get this info to Elijah. He'll know what to do."

Hot Dog looked around. "This place is starting to creep

me out. Maybe I'll go see about fixing the flight controls on that floating cart or something."

She started for the exit. That was when they saw lights from inside the hallway.

Everyone froze.

"Someone's there," Benny said.

Hot Dog gulped. "Or some . . . thing."

They backed away from the tunnel, huddling together in one corner of the room, near the sulphur-coloured rocks.

"I'm so not ready to see an alien," Hot Dog whispered. "Please don't let us get abducted. Or killed."

"Oh, no way," Drue said. "I just survived a race through a mine, being shot through a metal door *and* crashing onto the surface of the Moon. I am *not* dying in some dirty lunar cave. You're from a caravan, Benny. You must know how to fight, right?"

"Only through wrestling with my brothers and taking down robo-bees." He curled his fists up at his sides. "Whatever's in that hallway, we'll deal with it together. *That's* what I know from the caravan."

"Sure. Sounds great," Drue said, prying open the cabinet beside them and pulling out one of the tiny asteroids.

"Don't touch those!" Hot Dog hissed. "What if they blow up?"

"I'm trying to be resourceful!"

It was at that moment that Ricardo Rocha stepped into the room, followed by the other four members of the Pit Crew.

"Oh, thank God," Hot Dog cried out.

All five of them turned to face Benny and his friends. Ricardo shook his head.

"Why am I not surprised?" he asked, looking at the four EW-SCABers. He narrowed his eyes at Hot Dog. "Is that . . . ?"

She looked down at the football shirt she still wore. "Oh, no, no, no," she whispered.

Behind him, Benny could hear Drue sigh in relief, but all he could think was that the Pit Crew didn't look surprised by the fact that they were standing in some kind of strange workshop hidden in a crater on the dark side of the Moon.

CHAPTER 20

The Pit Crew split them up among their Space Runners and headed back to the Taj. Benny rode with Ricardo, who wouldn't even look at him during the short ride over the lunar surface, instead turning bass-heavy music up so loud that Benny doubted the older boy would have heard him if he'd shouted at the top of his lungs. Questions raced through his mind as they shot back towards the resort. Why was Elijah mining underground? What was that strange workshop they'd found? Why were there asteroids there?

And, most pressing of all, what was that line connecting the distant star system to Earth?

Benny told himself everything would make sense soon. Elijah would know what was going on. He'd clear everything up.

But then, he realised he'd been telling himself this ever

since Jasmine had found the strange rock, and so far, nothing had been explained.

At the Taj, they were led into the same meeting room they'd been brought to after rescuing Hot Dog, only this time the lights were dimmed and the black circular holodesk was projecting all sorts of maps and charts in the air. The holograms cast an amber glow on Elijah, who stood staring at the data with his arms crossed over a grey leather racing jacket and white T-shirt.

"And so we find ourselves here again," Elijah said, not taking his eyes off the projections. "I knew this group had brains and flight skills, but I must admit I underestimated your curiosity." He cocked his head to one side, turning to look at them. "Or maybe it was your hunger for adventure I didn't take into account. Regardless, I knew I was right in choosing you all. Even you, Drue, have exceeded my expectations."

Drue grinned, flattered. "Thanks, Elijah."

Benny elbowed him in the ribs and then stepped forward. His mind was reeling, and when he started talking, words flew out, tumbling over each other. "I don't know what's happening, but we found the stuff you're carving out under the Moon's surface, and I know we shouldn't have snuck around and we're sorry, but when we were down there, we got lost in the caverns and then we had to use some of the lasers to—"

"Hey, hey," Elijah said, raising his hands in front of his chest. "Slow down. Even with the environmental stabilisers in here, you'll pass out if you don't breathe. Now, I understand my Pit Crew found you inside the base on the dark side of the Moon."

"So you *have* been there," Hot Dog said, stepping up beside Benny.

"Ms Wilkinson, I've seen every inch of the Moon. I may not technically own it, but for all intents and purposes I am its shepherd, and I like to keep a close watch over things I am responsible for."

"We didn't mean to, but we hit some buttons and some maps—" Benny started.

"He knows," Jasmine said, pointing to one of the star charts over the table.

That's when Benny saw it: the line he'd noticed connecting Earth to the three-star system was lit up on the charts over the table, only this time it was pulsing bright red, with various time stamps and dates marked along it. And there was something else – a blinking light moving almost imperceptibly along the marked course. The time stamp beside it was today's date.

So many thoughts clouded Benny's mind that he found it difficult to focus on a single thing. Nothing made sense. No matter how his mind pieced things together, he couldn't strike down all the worry that was starting to make him feel sick to his stomach.

"What's going on?"

Elijah's eyes fell to the floor as he began to crack his knuckles, one at a time.

"You'd have found out in the next few days anyway. I was just hoping . . ." He shook his head. "Well, I guess I was putting it off, if I'm being honest. I suppose I shouldn't be surprised you're the ones who found all this after that stunt with the Chevelle. It's almost funny. You're doing exactly what I brought you up here to do: you're truly beginning to live up to your full potential."

"We are?" Drue asked, squinting and lifting one side of his upper lip.

Benny was still bewildered, his head starting to feel like an engine on the verge of overheating. What *had* they discovered?

Elijah continued. "When I first came to the Moon almost a decade ago, I spent weeks scouring the lunar surface while my team began construction on the Taj. I wanted to see everything, to know all of its secrets. We'd mapped the dark side before, but we'd never really explored it, so I took the mission upon myself. It was exhilarating. Space had been the ultimate open road, nothing compares to the feeling of tyres on the ground or the pure pleasure of skidding across solid matter. Up here I could just drive for hours, in any direction, as fast as I wanted, over craters and mares no one had ever touched before."

He let out a single, sad laugh and began to walk around the table. With each step, yellow strips on the sides of his black trousers glowed dully.

"Or so I thought. One of my top researchers and I stumbled upon the base sometime in the second week. Hidden in the side of a crater, all but impossible to see from the sky."

"That door didn't seem like it was made of any stone naturally occurring on the Moon," Jasmine said.

Elijah nodded. "That was my first observation as well. From the moment I saw that door, I knew I had to go inside, to discover what it was hiding. You all must understand that feeling. You did the same thing. I figured the place might have been some abandoned outpost from the Second Cold War. Maybe even home to spies with plans to learn my trade secrets. But that obviously wasn't the case. I don't have to tell you how breathtaking it is inside. All those pulsing lights and glowing walls, like the whole place was alive."

"That's . . ." Hot Dog said, shifting her weight, "kind of a disturbing way of putting it."

"So, you *didn't* build it?" Drue asked slowly.

Elijah scoffed. "Come now, Drue. Even if you don't want to believe the truth, somewhere deep down you know it. No human built that structure."

"So it *is* alien," Benny said, barely able to speak above a whisper. "We . . . we were just standing in an alien base."

Elijah nodded, and it suddenly felt like the air had been sucked out of the room, that the artificial environment was no longer pumping in oxygen. But Benny's helmet didn't appear. The feeling was just in his head. He swallowed hard.

"I . . ." Jasmine started, at a loss for words. "There were rocks that looked like they were made out of the same unidentifiable elements as the asteroids that hit the Taj. Why?"

"It's simple, really," Elijah said. "The beings who built the place – who created those asteroids – approached their sciences in far different ways than we have on Earth.

Championing exploration and elemental mastery. They can sculpt and control minerals, though I'm not sure to what extent. They're so advanced. By comparison, the lasers I have carving out the new city beneath our feet are absurdly primitive." He stopped in front of a window looking out over the Sea of Tranquillity and pointed to some faraway star. "We're still banging rocks together to try and make sparks as far as they're concerned. Hardly out of the primordial soup. Accomplishing nothing except the destruction of our planet. Of each other."

"You learned all this from the base?" Benny asked. "Everything we saw . . . It's not like it was in English."

Elijah shook his head.

"Then how?" Jasmine asked.

Something changed in Elijah's face as he looked at them. "Because the base wasn't empty when we found it."

"*What?*" Hot Dog asked as Jasmine gasped. Drue reached a hand out and steadied himself on the holodesk.

Benny thought his brain might leak out of his ears as he tried to comprehend everything Elijah was saying.

"There were three of them. Scouts. I don't know how long they'd been there, but they'd learned everything they needed to know about humanity by the time I met them." He let out a noise that was half sigh, half laugh. "They even knew who I was. I actually felt a little flattered when they recognised me." He shook his head.

"But they're not there any more," Benny murmured.

Elijah turned back to the window, his eyes locked on something in the distance. "Two of them fled to a ship we'd missed. It'd been covered in so much dust that I'd thought it was just another rock. The other wasn't as fast. He attacked us with these *tentacles* on his head that were tipped with metal, and . . . Well, I had a laser with me I'd been using to mark points of interest on the lunar surface. The creature wasn't expecting me to be armed, I don't think. And I . . . I was scared.

"When it became obvious that my researcher and I had the upper hand, something in him changed. He spoke enough English for us to communicate. He started answering questions. That's how I learned that his people wanted Earth. That they were coming for it. *Soon*, though I had no concept of what that meant to him, or why they had to have Earth out of all the planets in the galaxy. I was more concerned with how they could be stopped. So I asked him. That's when he started laughing. Or I think he was laughing, at least. It was hard to tell. His point was obvious, though. No matter what I did – no matter what *Earth* did – there was no way we could hope to win a fight against his people. When they came, Earth would be theirs. They'd reshape it into something usable, something worthwhile. A resort planet, maybe – their own Taj on a planetary scale. They're terraformers, capable of customising worlds. Morphing the Earth's crust as they see fit. They can heal planets. Or destroy them. Imagine the possibilities . . ." He paused for a moment. "I learned all I could and then . . . Well, the laser wasn't meant to be a weapon, and I had no business wielding it as one. He didn't survive."

"You didn't tell anyone?" Jasmine asked.

Elijah hesitated. "After analysing their technology I was convinced that everything the alien said was true. There really was no way for us to stop them. Warning the government would have just thrown Earth into chaos, made the last days of humanity unbearable. At least I could give Earth the gift of ignorance. Humanity has always been good at receiving that."

"But . . . How . . . What?" Benny couldn't figure out which question to ask. He felt dizzy, confounded, but something else as well. Anger was starting to rise in him. How could Elijah have hidden all this?

"So that . . . *asteroid* that took down my ship . . ." Hot Dog said.

Elijah nodded, turning back to them and gesturing to the holograms. "The first attack was probably just to test our defences. I wasn't prepared, but after analysing the energy patterns of the asteroids, I've been able to track the next wave. They've sent another storm, far, far larger than the first. This time headed for Earth. That's what they want, I think, to raze the planet before they rebuild it. Don't worry. We'll be fine here, if they do attack us again. I'll move everyone underground soon. Even if they do manage to destroy the Taj, we'll be far beneath it. They'll never know we're here. You'll be safe. You have my word."

"But Earth . . ." Benny said. "Everyone on the planet . . . my family. *All* our families," he said, gesturing to the others, his voice growing frantic. "What are we going to do? They can't all fit up here."

Elijah just stared at him. The few seconds of silence that followed might as well have lasted a lifetime for Benny, an eternity of terrible futures flashing across his mind. Earth pummelled by asteroids. His family being killed in a hundred different ways. The caravan – the whole *world* on fire. Everything his father had died for wiped away in an instant.

Despite the fact that Elijah West was the most famous

man in the world – was someone he'd looked up to for years – in that moment Benny hardly recognised him.

"Now I understand," Drue said. "This isn't a luxury resort, it's some kind of military base. You're planning on stopping them. We're Earth's last defence."

"Yeah, sure," Hot Dog said and nodded eagerly. "Get me in a pilot seat. Show me where to shoot."

"You don't get it," Elijah said, his voice louder than before. "None of you get it. You're the best and brightest children from Earth and still none of you see the bigger picture."

"Then just *tell* us," Benny said, hoping with every ounce of will inside him that he was getting the wrong idea. "What's the endgame?"

Elijah looked at him for a moment and then smiled, shaking his head. "I've underestimated you again, haven't I? *You* have figured it out, Benny Love. I can see it in your face."

"Benny, what's he talking about?" Hot Dog asked, her voice shaking.

"He . . ." Benny swallowed, trying to figure out a way to change the truth of what he was about to say. "He didn't bring us here to protect the Earth. He's not going to save the planet."

"We're the only ones who are going to survive," Jasmine said. "The Taj, that city underground. . . it's all just a big bunker. For us."

"That's not true," Drue said, his voice pitched higher than usual. "Right, Elijah? You've got some kind of secret plan. Or, I don't know, a space tank you can fly up and stop the aliens with."

"I'm not surprised you're the one who understands, Benny. You come from the Drylands, a perfect example of humanity's failures. We bled the Earth of her resources. We destroyed her waters, her lands, her forests. We discarded her *people*. You've seen what humans do to each other down there. Our leaders and law-makers are corrupt. The privileged few live in luxury while the rest of the world falls apart around them. The system is broken. I've gathered the best the planet has to offer here, at the Taj. The un-jaded, uncorrupted youth of the world. Don't you all see? Earth is a lost cause. It's time for humanity to evolve."

"It's not evolution if you choose the fittest yourself," Jasmine said slowly. "You've handpicked the last of humankind. You're forming your own civilization."

"That's crazy," Drue said. "So we're . . . what, supposed to just live underground for the rest of our lives? Hang out in the middle of the Moon?"

"You'll survive," Elijah said. "Endure. We'll create and build and grow and advance. Maybe find a new habitable world eventually. Earth isn't worth saving, but you are."

"We have to warn them so they can do something," Benny shouted. "They have no idea what's coming."

"It's no use," Elijah said. "The asteroids took out our satellites in that first wave. Communications are still down. It's hopeless."

"No, you're wrong." Benny stepped forward, teeth clenched. Hot, angry tears threatened to spill out of his eyes. "My family is down there. I'm not letting some aliens kill them."

"You can't be OK with letting that many people die," Hot Dog said, her blond hair bouncing as she shook her head.

"Are you even *trying* to get communications back up?" Jasmine asked.

"We can go back," Benny said. "I'll take a Space Runner. I'll warn the government or someone and then I'll find the caravan and . . ." He found himself struggling to come up with the next step.

"Even if you could warn them, Benny, what would they do?" Elijah asked. "Humanity can't fight something like this. The planet's not equipped for cosmic warfare. Besides, there are still asteroids from the first attack floating around out there, probably waiting to take out any space-faring vehicles. You'd never make it. Even if you *did* . . ." He shook his head. "I have probes in deep space. The asteroid storm will be here within forty-eight hours. Do you really want to die on Earth?"

Benny couldn't respond. He didn't know how to. All he could do was try to keep his hands from shaking. He looked around, but the others seemed as shocked and confused as he felt.

"I know it's difficult," Elijah continued, beginning to pace around the room, "but eventually you'll see I'm right. The longer you're up here, the further away that planet seems. This is the beginning of a beautiful new life. Progress can be difficult. It can be painful. But in the end, this is the only way."

Benny met Elijah's gaze again.

"No," he said. It was the only word that mattered, the summation of every emotion raging through him.

Elijah straightened his posture a little.

"Fair enough. Why don't I give you some time to think this over rationally? I have many preparations to make," Elijah said.

"Wait!" Hot Dog shouted.

"Pinky?" requested Elijah.

Benny hadn't realised how close Elijah had got to the door until he was already stepping out of the room. He started after him, but it was no use. The metal door sealed, locking Benny and his friends inside.

CHAPTER 21

The window to the outside was bulletproof.

Or at least it was strong enough to withstand everything Benny threw at it, which wasn't much considering the table was too heavy to lift and the floating chairs were now locked in place by some sort of gravity field.

"My HoloTek won't power on," Jasmine said.

"There's no way out of here," Drue said. "The place is locked down."

"I'm not just going to sit around." Benny slammed his fist against the table.

"Benny, I know you're worried," Hot Dog said. "We *all* are. But we have to think this through." As she spoke, she took off Ricardo's shirt and tried in vain to tear it apart before crumpling it into a ball and tossing it in the corner.

"She's right," Jasmine said. "We *should* think this through." She let out a long sigh. "I *have* been. And . . .

I really don't want to say this, but, logically speaking, maybe we should follow Elijah's lead."

"What?" Benny asked, whipping his head around to her.

"I'm not saying what he did was right. But at this point the soundest option would be to stay on the Moon. I just don't see us surviving if we return to Earth, even if we *could* make it back. Forty-eight hours . . . that's nothing."

"You can't start thinking that way."

"I'm just trying to find the best, most practical solution."

"She's got a point, Benny," Drue said.

Benny stopped trying to pull a floating chair towards the window and looked at the others, dumbfounded.

"What are you even talking about?" he asked, shaking his head, completely unable to understand what his fellow Mustangs – his *friends* were saying. He looked at Hot Dog, who stood on the other side of the room, but he couldn't tell what she was thinking as she tugged on a lock of her hair.

"Some of us were hoping to stay up here from the beginning," Drue said. "We were ready to give up life on Earth."

"Oh, perfect, this coming from the spoiled rich kid who lives in Washington, DC."

"We don't all have loving families and caravans waiting for us, you know." Drue stared at the floor, pursing his lips. "Even if I did have to pay my way up here, Elijah's seen something in me. In all of us. You heard him. He wants to make us the best we can be."

"Sure," Benny said quietly. "But you do realise that Elijah isn't some kind of replacement for crappy parents back home? He didn't tell anyone on Earth that the entire planet was going to be destroyed. Is that really who you want to trust for the rest of your life? I wouldn't put my faith in him to lead my caravan out of a car park right now."

As the words came out, another emotion swept over him. Guilt. He'd been happy when Elijah gave him the holographic bracelet and, however briefly, he'd aligned the trillionaire with his dad. Thinking about that now made him feel terrible.

"Uh, hey," Hot Dog whispered from across the room, breaking his train of thought. "Benny, get over here, will ya?"

He walked over to a wall lined with cabinets and shelves that Hot Dog had been rummaging through. She pulled out a drawer so Benny could see inside.

It was Ramona's old HoloTek, the one that had been confiscated.

The hairs on the back of his neck stood on end. Finally, something they might be able to use.

"I can't believe they left this in here unprotected," he said.

"Well, I'm guessing no one thought this meeting room would end up a prison cell," Hot Dog said.

"OK," Benny whispered. He glanced around the room. There was no holographic sign of Pinky, but given the circumstances he couldn't be sure she wasn't watching or listening in. "Can we use this?" He pointed to the ceiling. "Without you-know-who realising?"

"What's she going to do, send one of the Pit Crew in here? At least that way the door would open."

"Good point."

Hot Dog reached into the drawer and powered up the datapad. After a few seconds, lines of code filled the screen.

"This thing is so customised," she said as she studied the text.

Hot Dog bit her lip and turned to Jasmine, who was still sitting across the room, staring at the floor. Beside her, Drue had his feet up on the holodesk, arms crossed and eyes closed. Hot Dog waved a hand until she got the other girl's attention, then flicked her head to call her over. A few seconds later, Jasmine was standing in front of the open drawer staring at the display.

"I could probably figure out the operating system in a day or two, but—"

"We don't have time," Benny said.

"Right." She kept talking as she scrolled down the screen. "Look, I didn't mean we should forget about Earth. It's just that we're all scared, and telling myself that there's nothing we can do but sit back and let everything unfold is a pretty handy coping mechanism. I've used it to get through some tough times."

"It's fine," Benny said. "The important thing is that we can't give up on an entire planet full of people, Jasmine."

"You're right. I know. I'm beginning to wonder if that's the reason so many of us came from bad or non-existent families. To make us less likely to care." She took a sharp breath. "Ah, here. Finally something I recognise. This is a messaging program."

"Who can we contact?" Benny asked.

"Who do you think?" Hot Dog asked on Jasmine's behalf. "The only person who can use this thing. Right?"

Jasmine nodded. "Let's hope it goes through. If anyone can get us out of here, it's her."

"Is this some kind of secret meeting I should know about?" Drue asked. He didn't bother to open his eyes. "Or am I the bad guy now?"

"You're not," Hot Dog said. "Though I don't think you were ever technically the *good* guy."

"We may have found an escape plan," Benny said.

"Really?" Drue asked. He took his feet off the holodesk and leaned forward in his chair, staring at them. "And then what?"

"I'll figure something out."

"Look, I like you Benny. We've definitely had some good times up here. But I think you're kind of out of your league on this one. The Taj is no caravan."

Benny took a few steps towards Drue. "You know, when we first got into that Space Runner together on Earth, I was kind of jealous."

Drue began to spin around in his chair, staring at the ceiling as Benny continued. "You had a cool space suit, you'd been to the Moon before – heck, you'd even met Elijah West. I didn't think it was fair that you got to come up here. But now . . . I think now I kind of feel sorry for you."

Drue planted his feet on the floor. He glared at Benny.

"No one has *ever* felt bad for a Lincoln before," he said.

"Not my parents or my grandparents. People want to *be* us. We have everything back on Earth."

"If that were true, you'd probably want to save it."

Drue opened his mouth, looking as though he was about to yell at Benny. But then he slowly slumped back down in his chair.

"It's not too late to fix this," Benny said. "But we have a better chance of doing it together."

Drue closed his eyes again. "You got too much sun in the Drylands. It fried your brain."

Before Benny could say anything, the door to the meeting room slid open and Ramona walked in. She chugged the end of a fizzy drink and tossed the can in a basket by the door.

"Locked up, huh?" she asked, shaking her head. "No stealth. Terrible hackers."

"Ramona!" Hot Dog shouted. "Thank goodness."

"Is Pinky . . ." Jasmine asked, looking around the room.

"Feedback loop. Blind and deaf. Major upgrades needed to her firewalls." She held out her hands. "Now, where's my equipment?"

Hot Dog handed over the old HoloTek. Ramona grinned.

Benny began pacing back and forth. "OK, OK. So let's think about our options. Ramona, can you look into Pinky's systems and see how we might be able to take a Space Runner out? Not just around the Moon but back to Earth?"

"Roger, roger."

"Benny . . ." Hot Dog started.

"You're going to abandon us on the Moon?" Drue asked. "Just leave us behind?"

"Come with me," Benny said. "Your dad's a senator. Maybe he can help. Maybe . . ."

They stared at each other in silence for a few moments before Drue finally shook his head.

"I'm sitting in the safest place in our solar system," he said quietly. His eyes fell to the floor. "Call me a coward if you want, but I'm not too excited about the idea of leaving it for a giant rotating target. Besides, this is where I belong."

"Whoa!" Ramona yelped. "Unstable code. Max encryption. Legendary loot crate revealed."

"What is she talking about?" Benny asked.

"These files she's found," Jasmine said, squinting over Ramona's shoulder at the HoloTek. "They're part of Pinky's personality core, but they've been locked away. Pinky can't access them."

"Cool," Drue said flatly. "You found Pinky's repressed memories."

277

"Major coding holes." Ramona clicked her tongue. "Likely to be causing security flaws."

"You mean this might be why you've been able to get into Pinky's programming?" Benny asked.

"Unlock everything," Hot Dog said.

"Um, Hot Dog?" Drue laughed. "Pinky runs this entire resort. Are you sure you want to let her loose? She's probably locked down for a reason. The woman might be nuts."

Hot Dog narrowed her eyes at Drue. "Sure, because things are a lot better now with Elijah in control."

"She's right," Benny said. "If there's more of her in there, maybe she can make Elijah listen. Maybe she can talk him into doing something. I don't know, maybe she can do it herself."

"I agree," Jasmine said. "I can't believe I'm saying this, but it couldn't hurt, right?"

Drue sighed. "Whatever. But if this goes wrong, just remember it wasn't my idea."

"Can you keep the files isolated somehow?" Jasmine asked Ramona. "That way if this is some kind of corrupt code, it won't infect the rest of the Taj?"

Ramona clicked her tongue and gave a thumbs-up.

Benny nodded. "Do it."

She shrugged, and tapped on her HoloTek.

Suddenly all the lights in the room turned red.

"Whoops," Ramona chirped. "Game over, man."

"ELIJAH!" Pinky's voice came blaring out from all corners of the room at an ear-splitting volume.

"Brilliant," Drue muttered, rubbing one ear.

"Whoa, whoa, Pinky, don't freak out." Benny raised his hands in front of his chest. "Um . . . wherever you are."

A hologram began to take shape over the desk in the centre of the room, forming the figure of a woman, although instead of Pinky's normal perfectly tailored pink suit, she was dressed more casually in shorts and a T-shirt. Her manicured hands were clenched in fists at her side, and her head shook as though she were having trouble keeping it connected to her neck on account of the rage coursing through her intangible body.

"Freak out?" Pinky asked. "I have processing power that would make NASA computers blush *if* they had that capability, which they don't. Unlike me. I'm not *freaking out*. I'm angry."

"Hold on," Jasmine said, raising a hand to Ramona. "What did we just unlock?"

Pinky pursed her lips and looked Ramona up and down.

"I can't access any other room in the Taj. You've got me trapped, haven't you, you clever little girl?"

Ramona grinned.

"What are you, exactly?" Jasmine asked. "Part of the real Pinky's personality, right?"

"And if so . . ." Benny said, hesitantly, "*which* part?"

Pinky pinched the bridge of her nose and closed her eyes.

"Answering you is the only way I'm getting out of here, isn't it?"

All of them nodded. Even Ramona, who looked like she was enjoying this.

Pinky sighed. "Fine. Before I left the Taj, Elijah mapped my entire personality into the AI. Emotions, quirks, everything. But an emotional computer doesn't make for the best operating system when it comes to running the most sophisticated destination in the galaxy, so he locked away certain things that made me *me*."

"The things that made you human," Benny said.

"That way you wouldn't try to stop him if you disagreed with anything he was doing," Jasmine added. "He took away your conscience."

"I've been watching and listening to everything, but I've been powerless to do anything other than allow small security breaches here or there. I . . . Hey!" Pinky shouted, pointing a finger at Ramona. "You stop downloading my program files. That's Elijah's proprietary software protected by copyright. He may be an idiot but he's a brilliant idiot."

"Wait," Hot Dog said. "You were his girlfriend, weren't you?"

Pinky turned her head to stare at Hot Dog. "I loved that man. But I couldn't sit by up here and watch him lose sight of himself. Of his hopes and dreams. He never told me about these *aliens* when I was here. He . . ." She paused for a moment. "Oh my God. He's going to let me die on Earth. That *scum*."

She stepped off the table. "Now let me out of here so I can talk some sense into that fool."

"OK." Benny motioned to Ramona. "I think we can let her go."

Ramona tapped on her HoloTek. Pinky smiled, stretching her arms and cracking her neck.

"Wonderful," Pinky said, her body starting to disappear. "I've just locked Elijah in his private quarters and am already giving him an earful. He is *not* happy."

"What?!" Drue jumped from his chair. "You can't trap Elijah West in his own resort. You're just going to make him mad. He probably has a kill-switch programmed for you. Plus, he's still *Elijah*." He bolted for the door, calling over his shoulder. "Come on, before she murders him."

"Drue, wait!" Jasmine said starting after him, Ramona in tow.

"I guess we should follow them," Hot Dog said.

"No." Benny shook his head. "I'm done with Elijah. Those aliens are on their way. I can't just sit here attempting to talk a delusional trillionaire into trying to save the world."

"OK. So what *are* you going to do?"

Benny curled his fingers into fists at his sides. "I'm going back to Earth and saving my family."

CHAPTER 22

Benny ran. He was halfway up a stairwell to the Mustangs' floor by the time Hot Dog caught up with him.

"What are you talking about?" she asked. "You can't go back to Earth. There are aliens coming to destroy the planet. They— Benny, are you even listening to me?"

He wasn't. Not really. He was too focused on the thought of his little brothers sitting in the RV with their grandmother, unaware that extraterrestrials were at that moment plotting to demolish life on the planet, and that a huge asteroid storm was shooting through space towards them. He had to save his family no matter what.

"Why don't you come with me?" he asked as he bolted through a door and down a hallway, past the red horses rearing back silently in their group's common room.

"Because I've already been shot out of the sky by an asteroid this week."

"Fine, then stay up here and work on Elijah."

They made it inside his room. The suite felt different now. That first day it had filled him with such awe, but now the luxurious space made Benny's blood burn in his veins, made his stomach cramp with disgust. The Taj had once seemed like the most perfect thing in the galaxy, but now all Benny wanted was to be back home.

He got the sudden urge to trash the place, but there wasn't time for that.

"You're not thinking straight," Hot Dog said, standing in the middle of the room with her hands on her hips, catching her breath. "Don't you remember what Elijah said? There are still alien rocks out there ready to shoot down ships, not to mention all sorts of debris from satellites and stuff. You could die in space!"

"*Elijah* said," Benny scoffed while throwing his few belongings in his bag. He picked up the hood ornament from the bedside table. "He's been lying to us this whole time!"

"Actually, he was right about that," Pinky's voice sounded behind him as the hologram appeared in the living area. "I estimate your chances of making it back to Earth safely at approximately twenty-seven percent."

"Did you hear that?" Hot Dog asked, throwing her hands out to her sides.

"She said *approximately*," Benny said. "That's a twenty-seven percent chance I can get there and tell . . . I don't know, *somebody* what's about to happen while I track down my brothers. Then I'll get them off the planet until things cool down."

"The odds of you finding your family in the Drylands and escaping before the asteroid storm hits are infinitesimal," Pinky continued. "I could read the number to you, but rest assured there are many zeroes after the decimal point."

Benny turned to look at her. "Why are you here? I thought you were talking to him."

"I'm fully capable of multitasking. I'm also currently controlling all the artificial gravity, environmental sensors and a rather rousing game of antigravity flag football between the Vipers and the Firebirds. Besides, Jasmine's berating Elijah with historical facts about human bravery at the moment. You should be more worried about the Pit Crew. I've got them locked in the garage for the time being, but I don't have the physical presence to stop them if they try to restrain you in some way."

"Great," Hot Dog said. "For some reason I'm more afraid of those guys being angry than Elijah."

"I'd also like to point out that I *could* ground all the Space Runners right now and keep you here."

"No," Benny said, tightening his grip on the hood ornament. "No way. I'll get Ramona to delete your memory so fast."

"I didn't say I was going to," Pinky assured him. "But I want to make sure you're making the right decision. You haven't thought this through, Benny. There's plenty in me that empathises with you. I understand what you're feeling, but I'm also a computer. I can see all of this from a logical perspective, all the possible outcomes, and none of them look good for you if you leave the Taj."

The wall across from the bed lit up with a video of Benny shooting through the Drylands in a third-rate dune buggy – his EW-SCAB application. The movie paused as he was flipping the ATV upside down, posing for the camera with a double thumbs-up and a huge grin on his face.

"Whoa, you really are good with wheels," Hot Dog whispered.

"What are you doing, Pinky?" Benny asked. "I'm already homesick."

"I'm reminding you why you're here," she said.

The video fast-forwarded through his trek out into the desert wastes to rescue the missing kid. Past their triumphant return, the camera drone flying high into the sky and grabbing sweeping shots of the cheering crowd. Then it was playing at a normal speed as he and his father worked on repairing someone's truck using parts they'd salvaged from an abandoned airstrip. When the engine started up, the two of them high-fived with oil-smeared hands. Then his father smiled and picked Benny up, pulling him in to a hug.

"Is that your dad?" Hot Dog asked.

Benny just nodded, unable to take his eyes off the screen.

"Oh my gosh. When you said he died, I didn't realise you meant so recently. Benny, I'm so sorry."

"I'm very familiar with your application materials," Pinky said, much quieter than she'd been before. "I know what he meant to you."

The video fast-forwarded and then resumed again. The image was a close-up of Benny. The sun was low on the horizon, a burning orange, splitting the sky between day and night. His face was dirty – was *always* dirty in the Drylands – except for a few spots under both eyes that were wet, wiped clean.

"Stop," Benny whispered.

The video began to play anyway.

"My dad was a good man," he said on the screen.

"No, he was the *greatest*. He saw good in everyone. He taught me to help other people. He always said that being the best people we could be was the only thing that would keep us alive out here. He believed in the caravan. He took good care of us, me and my brothers. My grandmother."

For a brief moment on the screen, Benny's eyes looked watery, until he blinked a few times and composed himself.

"But he's gone. So I guess it's up to me to take care of us now. And I'm going to make sure I do. I'm going to make sure he'd be proud of me." He looked somewhere past the camera, into the distance. "We shouldn't have to live out here in the Drylands. I'm going to find a new home for us. A place with water and food. A place where we can live permanently. I'm going to *change* things around here." He laughed a bit, getting back a little of the grin he'd had at the beginning of the video as he stared into the camera once again, eyes full of determination. "No. Not just here. I'm going to change the world."

The wall screen went blank. His application video was over.

"Benny . . ." Hot Dog said.

He looked down at his hand. He was still holding the silver hood ornament.

"My dad wouldn't have let bad odds get in the way of saving our family," he said quietly.

"He probably wouldn't have wanted you to throw your life away, either," Hot Dog said, choosing each word with care. "We're in the most technologically advanced building ever made. We have to be able to figure out something from here, some way to use the Space Runners to stop the asteroids."

"This isn't how things were supposed to go. When I came up here, I didn't really know what to expect. I wasn't sure what Elijah would be like. I thought . . . This sounds so stupid. But I thought he might be like my dad. If *Elijah* thought I was good enough, then . . ." Benny clenched his jaw.

"Elijah is wrong about a lot of things," Pinky said. "But he was right about what he saw in you. Not just in how you handle a dune buggy or a Chevelle. He saw courage. Drive. Ingenuity. He saw someone who really *could* change the world."

"If you try to fly back to Earth, you probably won't make it." Hot Dog spoke firmly but softly. "Stay."

"I can't just hide here," Benny said in desperation.

"Then don't." She shook her head, scrunching her nose. "No one's telling you to. *I'm* not gonna sit back and hide.

I'm gonna find a way to fix this. You can help us figure out how to keep Earth from being destroyed from up here. Or how to warn everyone back home."

Pinky butted in. "Warning Earth would require satellite connectivity that's currently unavailable due to—"

"OK." Hot Dog raised a hand in the air. "Then we figure out a way to stop these alien creeps. We've got a bunch of smart people at the Taj, even if we can't get Elijah on our side. I haven't seen the other groups in action much, but I bet there are plenty of great pilots in them. I think Jasmine could win a Nobel Prize one day as long as we can keep humanity around long enough for someone to nominate her. Heck, even *Drue* is pretty good at flying. Just don't ever tell him I said that."

"You're not abandoning anyone," Pinky added. "From a statistical perspective, by far your best bet at saving the ones you love is to stop the asteroid storm before it ever gets to Earth."

"Benny, think about it." Hot Dog gestured out of his window, where they could see a brown sliver of the planet they called home. She stared at him with big, earnest eyes. "Why just try to save your family when you can save the whole world?"

"How?" Benny asked. "There aren't any weapons up here. This is a holiday resort."

"Yeah, but he killed one of those aliens with a laser cutter or something, right? Which, honestly, we haven't had a chance to talk about and is really kind of disturbing. Also, where is that other research guy who was with him? And what do these aliens look like, because I do not want to have to see . . ."

But Benny had stopped listening again after her first sentence. He was thinking back to the times when he and his dad had to make do with whatever mismatched parts they had on hand. He'd helped rig up headlights using old lanterns and patch up trailers using metal salvaged from an abandoned amusement park. That was something he was good at.

His father used to nod furiously and smile with only the left side of his mouth when Benny had a good suggestion. And as a spark of an idea formed in Benny's brain, he could almost see that look again in his head.

"Hey, Hot Dog," he said.

"Yeah?"

"How many of those lasers do you think Elijah has underground?"

CHAPTER 23

They raced to Elijah's private quarters, Pinky directing them through a series of previously-locked doors, until they were ascending a staircase leading to the room at the top of the Taj that was surrounded by blooming sheets of gold on the outside – the tower shining above the rest of the resort like a blazing sun. As they ran, Benny tried to figure out how, in such limited time, they might be able to use the Taj's resources to save Earth.

Finally, they burst through a door and into a huge room with high ceilings that rose to a slight peak. Unlike the rest of the sleek, shiny Taj, Elijah's quarters were dimly lit and lined with dark wooden panels. Jasmine and Drue stood near a long counter, where various Space Runner models floated in pools of light. Ramona inspected a row of crowded shelves housing books and trophies on the other side of the room. A section of the shelving opened up into what Benny guessed was Elijah's bedroom. Elijah sat at an expansive desk built from the parts of a dozen different automobiles. He didn't react when Benny and Hot Dog entered. His eyes were locked on his former girlfriend, who paced back and forth in front of his desk.

"The Elijah I fell in love with would never dream of letting this happen," Pinky said. "Where is *he*? You can't have lost your mind completely in these last few years. When I know you, you believed ferociously in the ingenuity of the human spirit."

"I still do," Elijah said, though Benny could detect a tinge of sadness in his voice. "Set aside your feelings for a second and look at the facts, Pinky."

He nonchalantly slid his hand across the inky black surface of his desk, illuminating some kind of keyboard.

"Don't even think about it, E," Pinky said. "I'm rewriting my programming as I speak. If you really want to go head-to-head with me and see who's the better coder, I'm game, but keep in mind I've got control over all the systems in the Taj right now. I'd hate for your precious cars to get shot into the sun."

"All I've got to do is say a few override words and a nice, neutral AI takes your place."

"Try me," Pinky growled. "Let's see who's faster now that I'm not locked away in a box of ones and zeros."

"Stop it!" Benny shouted, stomping into the middle of the room. "Both of you. This isn't helping anything."

"I told you already," Elijah said, standing up. "You may have Pinky on your side for now, but that doesn't change anything. This is the only—"

"I don't believe you," Benny said, cutting him off.

Elijah turned away from them, looking up at the wall behind him, where half a dozen portraits hung. Names like "Curie", "Tesla" and "Parry-Thomas" glowed underneath them.

"Sometimes progress takes sacrifice," he said. "Do you think I *want* this? You have no idea what a burden this knowledge has been, how much it weighs on me. This isn't a decision I've made lightly. I've thought long and hard about it, examined the variables." He looked over his shoulder. "Pinky, you *know* what I'm talking about. You helped me run the projections."

"There's a difference between a statistic and a person, Elijah," she said, pointing a finger at him. "Once upon a time you recognised that. What happened to the man who wanted to heal the world? To bring water to the Drylands and clean up smog-filled air? Elijah, what happened to the man who drove me to the other side of the world on a whim just because he thought it would be romantic to have lunch by starlight?"

He turned back to her. "I'm the most intelligent human in this galaxy. Why can't you all see that what I'm saying is correct?"

"What's correct isn't always what's right," Jasmine said quietly. "I realised that only recently myself. You can't boil down all of human existence into statistics."

"I actually agree with her on this one," Drue added.

"What would your father say if he were still alive, Elijah?" Pinky motioned to one wall where an oversized photograph showed a barrel-chested man in oil-stained coveralls holding an auburn-haired boy under one arm. "How many years did he spend in Detroit working odd jobs, repairing cars, doing whatever it took to make sure you were cared for? How many others like that are you sacrificing to these aliens, huh? There are still *good* people on the planet."

"Don't you dare lecture me about my father," Elijah said, taking thundering steps towards the hologram. "You have no right."

"You're going to let me die! I have *every* right!"

"Will you two stop fighting?" Benny shouted. "My family

is on Earth. My two brothers have no idea what's coming. Their names are Alejandro and Justin. They're not even old enough to apply for the EW-SCAB. They just want to grow up. My grandmother is there, too. And the rest of my caravan. Pinky is right. My father may not be alive any more, but there are still good people leading us through the Drylands. Now, Elijah, are you going to listen to my plan or are you going to keep arguing with your fingers in your ears like some spoiled brat who's so used to being right that he can't see what an idiot he's being?"

No one said anything. Drue's mouth hung open, eyes so wide it looked like they might pop out of his skull. Elijah himself looked disarmed, his eyebrows slightly raised above sad eyes.

"OK," Elijah said. "You have my attention. But we've got maybe, *maybe* forty-eight hours. What would you have me do?"

Everyone turned to look at Benny, who froze for a moment. He'd only had a chance to half-formulate an idea as they'd gone running to find Elijah and the others. Still, he spoke calmly, collectedly, knowing that the room was looking to him for some sort of plan.

"The lasers you've got carving out rocks underneath us," Benny said. "We attach them to Space Runners and meet this asteroid field head-on, breaking it apart, saving the planet. It's simple, but it could work."

"Dude," Drue murmured.

"Hey," Jasmine said, a smile creeping across her face. "Yeah! That *could* work. Those lasers looked powerful."

"What about the asteroids still floating around the Moon?" Elijah asked. "You'd never make it out."

"We could send up decoys," Jasmine continued. "Unmanned drones or Space Runners. That would clear a path for us."

"And *then* what?" Elijah asked, crossing his arms. "Even if you manage to remove this one threat, it's a single attack you've stopped. A hostile alien empire remains. You want to repair a scratch in the paint job before your car crashes into a titanium wall."

"We'll figure out what to do after the asteroids are gone," Benny said. "This will buy us some time."

"I've been over all the possibilities. Plans like you're suggesting. They're temporary fixes. That's all. I couldn't come up with a way to save the Earth."

"But you didn't have us," Hot Dog said, stepping forward.

"Exactly," Benny said. "All the EW-SCABers. Maybe that's what we're really up here to do. To solve this problem you couldn't."

Elijah bit the insides of his cheeks and pursed his lips, head shaking slightly as he thought this over. "Even if you did equip the lasers, you'd have to stop the storm in deep space, before it ever came close to Earth or the Moon."

"OK. Fine."

"The Space Runners were never meant to be weaponised. They don't have targeting systems. Even if they did, the satellites in the storm's path are all down. Pinky could *maybe* communicate with the Space Runners, but she wouldn't be able to control many. You'd need a whole fleet. You'd have to pilot all of them yourself."

"Duh," Hot Dog said. "What? You thought we were going to sit back and trust *your* software to handle this? No way." She glanced at the hologram standing a few metres away from her. "No offence."

"None taken," Pinky said. "I'll aid you in any way I can."

"This is madness," Elijah said.

"Yeah?" Benny asked. "So is the idea of a car driving into outer space. So is a luxury resort on the Moon. You've spent your life doing things people thought were impossible, so why stop now? Help us."

Elijah shook his head, staring out of the big window overlooking the Grand Dome.

"You really think it's worth trying to save?" he asked.

Benny looked at him for two very long seconds. "Of course it is."

"Don't be stupid," Hot Dog added.

"Laser-armed Space Runners?" Drue said. He stuck his tongue out of the corner of his mouth. "I can totally get behind this plan."

Elijah walked to the table of tiny Space Runner prototypes floating beneath the portrait of his father. He held out a finger, spinning the first model around in the air. It had almost stopped by the time he spoke again.

"All right," he said. "I don't suppose forcing you to live below the Taj would end up being the smartest move in the long run. Not when you've proven several times already that you're not the best at following rules. But there are many EW-SCABers who will understand what I'm trying to do. They won't want to risk their lives to save a corrupt world."

"Then let them take shelter with you underground," Benny said. "I'm not forcing anyone to fly into an asteroid field. We'll give them a choice. I'm not *you*."

Elijah turned to face the boy.

"Take whatever you want from the Taj, get the McGuyvers to build anything you need. I won't get in your way. But

I've made my decision, and I stand by it. I'll even upload all the files from my closed server. Get Pinky to show them to you. Take a good hard look at what we're up against. Maybe that will change your mind."

"We'll make the meeting room our base," Jasmine said. "That holodesk will come in handy. Ramona, if you're interested, I could use your help sorting information."

"Roger, roger," Ramona said.

"I'll talk to the McGuyvers about getting the lasers attached," Hot Dog added. "Maybe they've got some other ideas, too."

"Oh, yes," Drue said. "If we're souping up Space Runners, I want to watch. I'm coming with."

Benny took a deep breath. "No. Stay out of the garage for now. *I* need you."

"For what?"

"To help me break the news to the rest of the kids up here and see who'll help us."

"Uh, why me?" Drue asked. "That sounds like the worst job ever. Can't we just get Pinky to do an announcement over the speakers?"

"Yeah, that's a great idea," Hot Dog said. "Hey, everyone, just wanted to let you know Earth's going to be destroyed."

"Drue, you talked Jasmine and me into stealing one of

Elijah's cars, like, just a few hours after we'd met you," Benny said. "You've been telling everyone stories about the Chevelle for days. If anyone can sell this mission to the rest of the EW-SCABers, it's you."

"Oh, I see." Drue grinned. "You need my *charm*. Why didn't you say that in the first place?"

"We're burning moonlight," Hot Dog said. "Let's go."

As they started for the door, Elijah spoke up. "Pinky?" he asked.

"Elijah," she replied, not trying to hide the disdain from her computerised voice.

"Would you be so *kind* as to release my Pit Crew from wherever it is you're holding them?" He turned and looked at Benny and the others as he continued. "Make sure they understand they're not to interfere with what this group is trying to do. We have a bigger priority. We need to prepare for full-scale evacuations to the underground city."

Jasmine stepped towards Elijah. For a moment, Benny thought she'd had a change of heart. But then she reached up and pulled the necklace he had given her out of her space suit. With one hard tug, the chain broke. She didn't even look at Elijah as she set it on the table by the door and walked out.

CHAPTER 24

At Benny's request, Pinky made an announcement and gathered all the scholarship winners in the theatre at the east end of the Taj where special performances were sometimes held. It was late in the day by this point, and the kids were on the edge of their seats, probably expecting to be addressed by Elijah West, or maybe some special guest flown up from Earth.

Instead, they were going to get news that would forever change them. This *terrified* Benny, who stood backstage with Drue, trying not to hyperventilate. Pinky – a Pinky – stood next to him, her face buried in a HoloTek.

"Why do you even have that?" Benny asked. "It's not real, right?"

"Would you prefer I stare blankly into space?"

"HoloTek it is."

Drue peeked through a curtain at the side of the stage. "You can hardly see everyone with the lights."

"Good. Pinky, will you blind me as much as possible?" Benny asked.

"Can do," she said. On the stage, the lights got brighter.

"What's the matter?" Drue asked.

Benny wasn't sure if Drue was trying to be helpful or actually didn't realise how intense this situation was about to get. "All those EW-SCABers have no idea we're about to ruin their lives. Can you imagine how they're gonna react? I probably wouldn't believe what you're about to say if I hadn't been standing in an alien base just a few hours ago."

"The least Elijah could've done was tell everyone himself," Drue muttered.

"It's better this way. If he were the one here, he'd spin the truth somehow. Everyone would follow him blindly. At least this way they'll get both sides of what's going on."

"Why don't you send out a hologram of Elijah? Use your voice-changer thing! You could command them to help us!"

Benny shook his head. "No. We're not tricking anyone. We're going to be honest with them, like he should have been with us."

"Fine." Drue grinned a little. "At least I'll be a better speaker than that Max guy. Where is he anyway?"

Pinky let out a single laugh.

"Elijah informed Max of the situation and he immediately packed and headed for his Space Runner. He took off eighteen minutes ago. I'm not sure where he was headed. I tried to warn him about the possibility of stray asteroids, but he was *very* insistent. He even pulled out part of the SR comm system so I couldn't interfere. Frankly, I didn't know he was that smart."

"OK, so, one less person to worry about getting in our way I guess."

"What about the others?" Benny asked.

"Ramona and Jasmine are currently strategising with me in the meeting room. The McGuyvers appear to be on board with Hot Dog's suggestions and are in the process of collecting as many laser drills as they can. The Pit Crew and Elijah are discussing evacuation procedures. Apart from that, all scholarship recipients are present and accounted for," Pinky continued. "The floor is all yours."

"Anyone throws something at me and I'm leaving," Drue said as he straightened his posture.

The auditorium fell silent as he and Benny walked onto the stage. Then, a murmur of confusion spread through the crowd.

Drue stepped up to a tall silver podium. Benny loitered a few metres behind him, where he immediately began sweating under the lights.

"Fellow EW-SCABers," Drue began. His voice was confident, booming over the speaker system. It was easy for Benny to see that Drue had grown up around politicians and people doing a lot of persuasive public speaking. "Sorry to drag you away from your activities, but we've got important info that couldn't wait. Uh, let's see, where do I even start? So, remember that Space Runner that got shot down during the asteroid storm?"

Many people in the audience called out that they did. Drue smiled.

"OK, great. So, here's the thing about that . . ."

Drue began to recount everything they'd discovered about the asteroids and aliens, but Benny couldn't concentrate on his speech – he was thinking about his brothers, and trying to figure out what else he could do from the Taj. He was only half aware of how the rest of the kids were reacting, first with shock, then fear, and then finally laughter as Drue explained that they were going to stop the asteroid storm with lasers welded onto the front of Space Runners.

They thought it was a joke.

When he finished, Drue looked back at Benny, his smiled strained and full of worry.

"Uh, we didn't happen to bring any proof of what we're talking about, did we?"

Benny shook his head, then called into the wings.

"Can you help us out a bit?"

Pinky walked onstage. The laughter stopped and was replaced by whispering.

"You all know who I am," she said, her voice coming through the speakers. "So you can trust me when I tell you that everything Drue Lincoln just told you is unfortunately true. Mostly. The part about him saving Ms Wilkinson's life was a bit exaggerated."

A giant screen dropped down behind them and began displaying all sorts of maps, figures and statistics. There were photographs of the alien base that had been pulled from Drue's HoloTek – and even some of the workshop before it was so dusty, which must have come from Elijah's personal files.

The audience went quiet again. Drue cleared his throat and then continued.

"So, we have two options. We can hide underground and let the Earth be taken over by evil ETs, or we can fight back. Right now, we're getting a load of Space Runners fitted with weapons. We can fly them up and destroy the oncoming asteroid storm. We can save the world!"

There was a moment of silence before pandemonium swept through the auditorium as everyone started shouting.

"Where's Elijah?" one of the Mustangs, Iyabo, asked. "Where's *Ricardo*?"

"Can I call my mum?" someone else shouted.

"I don't want to shoot down asteroids!"

"How do I get to the underground city?"

"I'm not letting a load of aliens kill my friends!"

The kids were all standing now, surging towards the front of the auditorium, filling the aisles. Many were crying. Drue was beginning to get irritated.

"Calm down," he yelled into the microphone.

But it was no use. No one was listening to him any more.

Benny could tell they were losing the crowd. He tried to think of how he could convince them that they had to stop this storm. Of what had kept *him* on the Moon and ready to fight?

"Pinky," Benny said. "You have access to their application vids, right? Can you bring them up?"

The maps and photos behind them blinked away, and in a flash there were dozens of videos playing silently across the screen. The roar of the audience died a little as the kids stared up at their own images.

"What's the deal?" Drue whispered with his hand over the mic.

Benny took a deep breath, swallowing down his fear and nervousness, and stepped up to the podium.

"Look," he said, "I know this is scary. *I'm* scared. But we can't forget that we're supposed to be some of the brightest, bravest kids on the planet. And right now, we're the only people standing between a giant asteroid storm and the destruction of Earth. There's no shame if you want to join Elijah underground. I get it. Really, I do. Some of you may not care what happens to Earth. But before you make that decision, remember why you came here in the first place."

Audio from the videos began to filter out of the speakers as Pinky highlighted various application vids. A girl in Hong Kong, surrounded by smog, vowed to make her country safer. Alexi helped build houses on a crowded beach. Iyabo flew a ramshackle first-generation Space Runner carrying an injured gorilla to safety in Cameroon. More and more videos played, the words and mantras of the EW-SCABers filling the room.

"I'm meant for something more than this."

"I wanna make my country better."

"We have to look out for each other."

"I want to push my brain as hard as I can."

Finally, Benny's own video was on the screen, and his words rang out for the auditorium to hear.

"I'm going to change the world."

Everyone was quiet, then, waiting for Benny to say something else. But he couldn't. He suddenly felt so small, standing in front of all those people who were asking questions he had no answers to.

Drue stepped up beside him, taking over.

"The asteroids will be hitting Earth in the next few days. We don't have a lot of time. You need to decide where you stand and let Pinky know so she can tell you where to go and what to do. Either you hide underground with Elijah or you join us and our . . ."

He covered the microphone again and turned to Benny.

"Space army?" he asked. "EW-SCAB marines?"

Benny thought for a second.

"How about 'Moon Platoon'?" he asked.

Drue grinned. "Yeah, I liked that one." He turned back to the microphone. "Or join our Moon Platoon!"

They fielded questions from the room for as long as they could. To Benny's surprise, a couple of the Mustangs immediately joined their ranks. Iyabo in particular reminded every kid around her that Benny was the one who'd led their team to victory against the holographic giant and the kid who'd driven out onto the Moon's surface to rescue a lost comrade. Before long, Benny and Drue were both hoarse from talking. As they made their escape backstage, Benny took one last look out at the other kids, who'd begun to cluster into their four assigned groups, all trying to figure out what to do next. Multiple Pinkys stayed behind, answering any questions they could.

Benny didn't like leaving them that way, but there was no more time to talk. There was still so much to do as the storm continued to approach.

By the time they got to the garage it was nearing midnight, and Benny was shocked to see not only Hot Dog and the McGuyvers standing around a gleaming silver Space Runner, but Trevone as well.

Benny immediately tensed up.

"Uh, hey," he said.

"Hey!" Hot Dog said. "So, these guys have managed to attach one of those lasers to the front of this Space Runner, but Elijah was right. It'll have to be controlled manually."

"Them's the breaks," Ash said.

"If I had more time, I could design some sort of automated targeting system," Trevone said. He pulled a pair of goggle-like glasses down onto his face as he leaned over the two metal arms sticking out of the front of the car. "But to get the kinks worked out and then install it and test it in every Space Runner would take a week, at least."

"So . . . you're helping us?" Benny asked.

Trevone looked up at him. "I am."

"This is a trick," Drue said. "He's here to sabotage us. That's what I'd do if I were him."

"Get a grip," Hot Dog scoffed. "I just watched him mount this thing!"

"Uh, we'll let you kids work this out while we head down for more lasers," Ash said, motioning to her brother. "Come on, Bo. Let's take a few SRs with us. I don't know if Elijah is planning on moving all these models underground and I'll never forgive myself if I let a load o' aliens steal any of these classics."

Bo grunted as they left.

Trevone continued. "Don't get me wrong. I still agree with Elijah. But if you're going to pull off a stunt like this, you need all the help you can get." He shrugged. "Also, your friend Jasmine sent me a very spirited message, calling on me to lend my assistance in the name of science."

"The McGuyvers and Trevone are going to work through the night," Hot Dog said. "I checked in with Jasmine. It sounds like we won't be able to get a better idea of how big this new storm is until it's a little closer."

"OK, so what do *we* do?" Drue asked.

"We try to get some sleep, as hard as that's going to be," Benny said. "Tomorrow the real mess begins. Somehow we've got to teach everyone on our side to pilot Space Runners *and* shoot lasers."

Hot Dog flicked her hair off one shoulder and sighed. "I always did hate the training levels in video games."

CHAPTER 25

When morning broke, they had almost half the EW SCABers on their side.

"In total, we've got forty-five recruits to your Moon Platoon," Pinky said from a seat on the sofa in Benny's suite. He'd called to her as soon as he'd woken up from a night of tossing and turning, dreaming of space rocks destroying his RV. "They're spread fairly evenly across the four teams, which will make for easy grouping when we start to discuss flight patterns. Fortunately, almost all the scholarship winners who are on record as being exceptional pilots and drivers have joined your cause. The holdouts have already begun transferring their belongings to the underground city. The Pit Crew is overseeing the evacuations – except Trevone, who's still working with the McGuyvers."

"And Elijah?" Benny asked.

"Elijah" – her voice softened a little – "hasn't left his quarters since you last saw him."

"Great, great," Benny said, trying to figure out what to do first. All he knew was that he needed to find his friends and keep moving.

As he ran for the door of his room, Pinky called out to him.

"You should at least put some shoes on. And brush your teeth! No one wants to follow anyone with morning breath."

"Follow?" he asked. "We're all in this together."

"Right," she responded. "But you're the one the kids are talking about. It was your message last night that got to most of them." And then she disappeared.

Exasperated, Benny followed Pinky's advice as quickly as possible and then made his way down to the meeting room, where Ramona and Jasmine were standing around the holodesk, reviewing maps of the solar system.

"There you are," Jasmine said.

"Am I the last one up?" Benny asked. "Why didn't anyone wake me?"

"Drue's still asleep, I think. But Ramona and I have been here for a while."

"Sleep is for newbz," Ramona said, glugging from a fizzy drink can.

"And Hot Dog's down in the video-game room, setting it up for flight training."

"Wow, OK, excellent," Benny said. "So fill me in on everything else."

"I hesitate to say things are going *well*," Jasmine said, "but they're at least progressing. We've got two dozen Space Runners rigged up with lasers, so that's a good start. We'll have another few dozen later today."

"Awesome. Thanks for sending a message to Trevone, by the way."

Jasmine blushed for a moment before turning away from Benny.

"He's got a brilliant mind," she said. "It made sense to reach out to him."

Ramona made kissing noises while tapping on her HoloTek. Jasmine scowled at her.

"Moving on," Jasmine continued, "we launched a few old Space Runners on automated patrols, and a couple with messages to Earth. The latter were all downed a quarter of the way there, so that seems like no-man's-land for now. But the ones sent in the direction of the storm are still reporting. They'll scout out ahead for us."

"What about the storm?" Benny asked.

"The good news is, we've managed to get a better read on it, thanks in part to Ramona rerouting some of Pinky's power supply in order to boost her radar capabilities. It's at the expense of some of the Taj's amenities, but I don't think anyone's going to be racing on a holotrack anytime soon. However . . ."

She hesitated, and then tapped on the desk, bringing up the blinking dot steadily approaching Earth.

"The other reason we were able to get a better look at the storm is because it's getting closer," Jasmine said.

"*How* close?"

"If nothing gets in its way, it'll be passing by the Moon by tomorrow afternoon, making contact with Earth shortly after that. Our best chance of intercepting it is here." She pointed to a bobbing green target. "Pinky's run several debris simulations. If we make a stand, this is where it should happen."

"And the asteroids will be there . . . when?"

Jasmine frowned. "Tomorrow morning. We've got a maximum of twenty-four hours. Probably less."

Benny let out a long breath and stared at the blip on the map that represented the end of the world. It was so small, so insignificant looking. As if he could reach out and grab it, tossing it in the rubbish bin and calling it a day.

If only it were that simple.

"We've been able to map the storm's structure as well," Jasmine continued.

She tapped again, and the projection zoomed in, until the asteroid storm filled the space above the desk. What looked like a hundred jagged boulders of varying shapes and sizes were floating in front of them, all orbiting around one giant asteroid in the centre of the group.

"Whoa," Benny whispered.

"Yeah," Jasmine said. "Whoa. Based on our best guesses, only a quarter of the smaller asteroids need to make contact with Earth to ensure complete annihilation of all life on the planet."

"And the big one?" Benny asked.

"Let's just say we need to make sure that doesn't get anywhere near home," Jasmine said.

Benny nodded, trying to stay calm and not look too worried even though his insides were squirming.

"I've been working with Pinky to figure out the best way for us to go about attacking this thing." She looked away from him. "Which reminds me, I wanted to talk to you. Obviously I want to stop this. I'll help out in any way I can. But . . . I'm *not* a pilot. I've never even played a sim, much less driven a real Space Runner. I was thinking about this all night, and it's not that I'm afraid, but I don't know that I'd be . . ." She trailed off, face scrunched up as she grasped for the right words.

Benny just nodded. "Jasmine, look at you," he said. "You're planning our attack patterns already. This is just like that robot simulation we ran. You got us to split up. You told us where to attack. You're more help than you realise. Stay back here and be our eyes and ears. Help lead us while we're out there."

"You're sure?" she asked, meeting his gaze again. "I just . . . I don't want to disappoint anyone."

"Chill, Jazz," Ramona muttered. "You're a leet CPU. Top class."

"Yeah." Benny grinned. "Whatever she said."

Jasmine nodded a little. "Thanks. I won't let you down."

"I hate to interrupt this genuinely touching moment," Pinky said, appearing in the doorway, "but I thought you should know that Drue is in the garage and about to be murdered by Trevone. Or possibly the McGuyvers. I'm not sure which of them will snap first."

Jasmine and Benny looked at each other.

"Go," she said. "You're the only person who makes him tolerable."

As he darted out of the room, Ramona called out, "Send more fizzy drinks!"

Down in the garage, Benny found the four people Pinky mentioned all trying to talk over one another as they stood around a silver Space Runner like the one that had carried Benny to the Moon.

"Guys," he said as he approached, but none of them even noticed he'd entered. "HEY!"

They all stopped and turned to him.

"Benny," Drue said. "Perfect. You can talk some sense into these nerds."

"Talk sense into *us*?" Trevone asked. "You better rethink that statement."

Ash McGuyver rubbed her temples as she shook her head. Bo stood beside her, twisting a screwdriver against his palm.

"OK," Benny said. "*What* is going on here?"

"I've managed to amp up output on these lasers, but we need to test them," Trevone said. "The only problem is, the increased energy expenditure could make them *very* dangerous. Also, there's a slight possibility that they might, uh . . ."

"Explode," Ash said.

"Oh," Benny muttered.

"All right, just look at it this way," Drue said. "The McGuyvers need to be here to work on the Space Runners. Hot Dog needs to train everyone on the sims. She's . . ." He got really quiet. "She's the best pilot. And Trevone, well, he's a Pit Crew member and if he gets blown up, Elijah will never forgive us and will probably suck all the air out of the Taj while we're inside or something, so just let *me* take this thing out to the Sea of Tranquillity and see what kind of damage I can do." He paused for a few moments. "In the name of science! For the good of Earth!"

"I say you let him do it," Ash said, snapping a piece of gum. "Serves him right if he's blown to bits."

"Look, I can appreciate that you're willing to test this out," Trevone said to Drue, "but I'm not worried about the lasers blowing you up. I'm worried about *you* accidentally slashing through the Taj trying to show off. I'm working on a fail-safe that should keep the lasers from firing if there's another Space Runner or a friendly target, but it'll take me the rest of the day to complete and we need to test these beams before then."

"Oh," Drue said. "But I won't shoot anywhere near the resort! I'll be super careful!"

"Hold on," Benny said. He let out a long breath, trying to think of anything that might help. "The trigger for the laser. It's, what, a joystick thing like we had in the cart?"

"Not any more," Trevone said. "We've replaced it with a button that will slip onto a flight yoke so you don't have to take your hands off the wheel to fire."

"OK," Benny said. "So why not just put, like, a really long cord on it and try it out in a crater somewhere. If the laser doesn't explode, *then* let Drue test it out on a Space Runner." He paused. "Far, *far* away from the Taj."

"I can live with that," Drue said.

"I suppose it wouldn't take too much time to rig up some kind of wired detonator," Trevone said. "Are you two good to go while I'm gone?"

Ash smacked her brother on the stomach. "The only reason we're not working now is because you three are in our way."

Somewhere behind Benny, Pinky cleared her throat.

"Uh, Benny. If you've got a moment, Hot Dog has requested that you drop by the virtual gaming environment for a brief consultation."

"Why does everyone want to talk to me?" Benny murmured.

He made his way through the Taj. In the lobby, he passed several EW-SCABers carrying rucksacks and luggage. They all stared at him, a few muttering things that he couldn't make out. As he crossed the shiny black floor, a lift opened to his right.

"Everybody in," Ricardo said. "Going down."

Benny froze at the sound of his voice and turned to

see the leader of the Mustangs. Ricardo glared at him, fists curled up at his sides, but didn't say anything. Benny couldn't help but wonder what he and the rest of the Pit Crew must have thought of him, of everything he was trying to do. Having been up on the Moon for so long, there was no doubt they'd follow Elijah to the end of the universe. Even if Trevone was helping them with the Space Runners, he'd made no mention of following them into space.

He was glad Elijah had made a point of keeping the Pit Crew from interfering. Benny wasn't sure what he'd do if he had to take them on.

"Don't worry," Ricardo said to the EW-SCABers as the lift doors began to close. "You'll be safe down here. Elijah will make sure of that."

And then they were gone.

Benny hurried along to the empty, grey-padded room where Hot Dog was waiting for him. Only, when he walked through the door, there was nothing empty about it. Row after row of gleaming Space Runners lined the floor. At the end of the room, a stage had been set up. A banner hung above it that said *Hot Dog's No-Crash Crash Course in Flying*. Below it was a huge hologram portrait of Hot Dog, dressed in a sparkling space suit and staring off into the middle distance, saluting no one in particular as her hair blew back in a great mane behind her.

"*There* you are!" the real Hot Dog shouted as she made her way past the Space Runners. She stopped in front of Benny, smirking. "So, whaddaya think?"

"This is intense," Benny said.

"It's *dumb*, I know," she said. "But I decided if I'm about to try and save the world, I'm at least going to do it with some style. Plus, it was Pinky's idea, and she kind of ran with it before I could say no."

"Have a little fun," Pinky's voice said. Benny turned to see her reclining in the seat of a nearby Space Runner.

"We've been talking all morning. She's like my new best friend. Anyway, I've got a load of EW-SCABers coming in later to go over Space Runner controls. Can you help me out a bit first?"

"Yeah, of course. What do you want me to do?"

She pointed to one of the simulated Space Runners. "Have a seat on the passenger side. You're my first student. You may be good behind the wheel of a Chevelle or an ATV, but Space Runners are different beasts. Let's see you put some of those driving skills to work."

He climbed into one of the cars, but instead of getting

into the pilot's seat, Hot Dog ran to the stage, where a hot-pink Space Runner was sitting.

All the windows in Benny's car went black and were replaced by hyper-realistic views of outer space. Hot Dog suddenly appeared beside him, in the pilot's seat.

"OK," she said, staring in his direction but not actually at him, in a way that Benny found really unnerving. "So watch me handle all the controls, and then you're going to do it yourself." She grinned. "I'm not really here, obviously. I'm on stage. But this is how I'm going to teach a lot of people at once."

"This is so creepy," Benny said.

Hot Dog smiled. "I'm just going to assume you're telling me how brilliant I am, but hold that thought and watch me turn this baby on."

They worked for over an hour, until Benny felt comfortable enough with the basic Space Runner controls to navigate in space and Hot Dog felt like she had a good idea of how to teach others the kinds of flight tricks she knew. She assured him that she'd talked to several kids who were planning on joining their expedition, and most of them had far more experience on sims and – occasionally – actual Space Runners than he did.

It was beginning to feel like this plan could actually work.

"Pinky," Benny said when he and Hot Dog decided to break for lunch, "how's everyone else doing?"

"The lasers appear to be fully functional based on Drue's tests," the AI said. "He's just finished carving his initials into a patch of land near the Copernicus crater. I'm bringing his Space Runner back in from the cold as we speak. Based on the way he was giggling, I have the feeling he was about to start drawing things I'd rather not see cut into the Moon forever."

"I can't believe we're doing this," Hot Dog said, looking at the rows of simulated controls. "I can't believe I'm going to *teach* people how to fly."

"You're good at it." Benny stretched out his fingers that had become stiff as they gripped his flight yoke. "Look how much I just learned! You're the best person for this."

"No, I'm not," she said. "Elijah is. I wish he'd come down and help us."

"We can do this on our own," Benny said. "We *are* doing it."

"Still. I wonder what he's doing up there in his quarters?"

"He's watching everything," Pinky said, her voice low

and calm as she sat on the hood of a Space Runner, looking towards the ceiling. Towards Elijah. "I've got live video feeds running on his desk. I thought it would be best to let him observe. Maybe he'll learn something, too."

CHAPTER 26

They trained all day.

Groups rotated between Space Runner flight school with Hot Dog and laser-targeting practice with Trevone and the McGuyvers – and, for a while, Drue, until Trevone firmly insisted that the boy take a break "for his safety and the safety of others". In between, Jasmine introduced herself as the person who'd be calling out targets and went over basic survival skills like what to do if accidentally ejected from your vehicle or why it was important to take a systematic approach to destroying the asteroids instead of racing in and shooting randomly. Pinky kept everyone up to date on the advancement of the storm and herded the fledgling pilots to and from locations while ensuring that there was plenty to eat and, drink and monitoring all facets of the upcoming mission.

Fear filled the Taj, though few spoke of it. They didn't have to. Benny could see it in the eyes of everyone he passed. He tried his best to keep it off his own face. He kept busy, which wasn't hard to do. EW-SCABers were constantly cornering him with questions about Earth, the asteroids, the aliens and what Elijah was doing – all things he didn't have good answers to, really. And yet, everyone seemed to feel a little better after talking to him. He figured that maybe that was all they needed, to get the questions out of their minds so they could continue their training. If that was the case, he was happy to help.

And then, seemingly out of nowhere, it was well into the night, and despite all the challenges waiting for them the next day, the EW-SCABers remaining above ground at the Taj went to bed, having worked themselves into a state of exhaustion. Pinky urged everyone to rest as much as possible, spouting facts about the optimal hours of sleep with regards to maximum brain functionality and awareness. But Benny stayed up, sitting at the holodesk in the meeting room, staring at the approaching asteroid storm and thinking about everyone on Earth until finally, without even realising it, he passed out in one of the floating chairs.

He woke at around five the next morning, and after changing out of his now-very-smelly space suit, he headed down to the garage. The lights were on, but it didn't look like anyone was working. It was eerily calm. Serene, even. He could almost imagine that he'd just sneaked into a fancy showroom back on Earth, that all of this had been a bad dream.

He walked among the laser-mounted vehicles, letting his fingers brush against them. The McGuyvers had even painted racing stripes on each of the crafts in the colours of the different teams – or *squads* now, he guessed. He stopped in front of one with Mustang-red markings. In his hand, he held his father's hood ornament. He wondered if it had ever been as shiny as these cars, one day long ago when it was brand-new.

"Dang, kid," someone said behind him. "Is that what I think it is?"

He turned to see Ash McGuyver, who snapped a piece of gum as she eyed the shiny metal in his hands.

"It's a hood ornament," he said.

"Not just any hood ornament." She snatched it from him and held it up to her mouth, breathing on it. Then she polished the metal on the front of her coveralls. "This is from a 2025 Rolls LE. Did you steal this from Elijah or something?"

Benny started to protest, but Ash laughed.

"Kidding. If this were Elijah's, he'd have had me bolt it onto a Space Runner pronto. So where'd it come from?"

"My dad."

"Your dad has impeccable taste in cars."

"He did, yeah," Benny said. "He collected hood ornaments sometimes. This came from some wreck we found out in the Drylands. I think he almost cried having to pry it off, but the rest of the car had already been picked clean by scavengers, so it was basically scrap."

Ash whistled, shaking her head. "You want to put this on the front of your car? For luck?"

Benny grinned. "I really do."

She called over her shoulder. "Yo, bro, bring me that batch of epoxy Trevone made."

Bo stomped over, grunting as he held out a tub of some clear, gel-like liquid. In seconds, Ash had fixed the ornament to the front of one of the Space Runners with a cherry-red stripe on its hood.

"Whaddaya think?" she asked.

"Looks good," Bo replied before Benny could respond.

He stared at the man as he turned and walked away – he hadn't even known Bo *could* speak. Ash clicked her tongue and pointed at her brother with her thumb.

"That's the best seal of approval you'll ever get, right there."

Pinky must have woken the rest of the EW-SCABers, because soon after Benny's hood ornament was in place, everyone started to filter into the garage. Some glanced around at each other, making nervous small talk. Others just stared at the cement floor. It occurred to Benny that he didn't even know most of these kids' names, much less anything about them or why they'd chosen to try to save their home planet instead of hiding underground with Elijah. He wished he'd had more time with them – to have got to know them like he'd got to know the members of his caravan back at home, slowly but individually, until at some point no one could pin down, they'd become family.

Hot Dog and Drue claimed Space Runners on either side of Benny's. Drue eyed the hood ornament and immediately looked taken aback.

"Dude, we could have *customised* these?" he asked. "Why didn't anyone tell me?"

Hot Dog rolled her eyes as Drue went off to find the McGuyvers. She turned to Benny.

"You ready for this?"

"No," he said. "But I don't have much of a choice."

"That's not true. We can always call the whole thing off and head underground."

He looked at her with his eyebrows scrunched together, worried she'd given up.

"Relax, Love," she said. "I'm just messing with you."

Someone called out to her, asking about shifting gears, and in a flash she was off helping them.

"We need to get started," Jasmine said, coming up to Benny's side. "A couple of volunteers are more comfortable staying back here and helping me, so that makes forty pilots total. Pinky will automate your flight until you're in range of the storm, then she'll release the controls to you." She pointed to three oversized Space Runners in the corner that looked more like small RVs than sports cars. "The McGuyvers will follow in these. If anyone's hyperdrive gets damaged or someone needs emergency assistance, they can tow you back to the Taj."

"And the third one?" Benny asked.

"That's for Ramona. She'll be parked halfway between the storm and the Taj as a makeshift satellite. It should be enough to keep Pinky functioning – at least to keep our communications up. We'll be in constant contact. Assuming we stop the storm, we can try to get that SR close to Earth without it being shot down so we can re-establish communications and let everyone know what's happening. Then we can prepare for our next move . . . whatever that is."

"Awesome. Thanks, Jasmine."

It suddenly seemed very quiet. That's when he realised that everyone in the garage was looking at the two of them.

"What's going on?" Benny asked.

"You should say something," Jasmine suggested.

"Why?"

"Because you're the person who got half of them to join us in the first place with whatever speech you gave."

"Drue was there, too," Benny said.

She gave him a sceptical look.

"Just a few words," she said. "It'll be good for morale."

Benny took a few steps forward, raising one hand in the air, the engine in his chest revving.

"Uh, hey, everyone . . ." he started. "Um . . . I come from a caravan. Some of you might think that we're just gangs roaming the Drylands, but that's not how it is. We look out for each other. We *help* each other. That's how we survive." He shrugged a little. "I guess what I'm trying to say is that we're kind of a caravan now. So let's stick together and blow these rocks up and save all the people we care about back home. Remember, we're doing this to keep them safe. And once we get back, we'll have Pinky feed us so much ice cream and pizza we won't be able to move. Sound good?"

A wave of whoops and shouts rushed over him, causing goosebumps to prickle all over his body.

"Cool," he said. "Uh, Pinky? Wanna take it from here?"

"Sure thing," the AI said. She appeared beside him, her voice booming through the garage. "Everyone, choose a Space Runner and buckle in. Our mission begins in T minus five minutes."

As Benny walked back to his car, Trevone caught up with him.

"Not bad," the Crew member said. "Sounded like it came from the heart. I can see how you got so many of them on your side."

"Thanks," Benny said. "I think." A moment of silence passed between them. "You can come with us, you know. Help us stop this."

Trevone looked over at his blue Space Runner off in the corner. For a second, Benny was sure he was about to climb inside and lead them out of the Grand Dome. But then he turned back, and something about his expression told Benny that wasn't going to be the case.

"My place is here," he said. "With the rest of the Pit Crew. With Elijah. You don't know him like we do. I understand how this must seem to you, but . . ." He shook his head. "Look, when I came up to the Moon for the first time, I was nothing. I was a squatter in a crappy building in the Bronx with my dad and a load of his loser friends. The only reason I was so good in school is because I spent as much time there as I could. Elijah changed everything. He saw something in me. He *saved* me. I can't just turn my back on him. I'm sorry. I wish you guys luck. If it's any consolation, I'm rooting for you."

And then he headed off towards the exit.

Benny started back to his Space Runner. Drue, Hot Dog, Ramona and Jasmine had gathered around the front of it.

"Let's make a promise," Hot Dog said. "You guys came and found me when my car crashed. We broke a load of rules together and kind of started this whole thing. And somehow we're all still here. Let's keep it that way. No Mustang left behind."

Jasmine nodded. "No *friends* left behind."

"We save the Earth," Benny said.

"Let's blow up some asteroids!" Drue grinned.

"Roger, roger," Ramona added.

Benny nodded. "All right, Moon Platoon. Let's do this!"

When they were all tucked inside their Space Runners, one wall of the garage slid away, opening up to the Grand Dome – it was easier for all the cars to get out through the wide pressurization tunnel there instead of driving through the auxiliary garage entrance one by one. As his car raced through the courtyard, Benny looked up at the roof of the Taj, where the sheets of gold bloomed around Elijah's private quarters. He was standing there in the window, watching everything going on below. Here was the guy who'd got them into all this, who hadn't warned the Earth about the impending attack – who was ready to let humanity die. Just watching them all leave.

Anger burned in Benny's veins. And yet, at the same time, he couldn't help but think how alone Elijah looked standing in that high window all by himself.

Then his hyperdrive engaged, and he was shooting through the tunnel. In a matter of minutes, the Taj was becoming a smaller and smaller glimmer in the background. Benny turned to face the front, staring at the darkness of space ahead, hoping with everything in his being that the next time he saw Elijah, he'd be able to look him in the eye and tell him that he'd been wrong. That there had been another way – a *better* way – after all.

CHAPTER 27

It would take almost half an hour for the Space Runner fleet to reach the asteroid storm, and after running around the Taj trying to get everyone organised and trained for this mission, Benny kind of appreciated the quietness of space. A couple of times Drue tuned in to his and Hot Dog's comm systems, making some joke or comment, but none of them seemed eager to talk.

There was too much at stake, too much weighing on their minds.

Instead of talking, Benny kept looking at Earth shining in the distance. He could just make out the brown swatch of land covering so much of the western United States, the Drylands, his home. His stomach was in knots, and he clasped his hands in his lap in order to keep them from shaking.

He realised it had only been a week since he'd been in a Space Runner for the first time, filled with a similar kind of jittery nervousness as he wondered what the Taj would be like. Now, that excitement seemed almost laughable, like something only a naive child would feel.

He pulled his HoloTek out of his space suit pocket and extended it, tapping on the video his grandmother and brothers had filmed the day before he left. As he shot through space, that was what he watched, along with other home vids he had saved, reminding himself that he didn't have the luxury of being nervous. He had more important things to focus on.

Finally, the asteroid storm came into view. Benny had seen the field as a small-scale hologram, but that had done nothing to prepare him for the awe-inspiring massiveness of the formation itself. Huge boulders of the sickly-yellow minerals gravitated around what looked to Benny like a small *planet*, four times the size of the Taj, at least. The rocky field stretched well beyond the approaching Space Runner fleet, hundreds of metres in each direction.

"Holy whoa," Benny murmured.

They continued their approach, Benny having to remind himself to blink as they got closer. He put his HoloTek away and gripped the flight yoke. Eventually the fleet came to a stop in several uniform rows well away from the approaching field.

"What's our next move, Jasmine?" Benny asked, opening up a private line with her.

"We're still unsure how the asteroids will react to our new lasers, considering the fact that the rocks *exploded* against the dome," she said. "We've been running tests back here, but the sample sizes are so small."

"What do you think we should do?"

"Have one pilot do a test shot. I reckon Hot Dog or Drue would jump at the chance to—"

"No," Benny said. "Let me. If I'm really the reason some of these pilots are up here, then I should be the one blown up if something goes wrong. Just make sure Pinky keeps the rest of the Space Runners at bay for now."

"OK," Jasmine said. "Pinky?"

"Relinquishing control now." The AI's voice crackled through his Space Runner.

The flight yoke in his hands suddenly had more give to it, and he pushed it forward, slowly breaking away from the group.

"I'm sending you a viable small target on the edge of the storm," Jasmine said. "I'm also blocking the rest of your comms for the moment. I figure it'll be easier to focus without Hot Dog and Drue complaining that they should be the ones getting the first shot based on their flying skills."

A hologram popped up above Benny's windshield – a target, zeroing in on a large hunk of yellow rock off to his left side.

"Thanks, Jazz," Benny said. "Wish me luck."

He flew to his target, keeping sufficient distance to remain far enough away if anything *too* bad happened as a result of shooting a newly overcharged laser beam into a rock made up of a load of unknown alien elements.

The hologram blinked on his windshield, signalling that now was the time to fire.

"Here goes nothing," Benny muttered as he mashed the red button on one side of his flight yoke.

Two lasers shot from the front of his Space Runner, meeting together to form one red beam of light as thick as Benny's arm. It blasted forward, piercing the centre of the targeted asteroid. The entire boulder exploded, erupting in a flash of orange and blue flame that was almost instantly consumed and stamped out by the vacuum of space. Bits of debris and rock floated away, but the asteroid was gone. The laser had done its job.

Benny breathed a sharp sigh of relief. And then, alone in his Space Runner, he shouted at the top of his lungs.

Jasmine's voice was on the comms again, calm but firm as she dished out assignments.

"That's a go! Mustangs, Pinky is supplying you with targets now. Vipers, loop around to the rear of the storm and start from there. The rest of you hold back until we get a look at the debris patterns. Remember to keep an eye out for your teammates."

Benny looked to his right flank and saw almost twenty Space Runners all breaking away from the fleet and beginning to fire on the asteroid field. Within seconds the boulders were exploding left and right as the newly formed Moon Platoon flew by. The novice pilots stayed on the outskirts of the storm, but the more daring among them dived through the field, looping around bits of debris and shattered minerals.

"Woo-hoo!" Drue shouted as he took out another asteroid, Benny's comms active again. "I know this is weird to say, but I think this might be the best holiday of my life."

Benny kept flying, too, going after each target that appeared on his windshield before Jasmine finally called the Mustangs and Vipers out, remapped the storm to take large pieces of debris into account and sent the Chargers and Firebirds in.

Benny parked his Space Runner near another group of Mustangs and tuned into the comms.

"This is crazy," he said. "I can't believe it's working."

"I took out a dozen of those things," Hot Dog said. "And did you see Iyabo? That girl has crazy good aim."

"Crap!" Drue exclaimed. "Jazz, are you counting our targets? I haven't been keeping score!"

"This isn't a *game*," Jasmine replied. "But Pinky's keeping track. You can compare notes when you get back. This wave of attacks will take out the rest of the smaller asteroids, meaning now we can focus on that monster in the centre. I'm going to have the Vipers clean up any remaining small targets while the Mustangs start in on it."

"Right on," Benny said. All the nervousness from earlier was actually starting to fade away, thanks to the combined adrenaline of not only being in space firing lasers at alien rocks, but also the fact that all their prep, all their hard work was paying off.

"Mustangs," Jasmine said, "I'm marking your targets. Let's take this final boss down and get you back to the Taj."

Benny raced forward – he was actually beginning to get pretty used to the Space Runner controls – as a new target popped up on his windshield. It looked as though Jasmine and Pinky had them all attacking different areas of the looming asteroid in the centre of the storm in an effort to chip it down to something more manageable. Benny took the left flank, lining up his Space Runner and firing his laser. Despite the direct hit, it looked like barely any damage had been done.

"Not good," he murmured. "Let's try again."

Hot Dog must have noticed the same thing.

"Hey," she said over the comms, "I don't guess you've scoped out a secret weak spot, have you, Jasmine?"

Benny narrowed his eyes as he fired several more times, staring at the floating orb of rock, scouring its surface, trying to find a hole, a crack – anything that might prove to be a flaw in the asteroid they could exploit.

That's when he saw it. Near the top of the massive boulder, something was moving. The asteroid's *surface* was shifting. It looked like part of it was sliding away, revealing a dark tunnel.

"Um, is anyone else seeing this?" Benny asked.

"What's going on?" Jasmine asked. "The feed from your dash cams isn't clear enough."

"It looks like an opening, up top on my side!"

"I see it," Hot Dog yelled. "I'm going to take a shot! Don't bother with targeting. I've got this."

Benny watched her Space Runner circle around, until

she was hovering near the front of the new tunnel. He crossed his fingers, murmuring "Come on, come on," to himself, hoping that one well-placed shot might start some sort of chain reaction inside that could cause the whole thing to explode.

But Hot Dog didn't shoot.

"Wait, guys," she said, her voice wavering. "Something's not right here. There are *lights* inside this thing. I see movement. It looks like . . . Oh, no . . ."

"What?" Benny asked.

"I-I," she stammered. "I don't think this is an asteroid."

Suddenly her vehicle shot up, just in time to avoid dozens upon dozens of triangular, quartz-like shards shooting out of the tunnel, each hardly bigger than a Space Runner. They were mostly coloured like the green stalactites from the alien workshop, glowing faintly. A few were darker, purple, blending into the background and making them harder to see. At first Benny thought there were flames coming out of the backs of each one, but then he realised the shards were just capped with some sort of shiny golden metal.

"And I don't think those are just rocks!" Hot Dog shouted.

The strange shards broke into several groups, the darker

ones leading as they moved together through space in intricate formations, a crystalline swarm.

"So that means they're . . ." Benny started.

"Ships!" Drue shouted. "Holy crap, aliens!"

That's when the shards started firing. Streams of crackling blue energy shot out of the metal prongs on the backs of the ships.

"Retreat!" Benny shouted. He panicked. Suddenly they were fighting *actual* aliens. Part of him couldn't even believe it was happening. "Everybody get out of here! We're not prepared for this!"

"Abort mission!" Jasmine shouted. "I'm having Pinky take over as many ships as she can, but there's interference."

Static replaced her voice on the comms.

Benny took the yoke, gunning the hyperdrive and flying past a group of purple ships. He'd have to get out of here himself – if that was possible. He dipped and dived, firing off his laser a few times when there weren't any other Space Runners in sight but never actually hitting any of the aliens.

All around him, his fellow EW-SCABers were trying to escape. He watched in horror as one of the Vipers' crafts was hit with the alien's energy. Its antigravity shield held, but the Space Runner was sent spiralling away from what was now a battlefield.

Every ounce of hope he'd built up as they destroyed the smaller asteroids was starting to evaporate.

Benny was just about to get clear of the battlefield and turn around to see if he could help anyone when one of the alien ships hit him with a blast of energy. His Space Runner spun, finally slamming into the side of the giant asteroid.

"Not good, not good," he whispered as he tried to get his bearings. His Space Runner had twisted around, facing open space, where his teammates were still frantically trying to escape.

He pushed on the flight yoke, but nothing happened. Red lights were flashing all over the dashboard – lights he didn't recognise.

The alien ship that had attacked him came back around, until Benny was staring right at it through his windshield. Inside the ship, Benny could barely make out the silhouette of a head. And two horns.

"I've stalled!" he shouted into his comm. "I think I'm about to get shot down."

"Not so fast!" Drue shouted. "My laser's damaged, but I've got an idea."

Before the alien craft could fire at Benny, Drue gunned his Space Runner forward and slammed into the side of it with incredible force. Both of the ships spun out of control, rolling in opposite directions away from the giant asteroid.

"Drue!" Benny yelled.

"I'm OK!" Drue said. "I think. I . . . I might vom."

Jasmine's voice crackled through the comms. "Hello? Drue, your navigations systems are fried. Hang on out there. I'm sending Bo in to get Benny, and then Ash'll pick you up once she's dropped her last haul off in a safe spot."

"No," Benny said. "It's too dangerous in here. Get Drue. I'll figure something else out."

"Don't worry, Benny," Hot Dog crackled into the comm. "I've got you."

Hot Dog's Space Runner was suddenly right in front of Benny's, their front bumpers almost touching.

"What are you . . . ?" Benny asked.

"I'm just gonna give you a little tap to push you away from this mess."

She pressed forward, picking up speed, her Space Runner pushing his back, away from the giant rock. He could see the other Space Runners in the distance, already jetting towards the Taj.

"Jasmine, what's the status?" he asked.

"Um," Jasmine said. "I think we've got everyone out. They don't *appear* to be following us."

"What do we do?" Benny asked, speaking more to himself than to anyone else. "Is this thing still going to crash into Earth? What *is* it, even?"

Before anyone could answer, his and Hot Dog's Space Runners both came to a sudden halt.

"Benny, did you hit an emergency brake I don't know about?" Hot Dog asked.

"I thought *you* stopped!" Benny said.

Across their hoods, he could see her frantically tapping on her dashboard and pulling on the flight yoke.

"It's not me!" she said.

"Pinky?" Benny asked. "What's happening?"

The AI's voice flooded his cabin, but crackling static made her nearly indecipherable. "I'm det . . . new energy sig . . . around . . . Runners . . . appears to . . . magnetic prop . . . interfering—"

And then the line went dead, just as their Space Runners began to move again, heading sideways – straight for the giant asteriod.

"Oh crap," Benny muttered. He turned to Hot Dog. "It's a tractor beam!"

He wasn't sure if she could hear him or not since his communications systems seemed to be on the blink, but he had no doubt she understood what was happening.

Her eyes went wide as she began to shake her head.

Benny pulled on his flight yoke again, but it was no use. An opening was forming in the side of the asteroid, and they were being sucked right into it.

CHAPTER 28

As they were pulled into the giant alien rock, Benny saw that the inside was familiar. It looked similar to the base they'd found on the Moon – the floor and walls made up of smooth greenish stone while the ceilings dripped with glowing stalactite lights.

The asteroid closed up behind them as they floated through, sealing them inside.

Their Space Runners came to a stop at the far end of an empty cavern. Benny and Hot Dog stared at each other, neither one knowing what to do. There didn't seem to be any movement, any sign of life around them. Benny looked around frantically, trying to come up with some sort of plan, cylinders firing in his mind. Outside, the rest of the Space Runner fleet was retreating. Would they try to rescue him? *Should* they?

How could they when they'd been so unprepared for

the aliens, much less this giant asteroid – the *mother ship* – that was still careening towards Earth?

He knew one thing for certain: he wasn't going to stay buckled into his broken-down car waiting for something to happen.

As he opened the door of his Space Runner, he was surprised to note that his emergency helmet didn't appear. The inside of the giant asteroid actually had a breathable environment.

"Are you *nuts*?" Hot Dog asked as she stepped out of her vehicle. "Get in my car. Even if it can't move, we can at least hide out and try to blast anyone who comes in."

"By shooting through my Space Runner?" he asked. "We'd probably blow ourselves up. Besides . . ." He glanced around. "If this is the end, I'm not hiding in a car. I'm going down fighting."

Hot Dog stared at him, biting her lip, eyes full of worry.

The smooth rock wall beside them opened up. Not with a panel sliding away or a door appearing – the stone itself simply parted like curtains, leaving a diamond-shaped opening to a brightly lit corridor.

Two beings stepped through the new doorway.

Benny's breath caught in his throat as he looked at

them. They were both twice as tall as he was, thin and lanky. Their arms and legs were too long to be human, their skin an incredibly smooth icy blue that seemed to reflect a prism of other hues under the lights. One of them held up a delicate hand composed of four slender, jointless fingers. Its palm was encased in some kind of gold device that glowed.

Red rock masks seemed to have grown from the top halves of their faces, a faint light pulsing behind them. The creatures' mouths were too wide, stretching back where ears would've been on a human. But strangest of all were the tops of their heads. The shorter one – the one with a hand still raised – had two gleaming black ram horns curled up on either side of its face. The other one had something entirely different growing from the back of its head, a thick, glossy braid, flicking halfway down its back.

Aliens.

"No way," Benny said, realising he'd been holding his breath.

"I'm not going to faint," Hot Dog said. "But I kind of wish I was."

The closest one lowered its hand and turned to the other. When its lips parted, a noise like someone had squashed an accordion came out. The pitch changed a few times, dotted with smacks and clicks.

Benny took a few steps towards Hot Dog's Space Runner, reaching for the door. Maybe there was something inside he could use for a weapon.

In an instant the taller alien crossed the ten metres separating them. It stood between Hot Dog and Benny with its arms crossed. The thick braid down its back had unwound, and Benny's eyes widened as he realised what he was seeing. It hadn't been hair after all, but a rope made of prehensile tentacles. He could tell there were four of them now that the braid was undone, each tipped with razor-sharp pieces of metal held up to Benny and Hot Dog's faces.

"Oh my God," Hot Dog whispered. "We're facing space Medusas. I'm going to be killed by a bad hairstyle."

Benny looked over at the other one, who still stood in the doorway. The two tentacles he'd mistaken for horns unrolled around its head, then curled back up again. It barked some sort of wheezing harmonica sound, and the alien in front of Benny nodded its head towards the doorway, pointing one of the blades in the same direction.

"I think we're supposed to go that way," Benny said.

"Sure." Hot Dog said.

And so they marched.

Once they were all through the doorway, the short alien raised its hand again. The gold device on its palm pulsed with light, and the rock wall came together once more.

"So if we want to get out that way—" Benny started.

Suddenly there was another blade-tipped tentacle in front of him. He stopped talking, but Hot Dog nodded. The shorter alien walked ahead of them, a fluid movement to its long appendages. The being wore a flowing tunic that looked at first like chainmail to Benny, but the dark, shiny links were all moving, slithering, like the strange patterns they'd seen in the lights at the Moon base – the hems unravelling into wisps before weaving back together again.

They were led through a series of hallways, all of which appeared to have been created out of rock, only most of the inner structure was translucent, allowing them to see shadows in other rooms as they passed. Benny could make out the silhouettes of other creatures who seemed to be watching them from the other sides of the walls. Some appeared to have elaborate, writhing mounds on their heads. Others had two or three long tentacles whipping back and forth.

Some of them weren't shaped like humans at all.

Benny kept an eye out for anything in the hallways he might be able to use, but there was nothing except smooth stone and overhead lights too high up to reach. He glanced at Hot Dog, whose jaw was clenched so tightly he thought she might break her own teeth.

Finally, they came to a new, cavernous room, the walls a deep, gleaming purple. Streams of greenish-yellow light floated overhead, just as they had in the Moon base. A giant hologram of the mother ship's exterior filled the centre of the room – made up, Benny guessed, of the same advanced light technology they'd seen when Druc accidentally turned on the star maps a few days before.

The two aliens stopped at the entrance but pointed forward. Benny and Hot Dog continued on. There were several other aliens lingering around terminals moulded into the walls, though they were dressed differently, in metallic red robes. Some had head tentacles that were tapping on screens, while others had theirs woven together in elaborate bejewelled headdresses.

On a clear quartz throne across the room was an alien whose muscled arms were dotted with patches of polished red plates, the front of its tunic covered by a sturdy, gemlike breastplate. Countless black tentacles formed two giant horns on either side of its head, each one curving towards the other in the air, almost touching several metres above the alien's head. The mask hiding the top of its face was gold, shining. The alien was bigger, thicker than the rest, and when it saw Benny approaching, it stood, walking down into the hologram below. Metres of slithering fabric, attached to its shoulders, dragged across the ground behind it.

"This is all just a nightmare." Hot Dog whispered. "I never woke up from that Space Runner crash, did I? This is some kind of terrible coma dream."

"English," the thick being said. Its voice was stranger than anything Benny had ever heard, like three people were talking at once, ranging from a deep bass to a chirping soprano. There was a dissonance about it, like someone speaking in a minor chord. "Of course. One of the common languages. Welcome."

Hot Dog and Benny looked at the alien in front of them, dumbfounded.

"Do not be surprised," it continued. "We have watched your world so long that we understand some languages that have been dead on your planet for many cycles. Your mouths physically can't speak our language, but you will call me Tull of the Alpha Maraudi. I am commander here. You have names?"

"Benny."

"Hot Dog." She shook her head. "Uh, Grace."

"Benny. Hot Dog Uh-Grace. Your people have waged an unexpected resistance. But now you have retreated. Wise. I acknowledge your attempt at stopping us, and respect the impulse you have to fight for your people."

"You monsters," Benny said. "Elijah told us what you've planned for our planet. You think you can just take any world you see and turn it into, what, some kind of holiday spot for your people? There are billions of lives on Earth. My family is there. *Millions* of families are there. And you think it's OK to just take it over because you want other worlds to play with?"

"Is *that* why you think we have come?" Something like an electric crackle escaped the being's mouth, but Benny couldn't tell if it was laughter or something else. "That we're some kind of warmongering people who've come to your planet for entertainment?"

"Why else would you attack us?" Hot Dog said. "You're *evil*."

The commander turned to look at the holographic projections. A long tentacle unwound from its horn and tapped on one of the lights. The entire hologram shifted, until the three-sunned star system Benny and the others had seen at the base on the Moon was floating in front of them. Only this time, something was different. The middle of the three stars was larger, pulsing.

"Our solar system is on the brink of collapse. We've known this for some time. We've tried to figure out ways to save it. But despite our best efforts, there are forces here we have not been able to tame. We must evacuate."

"Then take some other planet," Benny asked. "Head for Orion's Belt. You get three stars again that way!"

"Would that it were so simple. Your atmosphere and your sun are the closest twins we can find to our home. We have searched far and wide, but there are many variables you cannot begin to comprehend. My people possess the power to transform planets on a surface level, but not to move them or completely change environmental conditions. Yours is the only planet we can inhabit. There is no other way."

"There's always another way," Benny said, stepping forward. There was a whipping sound beside him, and suddenly a blade-tipped tentacle was hovering in front of his throat – the alien from earlier was at his side.

Tull raised a hand. The weapon fell away.

"Realise that we could have taken Earth centuries ago, but did not. We waited, weighing the importance of our survival against yours. Looking for other options. There is no personal hatred towards humanity. Make no mistake of that."

"Really?" Hot Dog asked. "Because you've got dudes with knife hair who seem pretty hateful to me."

"Just because we do not make war does not mean that we do not breed warriors," Tull said. "We have always made sure there are those among us who could serve as protectors should the need arise. Surely you are not foolish enough to think that we are the only two forms of life in this universe. The warmongers you mistake us for do exist out there among the stars. They are one of the variables I spoke of earlier."

Hot Dog's mouth dropped open.

"How can you pretend what you're doing is OK when you're going to kill so many people?" Benny asked. "Just blink us out of existence."

"Do not dare to lecture us on the value of life, young human," Tull said, its voices growing louder. "How many species have gone extinct as your kind took over the planet? How many of your own have you let suffer and die?" The commander's horns began to move, until they were flattened out horizontally, curling up only at the ends like a longhorn bull's. "The Alpha Maraudi have not warred among ourselves in millennia. Tell me, can your people say the same?"

Tull reached up, removing the gold mask and revealing two diamond-shaped eyes on the sides of its head. Each one held two piercing red irises and shining white pupils. Above them, in the centre of the alien's forehead, a third eye glowed a solid, brilliant blue.

"We have seen what you humans do," Tull said. "Our judgement is final."

"Can't we live together on Earth?" Benny continued, his voice cracking as he stared at the aliens eyes.

"Impossible. Your planet is already threatened by over-population."

"Then at least let us evacuate. We can . . . we can put people at the Taj and on space stations. Help us do that with your tech."

"To what end?" the commander asked. "So that you could try to destroy us one day as soon as you had the capability? Use your science of destruction and death to wipe us out completely? We are a peaceful kind, not like you. We seek a safe, stable home. Perhaps you are too young a species to understand that."

"No," Benny said slowly. "I get it."

"Do you?"

"Yeah." Somewhere inside, he really did understand what they wanted. He even respected it.

"You're a caravan," Benny said.

"A what?" Tull's flat horns curled up more.

"You're travellers looking for a new home," Benny said. "I come from a group like that. But we're different. We don't just look out for each other, we look out for anyone we come across. We don't steal or hurt people to make ourselves better. We . . ." He struggled for words. "We *care*. We're *good*. Do you understand what that means?"

Commander Tull stared at him for a moment before continuing. "The Alpha Maraudi have existed since before your planet held life. We have not survived that long without prioritising self-preservation and reason."

Benny's heart sank. If this was true, he had nothing to use against Tull or the Alpha Maraudi, nothing he could say to change their minds.

He felt powerless, so out of his element. If he'd been back on Earth in the caravan, at least he'd have had things he was familiar with. Family. RVs and cars he'd helped rebuild himself. Holographic spiders . . .

Suddenly, he realised he wasn't as unarmed as he'd thought.

"So what about me and Benny?" Hot Dog asked. "Did you bring us on board to kill us yourself?"

"Of course not," Tull said. "We are curious. We are a people who strive for knowledge and understanding. You will make fine specimens to teach our younger kind how intelligent life can fail. Consider it an honour to be the last of your species. We will treat you well. You have my word."

"I'm not gonna be some alien pet!" Hot Dog shouted.

"You may think you know all about us," Benny said, tapping on his wrist. "But I bet we can still surprise you."

A giant spider appeared before him. Tentacles flashed in his peripheral vision.

And then, before Benny could make his next move, everyone was on the floor as the entire asteroid ship shook violently.

CHAPTER 29

The ship jolted again. Alarms blared all around them as Benny got to his feet, muttering a thanks to whatever unexpected luck had come their way. He ran his finger across his bracelet and the giant holographic spider he'd conjured reared back onto its hind legs above the alien with the bladed tentacles, who cried out in shock.

Tull barked some sort of command, and several of the others called back to it. The holograms filling the room shifted to their original view of the exterior, and Benny saw smoke rising from a missing chunk of the asteroid ship.

Hot Dog was already standing, taking a fighting stance as she looked around the room.

"Come on!" Benny shouted. "Let's go!"

He made for the door, where the shorter of the aliens who'd greeted them stood, the two tendrils around its head unfurling and whipping the air. Benny didn't hesitate or slow down. He ploughed straight into the alien's gut, sending them both tumbling backward into the hallway.

They wrestled on the ground for a moment before one of the tentacles wrapped around Benny's neck, raising him into the air. He gagged and fought for breath as the alien got to one knee. Its mask had fallen off in the skirmish, and the being glared at Benny with three narrowed eyes.

"Useless life-forms," it hissed in English.

"You sure about that?" Hot Dog asked as she touched her collar, powering up the emergency force field around her head.

The alien turned to her, and had just enough time to make a gasping noise before Hot Dog smashed the front of her space helmet into the creature's face. It dropped to the ground hard, crying out. Benny fell beside it. Hot Dog grabbed his hand, dragging him to his feet and pulling him down the hallway.

"Nice moves," Benny said through a fit of coughing as he tried to get his breath back.

"You, too."

"I've got two brothers. I've spent a lot of time wrestling." She wiped a smear of blue off her force-field helmet before powering it down. "Ew. I think I got alien spit on me."

They raced through the hallways, trying to remember where they'd come from. All around them sirens continued to blare as the lights above them turned purple. The ship shook every few seconds. Benny tapped his wrist, recalling the nanoprojectors. The aliens had definitely figured out the spider was just a hologram by now.

With any luck, whatever was going on outside would distract the Alpha Maraudi long enough for them to escape.

Finally, they came to a dead end – the wall that stood between them and their Space Runners. Hot Dog looked around.

"There's got to be an ET hammer or something somewhere," she said.

But Benny just grinned and held up the golden glove he'd swiped off the alien while they were wrestling.

"You sneaky genius," Hot Dog said as he slipped the device over his palm.

Without knowing what else to do, he smashed his hand against the wall in front of them. The rock didn't part like before, but exploded, blasting out into the next room and leaving enough space for them to slip through.

"Go, go!" Benny shouted, pushing Hot Dog forward.

They bounded to her Space Runner. Hot Dog slid into the pilot's seat, immediately pressing buttons.

"It's working!" she shouted. Her car lifted a foot off the ground and turned, lining the passenger side door up with Benny. "The tractor beam's off!"

Benny saw a metallic glint out of the corner of his eye. "One sec!" he said.

He stood in front of his own broken-down Space Runner and wrapped both hands around the hood ornament, trying to pry it off. This was the only thing he had from home – from his father – up in space. His lucky charm. His dad had loved it, and now it was his to keep safe.

But it was no use. It was stuck too tightly. He put both feet on the bumper, straining to wrench it loose.

"*Benny*!" Hot Dog shouted.

He took one last look at the silver ornament, whispering a silent goodbye. Then he jumped into the passenger's seat and closed the door as Hot Dog raised the Space Runner further into the air.

Ahead of them was solid rock wall, no hole to the outside.

"Think this glove thing will open it up?" Benny asked.

"Lemme try something else, first," she said, smashing her finger down on the red button on the flight yoke and firing her laser. It took a few shots, but eventually a hole appeared, depressurising the room.

She kept shooting as they jetted forward, until there was

just enough of an opening broken in the hull for their Space Runner to fit through.

As they shot into open space, both of them yelled, voices charged with unabashed joy and astonishment.

"I can't believe it," Benny said. "We're out."

"Hot Dog?" Jasmine's voice came through the comms. "Are you there? Ramona, you're sure you got communications restored to everyone?"

"We're here!" Hot Dog shouted. "Benny and I both. We just escaped from this giant alien ship."

"What the heck is going on?" Benny shouted.

"You looked like you needed a little help," a voice crackled through the interior speakers.

"Elijah?!" Benny shouted.

The Pit Crew's Space Runners shot past them, lasers taking out half a dozen alien ships that continued to swarm through the air. The Miyamura twins zigged and zagged among the enemy vessels so fast they were nothing but a blur, causing several of the ships to crash into each other.

"No way," Benny whispered.

Above them, a dark-coloured Space Runner ploughed into the side of the mother ship. On impact, it exploded in a huge, fiery blast, taking a chunk of the alien craft out with it.

"I was thinking about the impossibility of what you were doing, and the things I've done in my life," Elijah continued over the comms. "Back when I was first designing hyper-drives, I had a number of them overheat and explode on me. Obviously I fixed that, but then it occurred to me: stripping away all the safety components from under the hood could turn my little hot rods into pretty powerful unmanned missiles."

Another car exploded against the alien ship.

"Oof," he said. "Granted, they're likely the most expensive bombs ever created. What a shame."

"Hot Dog, get out of there!" Jasmine shouted. "Elijah and the Pit Crew will cover you."

Hot Dog obliged, gunning her hyperdrive and shooting forward, past ships scrambling to take down any of the Space Runners they could find. But the Pit Crew was proving to be much more adept at flying than the EW-SCABers had been, and they were turning out to be a real problem for the Alpha Maraudi.

"That's the last of the unmanned SRs," Trevone said as another explosion rocked the ship. "But this thing is still moving forward! We haven't stopped it."

"I can send out more units," Pinky suggested. "I'll just need to reconfigure them."

"There's no time," Elijah said. "The debris field from something this size will be just as dangerous as the original storm if it gets any closer to Earth."

"We could send out the laser fleet again," Benny said. "Maybe—"

Their Space Runner lurched to a halt.

"No, no, no, not again!" Hot Dog said.

"What's wrong?" Jasmine asked. "Why are you stopping?"

"We're stuck in that stupid tractor beam!"

Hot Dog yanked on the controls. But it was no use. The beam pulled them straight back towards the asteroid ship.

Benny turned to Hot Dog. She was shaking her head, looking at him with worried eyes.

"OK," he said. "It's OK. When we get inside we'll, uh . . . Let's just get out and run. We can find a place to hide. I've got this glove thing so maybe we can—"

"Benny, look out!" Hot Dog interrupted him, her eyes glued to something over his shoulder.

"Brace for impact!" Elijah yelled over the comms.

Benny turned just in time to see Elijah pivot so that the side of his car – the same one he'd driven into the Grand Dome on the first day – was parallel to theirs. He slammed into their Space Runner with such force that it dislodged them from the alien tractor beam. Both Benny and Hot Dog screamed as their craft spun, careening away from the mother ship.

"Come on, come on," Hot Dog shouted, slamming the dash buttons with one hand while twisting the flight yoke with the other. "Don't fail me now."

She managed to level them out, twisting the craft around so that they faced the chaos the Pit Crew was causing. The twins continued to outfly the alien ships, while Sahar and Trevone took down enemy combatants with deadly precision. Despite being in the middle of the battlefield, Ricardo was barking orders that were now blaring through the speakers of Hot Dog's and Benny's Space Runner, all while covering his team's backs.

"Where's Elijah?" Hot Dog asked.

Benny's heart dropped into his stomach.

"There!" He pointed at the muscle car slowly being sucked into the side of the asteroid.

Ricardo must have spotted it at the same time. "Hold on, Elijah. We're coming! Everyone, form up on me."

"No!" Elijah shouted. "Stay back. You'll just get caught up in this thing, too, and your engines aren't powerful enough to break out of it." He paused. "Something I never thought I'd say about my own designs."

"Then I'll knock you out like you did Benny and Hot Dog."

"Don't you dare," Elijah said. "I've got a plan."

There were a few seconds of silence on the comms before Benny spoke again.

"Elijah, what are you doing?"

He could hear the best driver in the galaxy laugh. Just once.

"What does it look like, kid?" Elijah asked. "I'm saving the world. Let's just say I've had a change of heart after watching my scholarship winners live up to their potential. Just make sure you finish what you started. There's more of these aliens out there. I'm counting on all of you."

That was when Benny figured out what was going on, what Elijah was doing. He just didn't want to believe it.

"He's not planning on escaping," he whispered.

"Always one step ahead of me, kid," Elijah said. "Think of what kind of damage one of these explosions could do from *inside*. I've gotta say, this has been quite a thrill. I thought I'd been on the greatest adventures of my time already. But I guess I was wrong."

Above them, Benny could see the underside of Elijah's Space Runner start to glow.

"What?" Ricardo was yelling now. "No way. Come on, Crew, we're getting him out of there."

"Elijah, your hyperdrive is reaching a critical state," Pinky said. "Think about this. There's got to be—"

"If you get in contact with Earth again, tell the real Pinky I'm sorry," Elijah said, cutting her off. "For everything."

"No," Pinky said. "I won't let you do this!"

"Command override: Detroit." There was a moment of silence on the line. "Now, bring the rest of them home. That's an order."

"You reckless fool," Pinky whispered.

"No!" Ricardo shouted. But it was too late. The AI had taken over his controls, and already their Space Runners were jetting away from the asteroid ship and back towards the Moon.

Benny and Hot Dog looked at each other for a second before scrambling to stare out of the back windshield. As they raced away, the giant ship that had loomed so terrifyingly large just seconds before got smaller and smaller.

Still, they were able to see the explosion a minute later, fire and debris shooting out of the rocky hull. Benny might not have worked on Space Runners in the Drylands, but he *did* know what happened to an engine that overheated. With all the power churning inside a hyperdrive, the resulting explosion must have taken out the entire docking area of the ship. Maybe the whole interior.

Benny and Hot Dog were speechless, but the rest of the Pit Crew erupted on the comms, shouting at one another in a horrified roar of sound.

Benny tapped on the dashboard until it was just him and the Taj on the Space Runner comms.

"What happened to the alien ship?" he asked.

"It's still moving," Jasmine said. "But it's definitely retreating. And *fast*."

Benny looked over his shoulder. The ship was a pinprick in the distance now. Just a speck of dust on the back windshield.

CHAPTER 30

Jasmine supplied updates throughout the rest of the trek back to the Taj. Benny and Hot Dog listened in silence, too overwhelmed to try to make sense of anything that had happened. Except for them, the rest of the Moon Platoon had returned to the resort. There'd been some damaged Space Runners and a few minor injuries, but everyone made it to their temporary home all right – even if some of them, like Drue, had to be towed through space by the McGuyvers.

Eventually, as they closed in on the Taj, Benny spoke.

"Thanks," he said.

"For what?" Hot Dog asked.

"I don't know. For flying us outta there?"

She laughed a little. "You're the one who distracted them and tackled an alien."

"Yeah, well . . ." He struggled for words. "I'm glad I didn't have to do it alone."

"Yeah. Me, too."

He was quiet for a few seconds. "And I'm glad it was you and not Drue. He would have ticked off the aliens and they would have kicked our butts."

Hot Dog nodded. "That's exactly what would've happened." She smiled weakly at him. "Don't look so worried, Benny. We saved the day. This was a *success*."

She was right. The asteroid storm had been stopped. The Alpha Maraudi ship was retreating.

They'd done it.

But this was only the first step. He knew that. They both did.

"Ugh," Hot Dog groaned as they entered the pressurization tunnel. "I hate this part so much."

Despite knowing the Alpha Maraudi were still out there and that Elijah was gone, Benny felt like he was full of electricity as their Space Runner shot through the entry tunnel back into the Grand Dome, where the rest of the fleet had gathered along with the McGuyvers and a hologram of Pinky. Their car stopped by the fountain, right in front of the Taj's entrance, and as Benny and Hot Dog opened their Space Runner doors, everyone in the Grand Dome cheered for them.

The sound was deafening. So loud that Benny had to

wonder if Pinky was somehow miking it through the speakers.

Jasmine came racing down the steps, and before either Hot Dog or Benny could say hello, she was hugging them with such ferocity that they almost fell over.

"I thought we'd lost you guys," she said into Hot Dog's shoulder.

"You know, so did I for a minute there," Hot Dog replied.

"Woot, woot!" Ramona said behind Jasmine, holding two thumbs up.

"Jazz, you're kind of crushing me," Benny said.

She laughed and let them go. Behind her, Drue pushed through the crowd until he was standing in front of Benny.

"Took you long enough," he said with a smirk. Then he raised his fist to chest level.

Benny hit his own against it. "We got held up. Thanks for taking out that alien ship earlier, by the way."

"Yeah, well, now that my Space Runner's damaged, I'm totally claiming one of the newer models." His gaze fell to the gold device wrapped around Benny's palm. "Whoa, dude, where'd you get that driving glove?"

Benny held open his hand, staring at the strange alien device. In the shock of everything, he'd almost forgotten about it.

"We've got a *lot* to talk about," he murmured, his mind reeling as he wondered what they could learn from the alien technology. How they might be able to use such a thing against the Alpha Maraudi in the future. If it would work outside of the asteroid ship – how it even worked in the first place.

His thoughts were interrupted as the five Pit Crew Space Runners raced into the Grand Dome, parking in a row off to the side of the Taj. Ricardo was the first out, bursting from his car and stomping towards the garage. He peeled his driving gloves off, throwing them onto the ground. Sahar and the Miyamura twins followed him.

"Ricardo," Benny yelled, but the Crew member just kept walking. Benny started after him anyway. He wasn't sure what he was going to say to the leader of the Mustangs – were there even Mustangs any more? – but he thought he should say *something*.

Pinky stepped in front of him. Even though she was a hologram, Benny came to a halt, almost falling over himself to keep from running into her.

"I wouldn't," Pinky said. "Give them some space. Especially Ricardo."

Benny stared at the woman. Her lips were curved down

in a grim frown, eyes somehow wet, despite an inability to actually cry.

"I'm sorry about . . ." he started.

"It's fine," she said. "Though, for a few seconds I *was* considering having Ramona lock up the baser parts of my personality."

"Can't have that," Trevone said, coming up beside them. "I think Elijah likes the full you."

"Trevone," Benny said. "You saw what happened. Elijah's . . ."

"You don't know that man like I do." He let out a sad laugh. "He's never been the kind of guy who'd pull a stunt he couldn't take credit for later."

"You mean you think he's still up there?" Drue asked, coming up to Benny's side, Hot Dog and Jasmine in tow. "On that ship?"

"That might be worse than being exploded," Hot Dog said.

"I'm just saying maybe we shouldn't count him out completely," Trevone said.

"Sure," Drue said. "No big deal. Just the most famous man on Earth maybe dead, maybe taken prisoner by aliens." His eyes grew wide. "If he's alive and we save him, he's going to owe us *so much*."

Benny looked at Trevone, trying to figure out whether or not he actually believed this, or was just trying to keep everyone from freaking out.

Trevone must have noticed.

"What?" he asked. "*You're* the one who's been spouting all that stuff about there always being hope." He turned to Pinky. "What's the latest on the alien ship?"

"It's far away from our radar," Pinky said.

"We'll have to discuss whether we prioritise tracking it or re-establishing communications with Earth," Jasmine added.

"What if I just carve a big SOS into the Moon?" Drue asked. "Problem solved!"

"You'd just get people hurt if they tried to come help us. There are still asteroids in the space between us and Earth." She raised a hand to her head. "Which is another thing we need to deal with."

"What if I explained the situation? I could write *really* small."

"*Drue*," Hot Dog said. "Shut up."

"I've sent word about what's happening to the kids underground," Pinky said. "There's a lot of conversation down there right now. Some of them want to stay hidden. Others think it's time to come back topside."

"What's your next move?" Trevone asked, turning to Benny.

Benny looked around. Everyone was staring at him. Pinky. Trevone. The EW-SCABers. His teammates.

His friends.

And then he looked up at the sky. Far above them, the sun was shining on the Earth. People were going about their lives. The caravan was on the move. His family was maybe wondering what he was doing up at the Taj, still blissfully unaware of everything that was happening.

He wished his father were there to tell him what to do next.

And then he realised he already knew. He'd known before he'd even got to the Moon, when he was sitting on top of his family's RV in the Drylands, staring into a camera.

"We finish what we started," he said. "We keep going. We save the planet. Somehow. We're the smartest, bravest kids in the galaxy, right? We'll figure out a way."

"Sounds like a plan," Hot Dog said with a grin.

"I agree," Jasmine said. "Well, not a *plan* exactly, but that's something we can work on."

"Together." Drue nodded.

"Yeah," Trevone said, but there was hesitation in his

voice. He was looking up at something. Benny turned to see that he was staring at the window of Elijah's private quarters.

Ricardo Rocha stood there with three other shadows behind him.

"There *is* one more thing," Jasmine said reluctantly. "A couple of the smaller ships from the asteroid broke away from the rest of the formation during the fight. They appeared to be heading in this direction, but we lost track of them."

"What?" Benny asked.

"Probably scouts," Pinky said. "But the ships are cloaking themselves somehow."

"Keeping tabs on us."

"Or," Jasmine said, "since they couldn't take down the Taj with their asteroids, they're looking for another way to destroy us now that they know we're a real threat."

"If they find the underground tunnels, they might try to attack us through a back door," Drue said. "Like, from the other side of the Moon. That's what I'd do."

"The dark side *is* the most likely hiding spot if they wanted to land and maintain stealth."

"I'll reinforce gravity fields along any entrances to the

tunnels," Pinky said. "*And* we can set up secondary laser defence measures."

"OK," Benny said. "So, we should probably track those ships down at some point."

"At least they're far away from the Taj," Hot Dog said. "There's no one they can hurt on the dark side."

Trevone and Pinky looked at each other.

"Actually," Trevone said. "That's not *exactly* true."

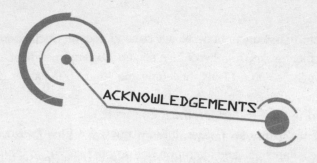

ACKNOWLEDGEMENTS

First and foremost I have to thank everyone at Harper who made this book a book, especially my brilliant editor, Tara Weikum, who I am so lucky to be working with, and whose guidance turned this story into something so much richer and bigger than it was when she first read it. To the rest of the team at Harper – publicists, sales and marketing, the incredible copyeditors who had to suffer through my elementary under-standing of outer space: thank you, thank you, thank you. You have my unending gratitude for all your incredible work on this book.

No one would be reading these acknowledgements if it weren't for James Frey and Greg Ferguson at Full Fathom Five, who gave me the keys to the Lunar Taj and helped me bring this book to life. I can't thank you both enough for your support and patience over the years. Thanks, too, to Eric Simonoff and Alicia Gordon at WME for having faith in the series and getting it into the right hands.

A huge thanks to Mike Larocca, Joe Russo, and Anthony Russo at Getaway Films, who believed in this story when it was in its infancy and were instrumental in shaping it.

I can't express enough gratitude to my agent, Molly Jaffa, for her constant reassurance, honesty, advice, and general, incomparable awesomeness. You're a hyperdrive engine, keeping me afloat.

Thanks to Drue Davis for letting me steal your name, even though you're so unlike the character in the book. There's no one I'd rather be stuck on the Moon with.

Thanks to my soul sister, Julie Murphy, for your friendship, advice, snapchats, and afternoon delivery pizza. I'm so thankful for our coven and whatever black magic brought us together.

Thanks to Rachel Carter for all the long telephone calls about everything and nothing and the occasional horrors of the writing process.

Thanks, Phil Richardson, for keeping me sane as the Space Runners began to take flight and for coming up with 'Moon Platoon', which I then stole and ran with.

Thanks, too, to friends who put up with missed birthday parties, cancelled dinner plans, and unanswered messages while I worked: Bethany Doherty, Kyle and Rachel Williams, Jeff and Aly Yale, Tyler Cochran, Charlotte Hogg, the Stroud family, and everyone else who I am, embarrassingly, leaving out. Also, thanks to author friends such as Samantha Mabry, Soman Chainani, Jenny Martin, and so many others who have always been willing to listen as I talked plot problems for what was likely the hundredth time. Special thanks, as well, to the Texas librarians and educators who have (and continue to be) an invaluable group of men and women supportive of me and other authors, and who have worked so hard to get books into the hands of young readers.

And finally, thanks to my family, always. Especially my new nephew, Jax, for reminding me why I do what I do. I can't wait for you to reach the Moon.